One American Robin

Eric Mancini

ISBN-10:0-9976818-0-2
ISBN-13: 978-0-9976818-0-2

Second Edition.

Brown Bird lyrics used with the permission of MorganEve Swain.

The Low Anthem lyrics used with permission from the band.

Best attempts were made to secure permission to lyrics by The Mountain Goats.

Van Morrison lyrics used with written permission of Alfred Music (invoice PR160823-2005)

Cover Design and Illustration by Holly Emidy

www.hollyemidydesign.com

Praise for *One American Robin*

Winner of the 2017 Independent Publishers of New England Award

Literary Fiction Book of the Year

"It's the realism of this story that I find so striking." - Motif RI

"Whenever I put this book down, I found myself thinking about Robin and wondering what would happen next - hoping for the best, as if she were a friend." - Jess Weil

"Eric Mancini perfectly captures that awkward stage of being in your mid-20s when the world expects you to be an adult but you still feel like an adolescent." - Chris Schneider

"Throw in humor, pathos and a great storyline and you may stay up all night, as I did, to finish it!" - Anne Foster

Dedicated to my wife Kristen, who made this possible.

And to my parents, who made everything possible.

Before Fall

"By concord little things grow great, by discord the
greatest come to nothing."
-Roger Williams, founder of Rhode Island

"Hey little bird / will you be the one /
to nest beneath my Gatling gun?"
-The Low Anthem

Chapter One

FOR THE LONGEST time, I couldn't visit my father without some small aspect of his nursing home bringing me to tears. There were men and women in the dementia ward who were really far gone, but for some reason, I was able to compartmentalize their suffering. I'd held the door for stretchers. Once, in the hallway, an ancient woman with a shrunken face grabbed my arm from her low chair and looked at me with the saddest, hungriest eyes. Somehow I could shrug that off. But then I would see something small: a paper-mâché duck made for a grandparent, or a photo collage printed on low-quality paper, and I would have to find a bathroom to compose myself. Never the big stuff, though. Just something small and stupid, like a paper-mâché duck.

That Sunday, a woman playing a Casio keyboard won the prize. I was early, and while I waited for Ariel and the kids, an orderly pushed the woman up to the front with one hand on the wheelchair, one hand trying to tamp down the woman's mop of electric red hair. She wore an aquamarine sweatshirt and red pants that contained a faded trace of former weekends spent on Martha's Vineyard. The guests wore their good outfits for Sunday brunch. Most of their ensembles harkened back to when life was normal for their families, before their loved ones' memories had been tipped into a bowl and scrambled with a fork. These outfits sat in plastic bags in the corner of the patients' pop-up closet next to their day-to-day, utilitarian apparel: shapeless housedresses, baggy white T-shirts, roomy slacks.

The orderly turned the wheelchair and gently shook it to tee the wheels up with the keyboard stand. I pulled out a notebook and wrote down everything I could see: the woman with the red hair, the orderlies, the families filing into the room to reserve chairs, pretending they weren't jockeying for the best tables, dragging their confused eight-year-olds and bored teenagers in tow. Mothers gathering up ketchup and syrup from other tables and stacking napkins. When I couldn't find a new piece of information to write, a tightness formed in my upper stomach and roamed like a searchlight. This obsession had started earlier in the year and intensified over the summer. I pressed my pencil tip into the paper until it almost tore through.

To keep the tight feeling at bay, I wrote backwards, through to the beginning of summer. I wrote about sweat-stained shirts, aimless walks. About waking up in a boy's dorm room with a fuzzy head and a blanket covering one breast. About stirring my last vodka drink of the night with a butter knife and being chastised for placing the wet utensil on a lacrosse magazine. About the salty ketchup of late-night drunk food. I wrote about the movers packing up my roommates' things, the boxes marked 'New York, NY,', and how through squinted eyes they looked like ants carrying large granules of sand. I finished by writing "May 27," the day we moved our dad into Shady Brook: Partners in Elder Care, and the first day of my current life.

The orderly unscrewed a series of knobs to adjust the height of the keyboard stand. I could sense the woman's nerves by the way she lifted her arms up toward her head; it carried a hint of a much younger woman checking her hair for bounce. In the dementia ward, these genuine moments appeared, to me at least, to be muscle memory. This same muscle memory would allow her to play a few simple keyboard songs from her past, while later at her table she would not be able to recognize any of her family members. She touched her hair again, her arms making parentheses around her face. The choreographed motions sputtered out unreliably, like garbled messages in static.

By the time the orderly had turned the keyboard on, triggering a tinny drum beat, I had already begun indulging myself in some private tears. Something about the drum sound: the sad thinness of it, and the way it separated the woman's movements into discrete parts. I reached into the pocket of my coat, which had been thrown across the table to reserve seats, and pulled out a few balled-up tissues. I never left the house without a few old tissues, not so much for me (I would just as well wipe a sleeve across my face) or for my father (who wouldn't register the tears anyway) but for Maddy and Emma, my young nieces. They didn't understand that what they were seeing should be sad, and their lack of understanding stood in beautiful defiance of the general mood of the dementia ward.

Maddy came around the corner first, a little bundle

of shoes and twirling tutu. She beat a path straight for me and jumped into my arms. I dropped the tissues on the table and raised her up a little, guessing her weight like a carnival barker.

"Ten pounds?" I asked her, shaking her so that her laugh bounced along with her. "Two hundred pounds??"

The rest of the family entered the room more slowly. The younger Emma stepped carefully, with an arm clasped to her father's pant leg. John, my brother-in-law, walked about as well as could be expected under the circumstances. My sister Ariel rushed past them both, unloading a half-dozen soft-cornered bags laced with dizzying patterns onto the table. Without acknowledging me, she immediately set to hunting down sugar, ketchup, and maple syrup.

"Is she still mad at me?" I asked John, with Maddy on my lap, her tutu splayed out on the table. John shrugged his shoulders and began removing containers and Ziplocs from Ariel's bags and arranging them carefully at the table. There were yellow slurries, green beans, snacks that looked like Cheerios mixed with cat food.

"Probably," he said.

John arranged the girls in their seats with their compartments of foods composed symmetrically around them. Maddy slipped off my lap and into her seat next to me. The room was filling up with similarly cobbled-together families. Some of the older folks had already lined up at the cafeteria line in advance of the official start of brunch. John took off his peacoat and carefully placed it around the metal-framed chair; then, looking with distaste at the shapes stressing the soft shoulders of the coat, removed it from the chair and laid it flat on the table. Even in this cafeteria, with walls painted a color blue whose very attempt to impose calm evoked sadness, John appeared in full control. He rubbed his closely shaved head, looking around in a way that said he saw under the surface of things, understood more about a situation than you did. I liked him immensely.

"What time does the band come on?" John asked. He looked at me conspiratorially, gesturing at the keyboard stand.

"Careful - that woman made me cry a minute ago," I said.

"Before the solo?"

Ariel, her condiments rounded up and arranged like Russian nesting dolls in ascending order, joined us at the table. She shook her ponytail out and put it back into a tight bun, stretching her hairband with laser precision. We sat quietly for a moment, the girls practically vibrating in their chairs.

"How's it going?" I said, breaking the silence.

"Not bad, pretty busy," she said. She smiled big but without her teeth, a smile propelled up through the cheeks. "Still find time for this, though."

"I'm sure Dad appreciates it," I said.

Ariel was mad at me because I had missed a few of these brunches lately, and was hungover at a few more. Also, there was an incident with our dad at the end of last winter which she still hadn't gotten over. Ariel can forget what you're saying to her as you're saying it, but she never failed to remember a slight. John looked at his watch. A few nurses and orderlies began arriving through the door with patients hobbling at their side.

"Time for the auction," he said. John called this portion of the brunch the auction because of the way the orderlies led the patients (guests, in nursing home parlance) in one by one as if they were being auctioned off. It never failed to make me giggle. This was, as far as I could tell, another token gesture of independence; you didn't have to go scoop up your loved one, they came right out to you by sheer free will. It was a nice place, and very expensive.

Our father came through the door. An orderly stood at his side but didn't need to assist him in any way. He still had a tall man's loping stride, the kind that looked as natural in a business meeting as on a basketball court. His height and his natural black curls stood him out from the crowd of slouched and white-haired patients.

John raised his arm, directing the orderly to bring Dad over to us. I giggled again, thinking of the auction thing, and Maddy and Emma giggled back in response, drawing a stern look from Ariel. The orderly helped Dad to his seat. John grabbed both of Dad's shoulders and looked straight into his cloudy blue eyes.

"Hello, Terry!" John said, loud enough for the deaf patients to hear. Even he, who understood the core of any situation, put on a mask for the initial greeting. I got the feeling he did it as much for himself as for Dad. "How are you? Let's get you in a chair."

"Oh hello!" Dad said to the group. "Pretty good."

Ariel walked over and laid a big hug into him. "How are ya, Dad?" she asked.

He thought for a moment, blinked his eyes to the

room, and responded "Pretty good!" Whenever he had to think before remembering a mundanity, his eyes lit up, ecstatic that the rules of conversation had suddenly come back to him. Within the first few minutes, I could usually get a sense of how good or bad a visit would be. The general trajectory of a dementia patient is down, but there are peaks and valleys along the way.

"Dad, you remember Maddy and Emma. These are your granddaughters." The girls looked across at their mother, politely bored by this weekly ritual they didn't fully understand.

"Of course!" Dad replied, after a pause.

Ariel glanced across at John. I looked at Ariel. We communicated the information with our eyes. 'Of course' was what our father said when he was confused. This would not be a lucid day. When this happened, you could feel the air going out of the room. We knew that the rest of brunch would proceed like a failed party with the guests too polite to leave. We all knew this and we didn't have to say a word.

By this time a few withered patients had walked past, each looking closely at my father's hair. A few said hello. One old woman, whose skin called to mind a walnut shell, stood by our table, smiling and not speaking until an orderly moved her along.

"Don't forget to leave a seat for Ma," Dad said. We had saved a seat, knowing he would ask. Ariel looked across at me. We talked more with our eyes. This week, to avoid drama, I raised my hand toward Ariel and said, "Sure thing, Dad."

"Well okay. Good."

I looked at Ariel with questioning eyes, and she very subtly shook her head. I took this to mean that she did try to contact our mother and that, again, she would not be visiting. Further details were beyond the extent of our telepathy.

John got up to start gathering food for the family, bringing back fruit, pancakes, and sausages, then making a second trip for glasses of milk poured from a brushed steel machine. First, he brought a bowl of sad, cut-up fruit and placed it in front of my father. That day Ariel, defiant, was not in the mood to accept our father's condition. Instead of cutting her losses and eating in silence, as I had planned to do, she prodded him with questions, acting like her job was to exercise his mind until the plasticides in his brain would so stretch and soften that he would, in a miraculous epiphany, remember all of us.

"Dad, Maddy's just started school this month. Do you remember Maddy?"

A pause. "Of course!" He smiled big in a way that gathered up all of his wrinkled skin and held it in his cheeks. On days like this, he was like a pitcher trying to survive nine innings without a fastball.

"Who's Maddy?" Ariel inquired innocently.

My father, so vibrant just a moment before, shrank in his chair, confused, unable to find a proper banality to keep the conversation afloat. Finally, he said, "Gee, I don't know" and began poking at the fruit with his plastic fork.

"Well, Dad, who's this?" Ariel said, tussling the hair of Maddy, who hadn't been paying attention for a while. This reframing of questions annoyed me to no end.

"Ariel, just let him eat, this always goes the same

way," I said.

"Butt out, Robin," she said. "Who's this, Dad? Do you remember her?"

"It's just, you know what he's going to say," I said.

"I don't know what he's going to say. We won't know unless we try, will we?" she said.

"Dad, who's this?" Ariel asked, again touching Maddy's tawny curls.

I waited for the inevitable answer. My insides seethed. He sat back in his chair, suddenly beaming, and relayed the information that had popped into his head.

"Why, it's little Maybel, Jerry's daughter." He reached across and gave her a tussle. Maddy looked at me, confused and irritable. In the early days of his illness, a chalk line had been snapped in time. Prior to this line, names and places still existed as words that could be pulled up at will. We tried to use the names and places he gave us to pinpoint this line, but the closest we could get was somewhere in his teens or early twenties, before all of us. Whenever an open-ended question was asked of him, the answer he supplied would originate from this early period. Maybel, Jerry's little daughter, was just one example, whomever the hell that was.

Ariel sighed. She turned and began fussing with him, fixing his hair. She wiped the crumbs from his shirt and, in wiping down his sleeve, took his arm and examined a spot on his index fingertip that was dark, as if permanently in shadow. He didn't respond when she rubbed her thumb over it.

The chair I sat on could barely contain me. Seeing Maddy and Emma innocently playing with little pink bits of toys on the table, I forced myself to contain my shaking, instead channeling the energy toward Ariel in a direct beam.

"That was six," I held myself from swearing, "six months ago. He's fine. Leave it alone."

She rubbed the dark spot once more and put his arm down. "Anyways," she said, and went back to her plate of eggs. I hated her so much in that moment.

"Dad, I have to go," I said. He looked back at me, blankly smiling.

I gathered my things, kissed him on the head, then kissed Maddy, then Emma, then walked toward the exit. Ariel smirked. She'd gotten what she wanted: she could be the responsible daughter, and I could keep filling the role of the emotional wreck. By the exit, I flashed a hand at John across the room, and he gave me his mischievous, conspiratorial look with a tall stack of pancakes tilting on his tray. Once I broke the plane of the double doors the keyboard playing began, tentative at first but quickly gaining in surety. I turned to look. The red-haired woman played in what appeared to be a trance. Despite the key being off, and despite the Casio's cheap excuse for an organ setting, it was impossible not to recognize the song. It was "She's Like the Wind" by Patrick Swayze. Some of the small things at Shady Brook can also make you laugh, thankfully.

Instead of going straight home, I idled past my apartment and got back on the highway, driving over the new I-195 bridge, blue and spindly, and worked my way to the east side of Providence to a familiar bench. It's a place that is everywhere and nowhere at the same time. I can sit and watch the black waters of the Woonasquatucket, the traffic over the Point Street Bridge. Across the river, the three smokestacks of the Narragansett Electric Company loom like relics of an industrial past. Brown and RISD students pedal by on colorful bikes. In nicer weather couples kayak past.

I sat for a while, scribbling thoughts into my notebook. Putting the notebook aside for a minute, my eyes fixed on a body bobbing in the river. I leaned forward and squinted, my pulse quickening. The body tipped and shuffled, but otherwise stayed in place in the river. I thought briefly that someone was struggling to tread water, and I reached for my cell phone. But then the sun glinted off its cowboy hat, and I could see that the body was nothing but a metal casting. An art installation. The hollow bust must have been chained to the bottom of the river, giving it a floating range of motion. I let myself be mesmerized by the body, bobbing up and down, listing like a buoy, floating downstream and snapping to a stop, then fading back. Green-headed ducks floated around the body. I watched them root their heads into the black water, using their bodies like pump handles to grope deeper for fish.

Downriver at the edge of my vision, real bodies kneeled on the muddy banks, dipping colorful bolts of cloth into the river. This was the city of tent dwellers that had cropped up in the depths of the Great Recession. At that point I'd only heard about them in conversations at bars. From where I sat, the decommissioned I-195 highway onramp, supported by rusted beams, hid the city from view. Still kneeling, they lifted their sheets from the black waters and slapped them back down.

I looked down at my notebook, where I'd written the words 'snowy owl' in triplicate on an otherwise blank page. I tried to visualize my emotions, and they resembled a tangle of cables and cords. I take a strange liking to untangling real cables, finding the work therapeutic. As a kid, I used to tangle up all our Nintendo controllers on purpose just to unwind them. Unfortunately, emotional cabling works a bit differently, and, sitting on the bench, I had trouble locating end points to work back from.

Chapter Two

INSTEAD OF TRYING to fix our relationship, Ariel focused with laser precision on Maddy and Emma, and I burrowed deeper and deeper into my world of books, a lone bright spot that summer. In the months since I'd started selling books, it had grown from a hobby to a full-time business that I could live on. Instead of taking phone calls all day in Woonsocket, I now spent my weekdays prostrate on the carpets of used bookstores, a postal bin at my side. I combed through each store, scanning bar codes with a custom PDA, one after another. The PDA, linked to the internet, flashed a book's market price. If the for-sale price at the store dipped below that by a fair margin, I put it in my bin, knowing it would fetch a fast profit online. In this way, the whole world of books was my grocery store checkout counter. Like any good business in an information economy, it didn't rely on the presence of information so much as on an imbalance of it. The bookstores where I spent my days were warm, charming, and mostly ignorant of their inventory's worth.

It was during one of these trips on a hot August day when I first saw Corey up close. Corey lived across the street from me on the west side of Providence in the tangled web of streets between Broadway and Westminster. I was scanning a row of design books, my postal bin half-filled with architecture tomes (always the heaviest) and a small pile of attractive hard cover fiction: Hemingways with a wallpaper-patterned dust jacket, Dickens with leather bindings. Cellar Stories, more than any shop in the greater Providence area, knew their books' worths, and I tended to visit rarely. A few of the books I bought at Cellar Stories I simply wanted to have, not because my PDA told me they were profitable but because of the more primal attraction that had made me a book lover in the first place. Some I might eke out a small profit on from the shipping rate, others I would hold onto, hiding them among my stacks of inventory where I could rediscover them later.

I turned the corner from physical sciences to the local zine section, bin resting on my hip, when I caught a glimpse of a white T-shirt at the end of parallel shelves. The pure, bleached cotton wrapped around the end of the aisle, ghost-like, leaving trailing spots in my vision. I hadn't seen a face, but I knew it was Corey. Before I had ever met him, I knew his name from some misdelivered mail that I'd held onto. And I'd seen that undershirt a hundred times, so white and clean that it reflected the porch light like a mirror held to the sun. He wore it like a uniform whenever he worked on his house, which was constantly. In fact, my first memories of Corey are tied up with the sounds of construction: of carpets rolled up and thrown out the window, of bags of asphalt shingles dragged scraping across the driveway. Drum sanders running past midnight. The sharp metal sound of hammer striking pry bar. I'd be out on the porch reading past midnight, and he would still be at it. His habits intrigued me, his looks more so, and I often wondered if he had a job beyond full-time, self-directed home repair.

I crossed the long row of international history books: Italy, Spain, Germany with its entire row of Hitler studies. He was at the far end of the Mechanical/Practical section with its yellowing books on boiler repair. It might sound strange that I remember this, but I've picked through Providence bookstores so thoroughly that I could walk blindfolded down their aisles, hands running across the shelves, and tell you from the spine textures which section I was in. Crouching down to the lower rows of Practical Psychology, I caught a sideways look at him through the shelves, his neck to lower torso framed like a movie still. I love the abbreviated glances possible at a bookstore, the dance of it.

He held a worn olive-green book in his hand, dictionary-thick. Turning each page, he ran his hand gently across it, bleeding the air out from between the delicate pages. Later that day, I wrote in my notebook that his arms were flecked with white paint.

I rose from a crouch, leaving my bin on the floor. Standing still, I tried to gather the courage to walk over and start a conversation. Being out of practice, I found more and more that I had to psyche myself up to approach people.

But before I could turn the corner, a bearded man walked around the aisle and stood in my way.

"What are you doing?" he asked. He looked like the type of older man seen in bookstores leering sideways at young women from books of poetry (a 'text,' he would probably call it). A professor, maybe. I let the scanner drop into my half-filled bin and looked up as if I hadn't heard him.

"Excuse me?" I replied.

"This is a small business, you know," he said. "Used bookstores aren't exactly raking in the lucre."

His sweater was, predictably, the worst.

"Well, I'm buying these, so..."

"I know what you're doing. You're making a dollar off the back of someone else. You're basically a, a..."

My cheeks reddened at the thought of Corey overhearing the scene. As the man stammered, I tried to look around him to see whether Corey was still standing by the bookshelf. I thought I had heard the hard snap of a closing book.

"You're a..a..."

"A scavenger?" I whispered. I used the word because I had been called it, among other names. One of the strange contradictions of being a bulk buyer with your own scanner is this: even though you are often a store's biggest buyer, people still treat you as if you're doing something wrong.

The man was still stammering when I lifted the bin to walk away. But instead of making a smooth exit I misjudged the weight of the bin and accidentally dumped a cascade of books onto the man's feet. Embarrassed, I started to pick them up, then abandoned that idea and left it all in a pile.

"Boo to you!" he said, backing away. "Boo!"

He literally booed.

I turned the corner to make for the exit, but Corey was gone. Looking behind from where he once stood, I watched him walk toward the front counter with a purposeful stride, the thick olive book held motionlessly. The entire row Corey stood in front of held the same style of worn, olive-spine books as he had been perusing. There was a hollow space in the middle, like a knocked-out tooth, where Corey's book had been. Still flush from my encounter with the sweater guy, my pulse racing, I quickly grabbed two of them and made a similar retreat down a long, lonely aisle of spirituality and sports books toward the front counter.

At the end of the day, I returned to my apartment with the two olive books my only purchase. They generated a mysterious power thumping around in the back seat. I didn't even bother to look at them before I had gotten into my car, but by the time I pulled into my driveway, it was all I could do not to pull over to the side of the road to inspect them. They were old home improvement books. The theme of each ran up the spine in blocky yellow text: there was one on heating systems and one on general home repair. The bottom of each read "Series: Ansel's *Build your Dream Home.*" The covers featured a prototypical 50's dad, line-drawn astride rough-hewn wooden beams, crew cut and all. I suspected their value to be nil, which the internet quickly confirmed.

I dropped the books into Karen's old room, which had begun to resemble the overflow space in a public library. The shelves in my room filled in July, and I had resorted to stacking books in waist-high towers around my low-slung bed. As each of my roommates had moved out, diplomas in hand with their eyes set on economically viable cities, their rooms had been colonized by medical books, genre pulp, self-help schmaltz and anything else deemed profitable by the all-seeing eye of my scanner. Though I lived alone, I still referred to the rooms as "Jen's room" or "Karen's room," unsure of what else I should call them. My landlord was M.I.A. He had never fixed so much as a light bulb since I'd been there. We had separate agreements with the landlord and mailed our checks separately. If the landlord noticed or cared that he was only cashing one check, he didn't let me know.

That night, like most, began with sorting and cataloging books, then moved on to boxing up units sold until daylight leaked away. My work done for the day, I poured a glass of wine, found a book, and dragged a chair out to the porch where I read, leg dangling over the railing. My porch light didn't work and I didn't have any inclination to fix it, so I had to turn on the lamp in the living room and position myself in front of the bay window to catch some light. After some time, I put the book down and pulled a spiral notebook from my pocket where I wrote facts from the day, ticking them off with dashes at the start of each line. These facts could be as small as a street name, a governor's wife, or they could be large, like my thoughts on Philip Roth (one of those restaurants you go to because you've never had a terrible meal). I wrote what I could about seeing Corey up close. I thought about my fight with Ariel at the nursing home and wrote "snowy owl" one more time, underlining the words with vigor. Some boys biked past, their voices vibrating as they absorbed the bumps of the cobblestone. A pack of college-aged students walked in a bubble of their own perfume, sights set on a party. It was a nice late-summer night.

Then, as if on cue, the metal screech of a circular saw tore the quiet scene in half. It ran for what felt like minutes, only to be replaced by something else: a hammer maybe, clanging on a long metal pipe. Its echo sent a mournful call across the city. I flipped my notebook closed and spied across the street. Corey's house, old and Gothic, vibrated with activity. Its paint wasn't just peeled, it was in the act of peeling. The house had one enviable feature: a circular turret anchoring one side of the house with a shingled spire roof. With all his house lights on I could watch him as he worked in one room, then another, moving between them at a frantic pace, safety goggles half-cocked on his head. It was like a lot of nights that summer, with one exception: I had now seen him up close. And now that I had gotten a pair of binoculars on him, as my birder father would say, I wanted to get another look, one good enough that I could have described him fully in my notebook.

The productive scream of the circular saw cut off around two in the morning, and for the Portuguese grandmothers that made up part of the street, the reign of terror ended for the night. Corey brought one last armful of scraps to his tree belt, sweat running down his forearms. He paused and squinted across the street, but he didn't see me because by then I had snuck back inside. Empty rooms greeted me as I trudged through the house turning off lights, and I said goodnight to each as I flipped their switches. Goodnight Jen's room. Goodnight Karen's room. Goodnight Violet's room. Lastly my room, filled with tall columns of books, precariously stacked. My window faced the street, and from my low-slung bed as I dozed off I could still see Corey, perched in the circular turret room of his house, hitting a piece of metal with a hammer, sending sparks into the night.

Chapter Three

THE REST OF the summer dribbled away. I remember discrete events, but the days themselves I can't account for. I visited western Massachusetts twice on book-buying missions, navigating around lush green mountains in search of quaint towns I had never heard of. I undertook a grand reorganization in the apartment, splitting the categories of non-fiction between Karen's and Violet's rooms, adding cheap shelving where I could afford it. Like a petulant child, I refused to split up the fiction, and as a result, my bedroom heaved with stacks of books. I had to walk carefully to bed; a quick turn or a swing of a bag would send the piles crashing like dominoes to the ground. By this point, the 'R' and 'S' stacks reached my belly button. I awoke each morning surrounded by towers of make-believe.

Ariel and I eventually made up, sort of. We had a phone call together where we spoke cordially, with neither of us addressing our fight, as close to a reconciliation as we'd get. A collaboration had brought us back together. Like adjacent countries under attack, we put aside our differences toward a greater purpose. That purpose was trying to get our mother to visit our father, which she hadn't done since Dad moved into Shady Brook in May. Throughout the summer, with all the decisions made about my father's care, it was about the only thing Ariel and I fully agreed on: we needed to get our mother over. On our weekly brunches we always saved a seat for her, and though she never showed up she was the largest presence at the table. Once she got there and saw our father, once she became inured to the horrors of the dementia ward, as we had, it would signal a sea change. What would change for us, day to day? We couldn't articulate it. But we'd decided that it was the solution to our problems, and that was all that mattered. In fact, by the end of summer I had convinced myself that it would fix all of *my* problems as well. We'd taken it as a mantra, spoken over and over again to ourselves and others.

Our attack would be two-pronged. Ariel would work toward getting our mother to visit, since she had a better relationship and granddaughters. I would work on Dad and the nursing home, making it mother-friendly. This involved making the room look more like a room and less like the hospital facility it was. I also wanted to prime my father's brain, if such a thing was possible, so that if she did visit he'd have a better chance of remembering her. I had my doubts. My father's repeated request to "save a seat for Ma" disturbed me, because he had always called our mother by name. I partly wondered if he was talking about someone else. He hadn't said our mother's name in months.

This led to a very memorable September night that I began in my apartment, collaging pictures of my mother. I got the idea from a dementia website that stressed the importance of family pictures in creating a "safe environment for remembering." Mentally walking through my father's room, I saw plenty of pictures of Maddy and Emma, one of myself and Ariel as kids, but nothing of our mother. So I set out to right this imbalance. I took a thumb drive to the drug store and printed out dozens of photos of my mother, brought them home, fanned them out on the table and began to wrestle with them. My mother is one of those people who make the same face in every photo. If you hold a stack of her pictures and flip through them, you can see time and space warp while she stands unchanged in the center of it all. Her eyes look forward, intensely. One side of her mouth rises, valiantly suggesting a smile, but the other side remains unpersuaded.

Making the collage required a craft basket that I hadn't used since high school. The crinkle-cut scissors, the heart-shaped hole punch. After thirty seconds of rustling around in the basket, my entire arm was covered in glitter. Working the scissors around the glossy card stock, I snipped out disembodied heads, whole bodies, signs of places my family had been. I wanted a big centerpiece for the middle of the collage, something with Dad and our mother next to each other. But in most pictures my parents had scattered themselves apart. Not on opposite ends, exactly, but asymmetrically across the photos. I didn't have any of their wedding photos or anything pre-Ariel and me, so I had to get creative, with a few glasses of wine helping to get the juices flowing.

During a break, I opened Facebook and through the course of scanning my main wall, I saw my friend Nizme's status: "Hanging with the boys in PVD!" with five guys tagged. Nizme was one of my only friends left in Providence, the last card spinning on my Rolodex. I'd known her since high school, and my trips to visit her at Brown were my introduction to Providence. I hadn't seen her all summer; she was away traveling to Thailand, or the Philippines - I forget which. Her new profile photo showed her standing humbly in front of a sacred-looking statue. I positioned the mouse cursor between her eyes and clicked.

The representative six friends displayed in her friend box were all dapper-looking guys. Did Facebook know that was what I wanted? I clicked on one of them. Curly hair. Standing by a body of water. Comments and clubs that implied boating. Large bicep muscles tapered down from the shirtsleeves. He had that puffy look that young boys get when they work out, like they're breaking out of their own baby fat. I felt a twinge of arousal, and my arousal sat like a drop of mercury at the tip of a knife's blade, not betraying which side it would roll down. I'm trying to be honest with myself. What happened was, I almost masturbated, but then I looked over at the collage work. I decided that if I stayed in and masturbated among photos of my mother, it would mark a new low in an already subterranean summer.

But the thought reddened my cheeks and left a lapping of energy in its wake. I shook my head and hit the back button, then closed the lid of my laptop. I texted Nizme, playing dumb and asking if she was out. Better to take the energy I had and direct it outward, I told myself.

I cleaned up the bits of cut photo paper littering the kitchen table. I put away the bottle of Elmer's glue and the vials of glitter. I left out the pictures of my mother, looking up at me in a sneering chorus of disapproval. Nizme texted me back with an address in Olneyville and a *"get over here - lots of guys!"* "Olneyville?" I thought. What would anyone be doing in Olneyville? I stood up too quickly and had to stand still for a moment with my hand on the table, letting the wine buzz settle before walking to my closet and changing out of my sweatpants.

Chapter Four

MY GPS DUMPED me in front of a derelict brick building adjoining an empty parking lot. I circled twice, confirming the address. Olneyville is built on block after block of these rambling factory buildings. Most are abandoned and none stood out from the others. I always got lost in Olneyville.

I found a small parking lot filled with bumper sticker-covered cars and pulled in. Finding a door proved difficult, as did walking through the rubble with my decent shoes. Seams of scrub brush turned the parking lot into a meandering hedge maze, which I tramped over searching for a door. Not finding one at first, I wandered around the brick exterior. My initial enthusiasm for going out began to fade. I thought about my warm bed, my towers of books, and my notebooks scratched with information.

But before I indulged these feelings I found a thick steel door propped open with a stone, a sliver of light issuing from the crack. I pulled the door open with both hands and walked into what resembled an airplane hangar. Clouds of twilight-lit dust churned in the empty ceiling, obscuring a set of parallel pipes that reached a vanishing point across the room. It was hard to make out, but I thought I saw a skate ramp and heard the rattle of their skate trucks echo across at me.

Nearby, a shipping container billowed smoke from a rusty hole in its roof. I stepped toward it and cracked open its crudely cut door. Figures sat on wooden benches, obscured by steam. I backed away, then heard, "entrez."

"Is this...a sauna?" I asked.

"One of them," a male voice said.

Along the walls, scrap pieces of wood had been fitted together to resemble a ski lodge as envisioned by an abstract artist. A small group of boys in beards, beautifully pale and almost hairless, sat in bathing suits. A few girls lay across the upper benches with one knee up, bangs over their eyes, revealing nothing except pouty lips.

"In a warehouse?" I asked.

"One of the guys that lives here made it," the voice said. "He's big into reclaimed wood."

"Oh."

The closest boy's face became clear. Condensed steam dripped from his beard, the expression on his face puckered and serious. He sat back with his weight on thin stick arms.

"Want to sit with us?" he asked. "We've got some extra towels."

What I noticed about this new crop of boys was how polite they were. Far from feeling threatened by them, I myself felt threatening just for having breasts.

"I was actually looking for a friend. Do you know Nizme?"

One of the girls, as if to respond to my question,

switched legs, laying one flat and sliding the other knee up.

"Oh yea," the boy said, throwing a towel over his narrow shoulders. "She was over by the bar in the far corner, next to the silkscreen station."

"Near the skateboard ramp?" I asked.

"No," he said. "Not that way."

I politely backed out of the steam room and closed the door. Nizme always made me meet her at places like these, and I would have complained, too, if I had another friend left in Providence. I don't know what bothered me so much about it. Breaking into an abandoned mill to make socially conscious art and mill grain? I think that my high school antics of smoking weed on golf courses and pouring beers out into the holes were a more pure act of rebellion.

The 'bar' consisted of a hodgepodge of ripped couches and a distressed red semi-circle bar underneath a tangle of antlers suspended with fishing line. A man in a bicycling hat worked the bar, and an assortment of art types sat around on the couches, some stretched out reading, others hunched together talking, their bike helmets on the table.

I ordered an IPA from the tiny-brimmed bartender and asked if he knew Nizme. Everyone did. But he shook his head.

Just then I heard "Oh Roooobin." It came from above, up in the rafters. I looked up, then spun myself around. I saw Nizme up there, hanging over a railing waving one hand up and down at me. I hadn't noticed – from a distance the pipes had obscured it – but there was an upper deck, crow's nest structure to the side of the bar, high up.

"Oh," the bartender said. "I know her."

"Get up here, girl!" Nizme said. I think that she was mocking the way a college party girl would say 'get up here, girl!'. I couldn't tell.

I walked under the supporting structure and found a rope ladder swaying in the corner. It was strong enough to support me, but not to maintain my dignity. I worked my way up slowly. My thighs rubbed as I hooked into each rung. I looked down at the poured cement floors, worried that the tiny-brimmed bartender might not be trained in emergency response. After what felt like an eternity, my sweat-slicked face emerged in the crow's nest where Nizme and a mixed group of attractive hipsters greeted me from their seats. I couldn't imagine a worse state in which to enter a group of good-looking people; I could feel my shirt riding up in the back, kept aloft by the same sweat that had helmeted my hair to my head.

I gave Nizme a hug and she kissed me on both cheeks, something I wasn't prepared for.

"I feel like it's been forever," Nizme said. She brushed at some stray hairs on my head. "Don't worry – we all looked like that after we climbed that ridiculous ladder."

"I don't believe you," I said.

"It's cool, though, right? This is where they used to keep the water barrels in case of a fire. Sit down, meet the boys."

She was thinner than when I first met her in high school, and more beautiful. I had watched her gangly height bend toward elegance, starting with trips to visit her at Brown. It accelerated when I moved to Providence and Nizme stayed to commute to law school in Boston. We were both book nerds in high school – that's how we first bonded – and I guess we both still were that day in the crow's nest, but she had found a way to transcend it, with her dark complexion and soft Asian features, and I had not.

The boys introduced themselves to me, placing their beers down onto the table before giving a slight, close to the chest sort of wave. They were a blur of tattoos, black shirts and pale, creamy skin. After greeting me, they reached back for their beers, arranged like a color wheel on the table. One of the boys, a clean-shaven one, looked very familiar, with round Harry Potter glasses, a small face and a redness in his cheeks. I couldn't place where I knew him from.

A bucket rattled up to the crow's nest and a boy grabbed my beer and handed it to me.

"The pulleys were in here when we first found the place," the boy said, settling back down in the circle. "Cool, right?"

The conversation ping-ponged from the economy to some crazy Crispin Glover movie they'd all seen, to spray painted stencils that had been cropping up around town, to housing, always housing during that period. Where the empty tracts were, who was squatting in what factory, where the basement parties were. "Basement parties" were held in the poured cement foundations of abandoned housing, and the boys talked about them banally, as though they had always existed.

I mostly sat listening, trying to keep up. I watched Nizme. She stressed her points by pushing her head forward into the shared space of the table; when she did this her hair lagged behind her face, revealing and then covering her bare shoulders. It clearly electrified the boys. I tried to drink slowly, but finding nothing to add to the conversation, I drained my first glass, then another just to keep my hands busy. The boy I recognized was similarly occupied with nervous drinking.

I perked up when the conversation turned to books. One of the boys claimed to be really into "this group of French detective authors in the 1800s who were all on opium." It was going to be one of those conversations. During a pause, Nizme graciously directed the conversation my way.

"You know, Robin's business is literature," she said. "She has a book selling business."

The boys shifted toward me. I hadn't noticed until then, but the boys had been angled inward toward Nizme and they had to shift their chairs to even see me.

"Oh, yeah?" one of the boys asked, casually fingering his plug. "Where's your shop?"

I explained that I didn't have a shop, per se.

"It's all online," Nizme said.

"Yeah," I explained. "I buy up books wholesale at shops around the city and sell them on Amazon and eBay."

"Right on," one said.

Another one said, "Wait. I recognize you. Do you walk around with those postal bins?"

"Yeah, sort of," I said. My face reddened.

"I saw you outside Symposium with this epic

mountain of books. I thought the postal bin thing was badass," he said. "It can't be legal to cart those things around."

"Thanks," I said. "I guess I'm kind of a badass."

"Yeah you are," Nizme said.

"Did you major in English with Nizme?" one asked.

"No," I said. "I didn't go to college."

"Oh, so where did you go then?"

"I didn't go to anywhere. Just some community college stuff where my mom used to teach, then I moved to Providence."

"Family stuff," Nizme said, as if to shut down the line of questioning.

"Right on. But why Providence?"

I thought for a moment. Like with any real life event, I didn't have a neat explanation for why I moved to Providence. Anyone who takes you through their life in a clear, linear narrative is trying to sell you something.

"Honestly," I said, "I visited Nizme a few times at Brown, and it was the only city I had ever been to besides going to the Boston aquarium as a kid. When it came time to move out of my house, I got a job at a bookstore and sort of just showed up here."

"I set her up with her first roommates," Nizme said. "You guys know Jill? The one from Trinity Rep? It was her roommate from freshman year. We were partying together a lot at the time. Her, her boyfriend, and another girl, I think she did Roller Derby?"

"An ideal situation you set me up for," I said.

"Hey, it got you out of middle-of-nowhere Mass."

"Could be worse," a boy added. "There are eighty

people living in tents under the old highway onramp. I went down there as part of a paper I'm writing. It's fucked up that it exists, but the place is pretty organized. They have a mayor and shit, and everyone chips in."

The gap between twenty-five, what I was, and twenty-two, what these boys probably were, felt as wide as a gorge. But I enjoyed the back and forth and the attention it afforded me. The tent city he mentioned was the same that I saw while watching the ducks on South Water Street. I put down my third beer, half drunk and still foamy, and prepared to respond.

"Wow," Nizme interjected. "I am going to miss these conversations when I'm in New York."

The group immediately reshuffled toward her.

"Niz, you're moving?" one of them asked.

"Since when?" asked another.

"Oh, it's not a big deal," she said. "It's this firm. I've always wanted to work for them and they actually recruited me. I'll start working there in January. I'm moving to Brooklyn next month."

"Congrats!" they all said, in their own way.

I polished off the rest of my beer, trying to quash an anger that had flared up inside me. I didn't care if Nizme moved away or not. That she didn't pity me enough to allow me my only conversation of the night spoke direly of our relationship.

"I thought you said you wanted to stay in Boston or Providence," I said behind gritted teeth.

"Yeah, you know," Nizme said, curling her straight hair with a long finger. Her combed-down bangs revealed none of her eyes while she spoke. "I guess I just kind of feel like Providence isn't a city you stay in. Like it was good for college, don't get me wrong. But I feel like if I'm serious, I have to move to New York. That's just me, though."

While I wondered how I could possibly follow this up, one of the boys, the one with the scrunched nose and the flip brim hat, asked, "What about Boston?"

"Yeah, I mean, Boston is cool, especially if you're doing medical stuff, but I just kind of feel like it's owned by the college kids. You know? Like if I stay there I'll feel like I'm still in college until I'm forty."

Though I should have found all this ridiculous, instead I felt shame for not knowing that these rules existed. Until that moment, I didn't know that I should hate myself for living in a third-class city and treating it like home. But after I did know, it was hard to un-know it.

During this conversation, I stood up and brought my empty pint glass to the basket, disregarding the empty glasses of the others. I lowered it down on its frayed rope and before long it rose back up to meet me eye level. I removed the full glass, my fourth, and surveyed the scene through the trapezoid of the rope. Skateboarders were still going at it; the ones waiting sat cross-legged eating oranges, dropping the peels into their helmets. Two girls left the sauna wearing vacuum sealed pants and neon camisoles, their heads wrapped in white towels. They walked up to a welded steel sculpture and pointed at it, making comments that I'm sure were so insightful they would have left me dumbly silent. The bucket dropped and the rope frame stuttered from view like a broken film strip. I had a clear thought, my last of the night: *If you're going to enjoy this place, do it now. Because you're never hanging out with Nizme again, and no one else is inviting you here.*

I felt a tap on my shoulder. Nizme sidled up next to me, arms on the railing. Her extra height forced her to hunch to avoid an angled I-beam pocked with rivets.

"Mind if I take a sip of that?" she asked. I handed it over to her. She smelled the air over the glass before sloping her neck down antelope-like and taking a small drink from the glass.

"Wow," she said. "That's really good. You always know the best food and everything like that."

"That could be taken as not a compliment," I said.

"Well, take it," she said. "It *is* a compliment."

She squinted her eyes and looked out onto the floor. Some of the day's last light cut into the factory through high windows that had been painted over then partially scraped clean.

"What a crazy place," she said.

"Did these places exist when you were at Brown?"

"Oh yeah," she said. "Less, though."

"The twilight really lights up the dust clouds," I said.

"Yeah, I guess," she said. "I'm going to miss Providence."

She took my beer and drank another big sip. When she turned, I could see her eyes behind her bangs the way you can see through a fence if you walk past quickly. They displayed more emotion than I had guessed at when they were hidden. The beer left a strip of foam across her upper lip that she wiped away with a bare arm. She didn't get it all at first and had to go back with a hooked finger to wipe the rest away. It was a real moment, the first from her all night.

"So, what've you been reading lately?" she asked. "I slept with my con law books all across Thailand. I don't think I've read a short story in three months."

"*Odd Sea*, again," I said, "I just keep going back to it."

"Ahhh, O'Brien, right?"

"Yeah. AP English - eleventh."

"Less weight," she said. And I couldn't help myself. I broke out laughing.

It was an old joke between us. We were watching *The Crucible* movie in class, the old one that everyone watches in high school. Nizme and I were mousy book nerds just getting to know each other; she had big glasses and wore her hair back in a shapeless ponytail with a rotating cast of scrunchies. I looked much the way I do now. Maybe I've gotten a little better looking. I don't know. It's not important.

There's a scene in the movie where the pure-hearted are crushing suspected wizard Giles Corey underneath a board piled with boulders. The Puritans added boulder after boulder, saying, "Confess! What say you, Giles Corey?" and in brave defiance, over and over he says, "More...weight." During this scene, with the lights low, a particularly zealous witch hunter on screen shrilled, "What say you, Giles Corey??" and I dead-panned, "Less. Weight." This being high school, the entire class did not break out laughing. The students, hedging their bets, ignored my outburst. Except for Nizme. She began squealing under her shirtsleeve. Her laugh rose and fell, stopped, then burst through her sleeve like a tidal wave.

Eventually she had to excuse herself. I could hear her running to the bathroom, her full-throated laughter echoing down the hallway.

After that day our friendship began a steady ascent, plateauing somewhere between her freshman and sophomore years at Brown, then gradually declining until, I guess, that very moment up on the ledge, surveying an abandoned factory together.

"You know," Nizme said, "I think James is into you - he kept looking your way. He's young, but he's a cool guy. He's the one with the black T-shirt."

"Niz, they all have black T-shirts."

"Plain black. Left from where you were sitting."

"Oh. With the glasses? I think I know him," I said. "I'm not sure from where, though. He's like Yoda small."

"Yeah, nice guy, though. Smart."

"So, congratulations," I said. "I'm proud of you, I'm sure you'll do well in New York."

"Oh. I have mixed feelings about it," she said, "but there aren't many good law firms in Providence, and it seems like the adult thing to do."

"You know," she added, turning her body carefully toward mine and looking straight at me, "you're so smart, Robin. Now, with the recession, it seems like it would be a great time to go back to school. I know there were reasons why you had to delay it. But it's not too late."

I doubt that she was trying to be patronizing, but that's how it sounded to me. I clutched the railing.

"I don't want to be a lawyer. And I don't want to be under a mountain of debt."

"It doesn't have to be law school. Anything."

"Our family's money is tied up in my father right now. I don't have anyone to pay my tuition for me or sponsor my trips around the world."

"Okay, Robin, you're being mean. I was just trying to be encouraging."

"It's none of your business." I was yelling under my breath, not wanting to get the attention of the guys. "I told you once that this was off-limits. Think of it like you're telling me I'm fat. It's not okay."

"I've never told you that you're fat."

"I know! That's not what I mean. I can't do this. I cannot."

I stomped away from Nizme, past the guys. Their body language lacked purpose without her at the table. I got the sense that they were like athletes resting between periods. I left the ladder swinging behind me and settled my bar tab with a crumpled twenty. When I was out of the bar area, Nizme yelled down, "Robin!"

At first, I didn't turn, but she yelled again, so I looked up exasperated and yelled, "What??"

"Can you give James a ride home? He took the bus here."

"Yeah, sure. Whatever. Send him down."

I walked across the space quickly with James working to keep up with me. I wasn't going to slow down and do him any favors. Daylight was gone and emergency lighting began to pop on around the factory. It didn't fully compensate and left large voids between the lit areas that made you disappear and reappear as you walked.

When we got to the car, James piped up.

"If it's too much trouble, I can take the bus."

"No, James. It's not you. Get in the car. It's fine."

"I could drive, too, if you want."

"Why? Oh. I'm not that drunk. I'm just upset."

James directed me over the highway to College Hill and down Thayer Street with neon signs and upscale, college friendly chains designed to look like one-offs.

"So how long have you known Nizme?" He was trying to make small talk. I guess he could sense the tension in the car.

"Too long. Why are you going home so early on a Friday night?"

"I have work tomorrow."

"You have a job? Rare among the privileged."

"I'm sorry if you had a bad night," he said, sincerely.

Thayer Street buzzed. The sidewalks ran over with packs of students. Even with the car windows closed, you could smell the clouds of perfume. I idled down, tapping the ball of my foot against the brake pedal. Blue public safety phones lit the quiet cross streets.

"Do you want to grab a drink?" he asked. "Vent a little bit?"

"Are you twenty-one, James?"

"None of the bars around here care. You just show your college ID and they let you in."

"Oh, fuck," I said, with sudden recognition. "You're the top hat guy."

"Umm?"

"That's your job. You do the tours. I've seen you."

"It's a work study gig."

"I went on your tour."

"Oh wow. Cool. I don't recognize you. You can park

wherever, my dorm's close by. And there's an English pub kind of place up on the right here."

The bar slinked up from its underground lair. A red awning with old-timey lettering announced itself at the street level. Parking off Thayer, I turned my rear view mirror down and slyly checked my makeup by the accessory lighting. I turned the mirror to show James. He looked held by the car seat like it was a large hand picking him up. The fucking top hat guy.

A pulsing heart attack of synths and drumbeats tripped up the stairs of the bar, audible from the car. The cardinal rule of Thayer street bars, which I had learned with Nizme and then forgotten, is that they're all the same. The signage – English pub, German bierhaus – is interchangeable facade. If the college students wanted techno dancing, then an English pub would give it to them.

I pictured the scene inside. Groups of sweaty bros moving through tight spaces with one polo shirt after another wiping across my arm like a human car wash. Shouting to be heard. Minutes of staring around in silence, the thoughts in those minutes confirming that life was not short, as the saying goes, but grossly, painstakingly long.

"Sorry, I can't do it," I said. "I'm done with those kinds of bars and I'm okay with being done with them. It's about the only thing good about getting older."

"Do you want to come to my dorm then?" He shifted in his seat, looking nervous and sort of surprised he'd asked. "I have some vodka leftover, I mean it's cheap..."

Someday, I suspect James will place that moment on an imaginary line documenting his maturation. "I was shy and puny in high school," he might say to his fiancée, "no girls would talk to me. Then in college, I sort of came out of my shell." But all he really did is learn that there is a small subset of people who will always say yes if you ask.

"How close do you live?" I asked.

"In the George street dorms."

"Is that close?"

"Pretty close."

"Okay."

The walk to his dorm proceeded hazily. I began a long, rambling story about Ariel, and how she's mad at me because I took my Dad out to bird watch in the snow and he got frostbite, and that I knew I shouldn't have but I just wanted to do something normal with him. And that I thought the snowy owl was beautiful but now I can see judgment in its yellow eyes when I picture it. It was one of those drunk-girl stories, aching with sought-after validation, that men endure when sex is dangling out ahead. Stories that even the teller knows aren't interesting because they contain prompts built into them. "Isn't that unfair?" "Do you see what I mean?" to which James responded "Yeah – definitely," afraid that answering too specifically would lead to more talking. At one point in the conversation he asked, "Does just one of your arms have glitter on it?"

We arrived at his dorm, a large brick building with grand stone steps. At the door, James turned his body and in one motion pressed his jeans pocket against the door's card scanner. The scanner beeped, and the door popped open effortlessly. He chuckled self-consciously, but in fact, I was awed at the ease with which this two-hundred-year-old building sprang to life, bowed, and allowed us in.

A few of the doors were cracked open, casting slices of television light onto the hallway floors. I ran my hand along the painted cinderblock walls. I had probably been in this hallway with Nizme years ago.

"Let me check for my roommate."

He cracked the door and pivoted into the dark room with the door open the minimum amount to allow his body through. The door shut behind him, leaving me leaning against the glossed walls of the hallway playing with the tassels of my purse. The hallway lights strobed fluorescence. A boy popped out of a nearby door wearing a towel and swinging a shower caddy. He glanced my way and continued down the hallway where he disappeared into another door.

"Robin," James said. I could see one eye in the crack of the door. "It'll just be one second."

"Listen," I started, "maybe."

"No, just wait," he said. "Please."

The tone of his voice startled me. "Okay," I said to the closed door. And that, in the end, is a perfect descriptor of my summer. A meek boy, with virginity still visible in his rear view, bossing me around because something in my body language told him that he could.

I waited for probably ten minutes, watching students enter and leave dorm rooms like floating specters. I could have left a hundred times. What kept me there for the full ten, more than James's instruction, was the thought of lying alone in my own bed, my mind spinning over Nizme, my father, Ariel, the snowy owl, with the only relief provided by Corey's mind-erasing construction sounds. Of warming up old coffee in the microwave and reading until dawn because good sleep, a finite resource, had all been reserved for people with college degrees, healthy relationships, and parents who remembered their names.

The door swung open, silent on its hinges, and instead of James, a bleary-eyed and bed-headed boy stomped out, a pillow held to his chest. I put a strand of hair behind my ear and entered the room, where James waited for me on his bed underneath his top hat hung from a plastic hook. A MacBook closed on his desk breathed light from its power indicator. I thought about another time, years ago, when I had visited Nizme and ended up in a boy's dorm. I remember that before I sat down on his bed with him, I commented on his computer monitor, which was thin and flat at a time when monitors took up half a desktop. "Present from the stepdad," he said casually. Then he sat down, tapped the spot on the bed next to him, and flipped off his desk lamp. Nothing changes, I thought, except the technology.

The only other light came from the hallway, and as I closed the door, it wiped across the room and extinguished. The last thing I saw was James swallow and relax his shoulders.

Fall

"And I'm conquered in a car seat,

Not a thing that I can do."

- Van Morrison

Chapter Five

MY DAD CHANGED a lot over the years; he wasn't one of those guys that got stuck in one particular era and froze. His jobs changed, his hair style changed, the sport he used as escape from my mother changed. But through it all, he watched and studied birds. A birder, he called it. When underlings at his company wanted to impress him, they would, when they discovered his love of birds, say with a puff of air, "Oh! An ornithologist!" But my dad never accepted that title. He never wanted anything from birds except to watch them.

So when I'd heard last February that a snowy owl had taken for its perch a desolate rock on a nature preserve in Middletown, I'd contacted the nurses and filled out the necessary paperwork to get Dad out for a day. This was his first, lower security nursing home near our mother in Massachusetts. I'd read about the bird in the Projo and ripped out the map insert that showed its current location. On the drive over, I'd pondered the similarities between the snowy owl and my father: both were away from their natural habitats, sitting stone-still in the same area for months, waiting away the day, hoping for night. For the snowy owl, night meant a chance to hunt for lemmings and rodents; for my Dad, it meant a chance to hatch a confused escape or some other mischief. The nursing home built a certain permeability into its spaces so that the patients wouldn't see or feel their bars, and my father, being younger and savvier than most of the dementia patients, often used cover of night to test just how permeable his cage was.

On the drive to the nature preserve, my father had tattered on and on about the snowy owl. Simply saying the words 'snowy owl' would cause a string of lucidity to spin out of him that is now, just months later, unthinkable.

"If a snowy owl is this far south, it's starving," he said. "Starving. The younger ones get pushed out if there's no food in the tundra."

He had his orange wool hat on, and an old pea coat. The nursing home had dressed him up for the cold, but they didn't know we'd planned to stay outside indefinitely. I still hadn't known all the rules of his nursing home and tended to give no more information than they required. The temperature had dropped that month, and in the uneven heat of my car our breaths escaped as streams of vapor that disappeared against warm pockets of air.

"I have the map from the paper," I said, handing him the ripped square of newspaper. "But I think we'll have to do a little searching to find him."

"Not even close," he said. "Birds are creatures of habit. He won't be more than twenty feet from this dot." He held the map gingerly at the edges, holding it up to careful examination with his tongue resting on the lower lip.

"He won't be hunting?" I asked. "Or at least scouting

out hunting spots for night?"

"If the bird is in Rhode Island, it's young, it's starving. It wants to be in the frozen tundra. Once it finds a spot on a rock, it'll stay there stock-still until nightfall." My father, in fingerless gloves, twittered his fingers in front of the heating vents as he spoke, nervous with energy. He occasionally touched at the side of his taut face, where a thin bruise ran from his sideburn to his chin. When he turned to me, I saw the thin bruise, a pale shadow of the larger mark that had once painted the entire side of his face. It was this patch of skin that had landed him in the nursing home. The last of many last straws. Problems even my mother couldn't ignore. Burned pans. Tumbles down the stairs. It's amazing how the clichés pile up at the end of a life.

We pulled into the small parking lot and opened the car door into a wide-open landscape. Several acres out ahead the ocean thrashed in the wind. My father's left boot was unlaced so I knelt down and tried to tie it as best I could. We trudged through the snow with the map out ahead of us, following along one of the old rock walls that stitch across the Rhode Island landscape. From the owl's perspective, we must have been no more than two smudges on the white landscape, making a pilgrimage to its altar. The hard snow made walking difficult, and we tried to step into existing footprints.

We arrived at an area stamped down to dirt by foot traffic. Seeing that it was a common watch point, we settled against a rock wall and had a quick breakfast of bagels and apple slices, all taken from the nursing home and wrapped in napkins. Sheltered by the wall, we were able to eat in peace with the wind whipping over our heads. Dad talked birds the entire time. He told me that he had named me for the American robin because I was born on an early spring morning. The deal he had with my mother was this: she would allow the name only if I arrived before my father saw the first robin of the season. He said he wanted my birth to be his first sign of spring. I obliged, just barely, because, in an oft-repeated bit of family lore, my father saw a real robin later that day in the garden of the hospital.

"From that day on, there was only one American Robin I cared about," he said, poking my jacket. "Just one."

I had heard this story before, of course, but he had lately told it with a growing frequency. It was one of the stories that I didn't minded hearing again and again.

I laid a blanket down over the slush. We turned around, knelt on the blanket and peeked our heads out over the rock wall. Until that moment, I hadn't realized just how dramatically the temperature dropped at the shore. The circling winds bit at the corners of my eyelids, and my hands grew stiff until I was forced to put gloves back on. The snowy owl sat still, a stuffed toy out on the glacial rocks.

My father, his face scarlet red, maintained his enthusiasm in the cold. He put the binoculars to his face with one hand and rested his chin on a rock to steady it. The whole time he talked at a manic pace about the owl. He sounded like my niece Maddy sputtering out amazing facts about dinosaurs.

"Wowie kazowie," he said. "He's a young male all

right. Look at that black barring around the feathers. He'll get whiter as he ages. Feathers on the talons, too. He doesn't feel a thing in this wind. He's probably warm. Robin, check out the yellow eyes."

Through the binoculars, the owl appeared in his true proportions, standing as tall as a toddler but wider. All those black-tipped white feathers. His beak, tiny by comparison to his size, pursed like disapproving lips. He stood and waited, yellow eyes motionless, as if he had waited for centuries and would wait for centuries more. He lifted one foot, then the other, playing a slow-motion game of potato on the frozen rock. Behind him, the ocean moved like a rioting crowd.

"Dad, he's incredible," I said. "He doesn't move an inch."

"He's a creature of habit," he said. "If he can find food here, in a month he'll try to make it back to his real home in the Arctic. This is a real find."

I had been so proud that I could give my father this pleasure that I allowed myself to ride on the feeling, eagerly letting a wave of it wash away my vigilance. It was easy to relax during spells like this when he looked and acted exactly like the father I knew. I asked him if he wanted me to try to get a picture of the owl before we left.

"Birders don't take pictures," he explained. "Once you start worrying about getting a good picture you stop seeing the bird. I'll write it up in my notebook."

"I don't think we have it, Dad," I said. "Should we wait until we get to the car?"

"It's important to do it now while we're really seeing it. Any paper will do. I can copy it later."

I dug a half-torn envelope and a pencil from my backpack and placed it on a hardcover copy of Jane Eyre that I had been carrying around. I gestured this makeshift desk setup toward him, and he replied casually with something that stopped me cold.

"Can you write it for me? I'm having trouble moving my hand."

I looked over at him. His right hand was on the rocks. Two of the fingers, exposed in fingerless gloves, had burrowed into a patch of snow between two of the rocks. Wind rippled over his red knuckles.

I scrambled over to him and pulled his hand out of the burrow. His ring and pinkie fingers were bluish. Bits of crystalline ice shook off and released their water onto the rock. I pulled my own gloves off and wrapped my sweating hands around his fingers, squeezing them.

"Dad, can you feel my hands?" I asked.

"What, honey?" he said. His face appeared serene and unlined. I tapped on the tips of his fingers.

"Can you feel this? Can you feel it?" I asked again.

"Feel what?" he asked.

"Feel this," I said, laying a quick punch into the palm of his left hand.

"Oh," he replied, "a little, I guess. Did you find my notebook?"

I released his hand and began gathering up our things, my hands moving slower than the brain controlling them. I threw the slushy blanket into my bag unfolded. Halfway through carefully picking up all of our food bags and placing them into small pockets, I shook myself out of it, took a breath to stop my tears, and attended again to my father who, to my surprise, had snapped right back into the same position, watching the bird while his hand rested in the same pile of snow. I pulled him off the rock by the collar of his peacoat and he snapped back surprised, as if he had noticed my alarm for the first time.

The snowy owl, with eyes that could spot a field mouse from the sky, must have looked out on us with equal wonder. An orange hunting hat peaked above the rock wall. A woman in a powder blue jacket flailing against a pristine white landscape. The two making a slow retreat back to the parking lot, marked by several dramatic pauses. The whole time, the owl moving no more than a single talon.

It wasn't until we were back in the car racing toward the nursing home that my father began to understand what had happened. I forced him to hold his fingers up against the car's air vents, and once the vents became full with hot, dry air, he recoiled in pain. He yelled that his fingers were itchy, that they hurt, that he couldn't feel them. He called me Ariel several times. He called me my mother once. I kept my hand on his knee the entire ride home, trying to soothe him as best I could with a low, slow voice. From the moment the hot air grazed his frostbitten fingers, his face puckered up with confusion and he lapsed back into the dementia patient that he was, in fits and starts, becoming.

When we arrived at the home, they wheeled him into the hospital that was thinly concealed from the residential section of the dementia ward. I thought this was a little dramatic. All they did was dip his frozen hand, which at the time resembled a claw, into bowl after bowl of warm water. It could have been done more comfortably in his room, but I guess they had their protocols. While I held his good hand, he wailed, as unaware as a child of what had caused his pain.

Once the seventh bowl of water had cooled, my father regained feeling and motion in his hand. In the end, he was scarred only with minor blackening at the tips of his pinkie and ring fingers. He lost feeling there, but it's just the tip, spots small enough that you have to work to find them. But there was a demarcation from that day. Afterwards, Dad tended to be worse, and his lucid spells tended to be shorter. Was his frostbite to blame? I can't say for sure. I wish I could say some positive memories remain from it, and that when I visit my dad, he won't shut up about the snowy owl. But he hasn't brought it up. I took a picture of the owl, as far in as I could zoom, when I knew he wasn't looking. I had it printed up and tacked onto the cork board in his bedroom, but after a while, it disappeared.

Chapter Six

THE SCRATCHING OF my notebook woke James. He had fallen asleep almost immediately afterwards. In a quick game of limb Jenga I untangled myself without waking him, sat up in his bed and wrote by the green light of the clock's LED. He slept with his face smudged into his pillow, a row of his curls fanned out in a seal around it. Sleeping the sleep of the innocent. I eyed the surfaces of the room, writing the details, the types of laptops, the brands of cologne. The name of every economics book stacked on his night stand, no matter how dry or nonsensical the title. I started to describe James. Was he a freshman, or a sophomore? Did I already ask that?

When James began to wake, I flipped my notebook and raised the lip of the sheet over my breasts.

"What are you doing?" he asked, his eyes slits. "Can't sleep?"

"Yeah."

He turned to me and propped himself up on one elbow. The row of curls bonneted his head.

"I had one of those sound dreams, you know?" he said. "Like when there's a buzzing fly in your dream, but it ends up being the sound of your alarm? This one had a tiger or some kind of big cat scratching on a stiff wooden post. Then I woke up and it was your pen."

"I was just writing."

"Diary?"

"Just some thoughts. Hey, are you a freshman or sophomore?"

"Freshman," he said. "This is a freshman dorm. What about you? Beside the book thing, are you in grad school or something?"

"Yeah," I said. Sure.

"I got the feeling you were older."

"Than I just said?"

"No. Older than me."

"Well duh, James."

"You know that stuff you said last night, no one's ever said those kinds of things to me before," he said.

He tried to play with my hand by placing his fingers inside my palm, but I shook him away.

"Let's not talk about it."

I pictured James below me, looking like the child he nearly was, his small hands fluttering over the new abundance he'd been given. Before we finished, something had changed. I found myself on top, and my mind started to wander. Sex stretches the boundaries of time while it's happening; it's amazing the number of things you can think about. I thought about Nizme and pictured her standing, then sitting, then standing again, with all of the boys following suit. A jolt of energy shuddered through me, and I began to go at James with a violent determination. Words came out of me that I had never said before. James's face changed as if something had fallen into his lap which he had long desired but not fully prepared himself for. It didn't take long after that.

But the words didn't sound so sexy running through my head in the pre-dawn hours. In fact, they made me feel pretty awful.

"Can I tell you something?" he asked.

"Depends. Is it about tonight?"

"No, and it's not a big deal really."

"So say it then."

"So...," he started. "I lied before. I do remember you from my tour. Only it was more than twice."

My body clenched.

"Maybe closer to three, four times."

"James."

"No, it's okay. I'm not judging. I just want to know: were you stalking me?"

"James."

"I've never had a stalker before. Or even have someone show interest in me, here anyway."

"I'm not a stalker. It's complicated."

"Okay. Sorry. I'm just saying, like, I wouldn't mind."

"Well, I would. I'm not a stalker."

The room had still been dark then, and I had the sensation that I was talking not to James but to a disembodied consciousness, or, even stranger, to myself. I squinted my eyes, trying to get a read on his face as he spoke, but there wasn't enough light for my eyes to adjust to.

"I've been going on a lot of tours lately," I said. "Not just yours. You know the lanky guy with the red beard?"

"Will."

"I've probably been on Will's tour more times than yours. No offense."

"He's really good – I can't hold a crowd the way he can."

"You're okay. You just need a smaller hat."

He chuckled. "Yeah, it's part of my shtick."

He let it sit for a moment, then asked, "Why so many tours?"

"I'm not entirely sure. After my work is done, I tell myself that I should walk over to Benefit Street and enjoy the weather. Then, once I'm there, I'm looking out for tours, and when I see one, I tell myself that I should go see who's doing the tour."

"Uh huh."

"Then once I'm with the group, I keep trying to peel myself away, but I get this pain in my stomach like a pebble is rolling around in there. Like I'm anxious that I'll miss a new fact. Eventually, I do peel off, and I feel like I've just had the wind knocked out of me. I sit on a bench by the river and try to write everything down. Then I go home, drink a bunch of coffee and write more. If I forget anything, I beat myself up about it. I don't know why. It's new. I don't understand it."

I waited for a response, but none came. Opening my eyes, I saw the same darkness as with my eyes closed. After quieting my body, I could hear faint rhythmic breath from James. He didn't gurgle, he didn't thrash on the pillow. He was freshly, brilliantly asleep.

I searched around the room, collecting my clothes by the light of my cellphone, then gathered my purse, necklace, two bracelets, earrings. Then, with extreme care,

I opened the door and slid out silently into the hallway, then to the street to my waiting car, which took me down silent streets back to my apartment. Cities are always waking up or going to sleep in stories, but at that hour, Providence wasn't doing anything. I didn't see a single person.

By the time I got to my door, I was so tired that I was already listing things that I wouldn't do before bed: brush my teeth, take off my clothes. I placed my house key into the rusted front door lock, leaning forward with exhaustion. The door responded to my turn with a disinterested click. I wriggled the key in the lock, then tried removing it fully and working it in. I pulled the key out and took a breath. Then I put its jagged end into my mouth to lubricate it. The metal felt cold and hard on my tongue. I put the key back in but the second try yielded no better results. I didn't know exactly how locks worked, but I pictured a rusted interior world, like an undersea shipwreck in miniature.

After a third try, I lost my patience and began beating on the door with my forearms and kicking the house's siding, channeling all of my frustrations into the uncaring wood. I threw open the storm door and let it slam closed, casting a hard echo out onto the street. Finally, deflated, I walked over to the wicker love seat on the side of the porch and collapsed into it. I curled my knees up to my chest and wrapped my arms together, warming one against the other. My forearms had thin streaks of blood from pounding on the door, the scratches making an apt memento of a sad night. I switched positions, hanging my legs over the arm rest. It felt like forever before I fell asleep.

Chapter Seven

WHEN I OPENED my eyes the next morning, Corey was standing above me with his head eclipsing a low morning sun. Light flared around the edges of his head, darkening his face and making any expression difficult to discern.

"You're alive," he said. "That's good."

"Where am I?" I asked.

"On your porch."

He shifted his body to one side, revealing the full power of the morning sun. I slung an arm over my face to block it.

"Move back to where you were," I whimpered. The sun triggered a hangover that scraped like rusty nails across my brainpan. Corey moved his head back into its position between the sun and myself.

"Are your forearms bleeding?" he asked.

I opened my eyes to slits and let them adjust.

"Please, whatever you do, don't move from that spot," I said.

"Rough night?" he asked.

My eyes felt cottony, a consequence from sleeping with my contacts in. I could tell from his body language that it was difficult for Corey to avoid being in motion. He shook in tiny increments that he actively worked to reign in.

"Your bed was so close," he said as if I hadn't realized it.

"It's my fucking door lock. It keeps freezing up."

I stretched my legs out and draped them over the wicker armrest. They had been curled all night, and I could feel the blood returning to where it had been cut off.

"Give me your key, I'll try it," he said.

I reached into my purse, which was draped over the arm of the love seat, and handed him the jagged cluster of keys.

"I'm going to have to move from where I'm standing."

"That's fine," I said. "I deserve it."

I closed my eyes. He pivoted toward the door, and my eyelids lit up with orange cobwebs of veins. Corey wrestled with the lock out of view, producing the same discouraging thuds that greeted me the previous night.

"What time is it?" I asked.

"10:45."

"Jesus."

"I waited a while before coming over here. I was worried you weren't going to wake up."

He grabbed the door handle and shook the door.

Corey muttered to himself. "Let's see: floors, trim, lunch...I have ten minutes." Then to me, "I'll be right back."

Corey came back shortly after leaving, holding a large cordless drill in one hand and a blue-handled screwdriver in the other. By then I had turned into the love seat, away from the sun, and pulled my small spiral notebook out of my pocket to finish what I had started in James's room. I tried to scratch as much down as I could, knowing I could always flesh it out later, but that soon the finer details would be gone.

"How anal is your landlord?" Corey shouted from the front door. I put the notepad aside.

"I met the guy once when we first moved in."

"Well, this lock is completely rusted up," he said. "Is he the kind of guy that fixes things quickly?"

"He's never fixed anything," I said.

"Okay, that's all I needed to know," he said.

I heard his drill fire up and begin to crush itself into the metal innards of the lock. Within the metal on metal screech, I heard a plink plink plink, like cans being shot off a wall. He progressed slowly considering the width of the lock. Plink plink plink. Finally, the drill made a sound like an animal unleashed, and he pulled it out with slow care. He inserted the flathead screwdriver and jiggled it until the deadbolt retreated into the door with a satisfying shloomp.

"So this is your new key," he said, handing me a flathead screwdriver and tossing my keys onto the love seat. I held the screwdriver by its milky blue handle, rubbing a thumb down the tapered edge like it was a rabbit's foot.

"Thanks," I said. "Wow."

Corey stood in front of me, his head resuming its planetary position. His phone buzzed inside his pocket, and he pulled it out.

"Hey, would you mind if I did some pushups on your porch?"

"Pushups?"

"It's just - it's time to do pushups. I know it's weird."

"Yeah, I mean..."

"Thanks."

He dropped down and began grunting. I swung my legs off the love seat and faced him head on, watching him lift his body until the space between his arms became a trapezoid. He grunted lightly each time his chin touched the porch.

"So do you always do this at the same time?"

He didn't respond, instead continuing to inflate and collapse the space between his arms. When he finished, he stood tall, a first bloom of sweat across his dark eyebrows. It was the first time I could see him up close without the sun darkening his face. He was all angles. It was the kind of face made to be clean-cut, but it wasn't, like a carefully spaced garden gone untended. He had bushy eyebrows, uneven stubble, and salt deposits from sweat outlining his sideburns. Specks of white, either paint or dust, coated his browned arms. Despite all this, his shirt was perfectly white and clean as a freshly washed sheet.

I have to admit that I found him as attractive as I thought I would when I could only see him from across the street. Visually at least, he was striking in the angles of his face and in the shape and proportions of his body. I say visually because there was something pedestrian about Corey that made him hard to connect with at first. He didn't make direct eye contact when he spoke, and his mind was clearly elsewhere. I thought that I could objectify as well as the next girl but for me, in the end, attraction lives and dies in the mind.

Just after it had become awkward that he didn't respond, he responded.

"I do pushups," he said. "Between house projects."

His phone buzzed again.

"Speaking of which. I'm glad I could be helpful. Take care."

"My name's Robin."

"Oh, okay. I'm Corey."

"Thanks again, Corey," I said, saying his name like I was trying it on, like I didn't know it already from the mixed up mail and light internet stalking.

"Wait," I said. "What are you working on today?"

"Crown molding in the bathrooms."

"Do you need help? If you don't-"

"You know, I've got it worked out. I set aside enough time to finish it alone. Thanks, though."

I started to talk, but he was gone, already halfway across the street. I'd watched him throughout the summer, and I knew that he was returning to a house where dozens of tools sat, foreign to me and uncatalogued in my notebook. Corey would take up those tools against hundreds of different materials, the names of which bloomed inside my brain. Words that are hard-nosed scientific but also mysterious. Gypsum board. Mastic. I rubbed my temples, keeping the hangover at bay. What I would have given to get up and run after him, or past him even, straight into the soothing cacophony of his projects. But instead, I inched back into the dead silence of my house, the door popping open at the turn of a screwdriver.

I napped off my hangover in bed, did a few hours of eBay maintenance, then went to bed for the night. Brushing my teeth in front of the mirror, I noticed that I still had indentations in my skin where I had slept across the wicker. The undersides of my arms and thighs showed complex braiding as if I'd lain across thick rope. But by the next morning, it had faded. It just takes time.

Chapter Eight

I SPENT THE next few days loafing around the apartment, feeling despondent. Any excuse to stay inside was embraced without scrutiny. More than once a mug of coffee twirled in the microwave late at night while I reorganized sales forms at the kitchen table. Emails came in from Ariel, colluding about our mother's upcoming visit for Thanksgiving. How could we get her to visit our father? Should we go too? Should we just drop her off? I ignored them. The clock on the wall ticked off seconds, and as the days passed, the seconds felt longer and longer apart until I feared time would stop altogether and I would be forever stuck in the fall of 2009. At one point, practically hallucinating with boredom, I pictured myself bobbing dangerously on a high, thin tree limb. Looking back to the trunk, far enough away to be obscured by fog, I could see hundreds of other branches, some of them more than sturdy enough. I stepped a foot onto one, felt its sway run up my leg, and took a cautious step backwards.

I pictured a fall morning a few years ago. I'm sitting at the kitchen table of the house I grew up in, packets of paper spread across the thick slab of oak. Their envelopes carry postmarks from every corner of the country. Glossy magazines inside show groups of beautiful, ethnically mixed students. I am poring over them, adding data to a spreadsheet, which I am very proud about, thinking correctly that I am being mature for my age. Like the materials in Corey's house, the words I write down are concrete but elusive: Symbology. Aesthetics. I write the word mythology and my cursor pulses at the end of the line. I say the words to myself, luxuriating in each syllable.

The rattle of teacups in the china cabinet means someone is coming down the stairs. That's what I remember most about our house: how the rattling of knickknacks pinpointed a person's location as precisely as GPS. Our mother placed cabinets and curios everywhere and as a result, each room contained over-stuffed worlds trapped behind glass. Was it my mother coming down the stairs? Once my father started to degenerate, my mother's sleep schedule slipped until 1 PM, then 2 PM. At her worst, she was getting up in time for me to put dinner on the table. Ariel? She was out of the house already, living in London with John on one of his temporary work assignments. I saw pictures of their travels through email, always with Ariel sideways, displaying her baby bump to the Eiffel Tower or whichever landmark she was visiting that weekend.

On this day, it's my father rattling the teacups. He has come down in a bathrobe. This was early in his decline when he was still lucid until proven guilty. Instead of watching him like a hawk, I decide to use the rattling of the knickknacks to keep tabs on him. When my spreadsheet is complete, I sort it by major, then ranking, then location. I'm looking at the locations; some of them

I've heard of and others I haven't. Their names make me think of mountains with snowy peaks, cresting blue waves, and wet forests lush with pine tar. Then I picture a guy that I've assembled from pieces of each catalogue, one that doesn't exist at my high school. I picture him wrapped in white sheets in a small, sunny room, a cup of coffee in his hand. And then I hear my father scream.

I snapped back to reality and banged on my kitchen table, sending sales papers floating to the ground. "Goddamn it!" I yelled aloud to no one. "Enough!" I'd spent the whole summer letting the world happen to me, and I was sick of it. Boys. Friends. Family. Providence. All were free to reach inside and reconfigure my insides to their specifications. Sometimes even my business felt this way: it wasn't me but my all-powerful scanner running the show.

The next morning, I walked over to Corey's house with a notebook in hand and a rare fire in my stomach. He answered the door holding a crowbar in each hand.

"Robin. What..." He was practically vibrating with energy, energy that he looked annoyed to be wasting at the door.

"Hi, sorry to bother you."

"What's up?"

"You mentioned the other day that you were doing some house work?"

"I'm working on a cracked ceiling today. Plaster."

"Oh wow. That's a coincidence. I have a similar issue over at my house. The ceiling above my bed is all cracked like a spiderweb. I'm afraid it's going to collapse on me while I'm sleeping."

"You don't have to worry - it won't collapse. The way the horsehair plaster mushrooms behind the lathe board is pretty strong. Worst that happens is it cracks and looks ugly."

"I'm pretty sure it's going to collapse. I just have this feeling."

"Okay."

"I thought that maybe I could help you and like, learn so that I can do it myself."

"It's not really a two-person job."

I wanted to point out that he was holding two crowbars, but I didn't.

"Or maybe I could just watch?"

He turned and looked inside the house.

"Yeah okay, fine. But come in, I'm behind already."

He turned around to enter the house, and I tried to hide a smile as I crossed the threshold. It wasn't seizing the day, and it wasn't taking fate into my hands. But it wasn't sitting alone in my kitchen or waking up naked in a freshman dorm room, either.

He led me through the foyer into a tall room with a framed entryway. Small piles of wood and mechanical junk covered the rough, wide-beamed wood floors. I saw springs and rusty gears. Every three feet or so a power tool waited to be picked up: circular saws, drills, Sawzalls. A rubber tube, extruding from a humming compressor, snaked around some tools, under drop cloths and onto a dusty chair, where a fully loaded nail gun vibrated like a purring cat.

"Is that nail gun on?" I asked.

"Oh. Yeah." He traced the line back to the air pump

and flipped the toggle switch. The room went quiet. "They don't fire unless they're pressed up against something," he said. "You weren't in any harm."

"Were you using it today?"

"I think so. What's in your other hand?" he asked.

"Notebook. In case I learn something." I smiled.

"No, the other hand."

"Oh. It's a French press. For coffee." I had brought it over with me.

"I always have coffee on."

"I'm a little picky about my coffee."

He just sort of looked at me.

"Okay. I'm going to head up and get back to work."

"I'll be up soon."

The kitchen, back behind the staircase, was a disaster. Fine sawdust coated an expanse of stained vinyl flooring. Paint-splattered drop cloths covered every surface except for the cabinets, which were chipped and yellowing. I found an aluminum pot, dusted it with the corner of my shirt, filled it with hot water, ignited the burner, and waited. The first days in Corey's house, I walked around on my tiptoes. I didn't touch things unless I needed to, and when I needed to open a cabinet or move a hammer I used the end of my shirtsleeve as a glove.

Industrial sounds greeted me at the top of the stairs. First, a sharp metal ping, then a gentle crumble, like a body folding to the floor. Ping. Crumble. Ping. Crumble. I balanced the French press on the banister and un-looped the mug from my thumb.

The room had been cleared, its contents spilled out into the hallway. Inside the door, Corey stood kabuki-style with a crowbar held over his head, a hammer hanging loosely in his other hand. He spoke from behind a cotton breathing mask.

"There's a mask in the dresser drawer in the hallway. Just don't stand over me while I'm working, this stuff is cement, and it falls hard."

A jagged piece of ceiling lay on the drop cloth next to Corey like an accident victim. On the ceiling above, an exposed swath of brittle pine lathe allowed a slitted view into the attic. I didn't know that it was pine lathe at the time - Corey taught me all that. Before I met him, I could barely identify a door handle. I tried to pick up the piece of ceiling but found it weighed even more than it looked. Small, stiff pieces of what looked like hair gave the cement a fuzzy edge.

"That's horsehair plaster," Corey said. "Any house built before the 50s not made out of stone or marble had it."

"And it's real horsehair?"

"Yeah, from the tail. Mixed in for strength."

He walked to the opposite end of the room. A piece of cracked-out plaster hung down like an angled stalactite.

"It probably won't fall on its own, but it won't be hard. So I put the edge of my pry bar into the crack, the side with the severe angle, and hit it with my hammer."

"God, that's so loud."

"I got some earplugs if you want" - he was shouting - "So you keep. Hitting it. Once you can fit your bar in there, put the other side in, the one with the gentle slope, and hit it away from you. See how it's coming loose?"

He kept whacking at it, generating a sound that

resembled hundreds of golf balls being struck in unison. Pieces of plaster the size of dimes and smaller pattered onto the drop cloth. I wondered then why a drop cloth would be necessary when the rubble could be swept and picked right up off the wood floor. As I wondered this, a small iceberg of plaster crashed to the floor, shaking my vision.

"Can I do that?" I asked. "I want to do that."

"I guess you could, but we have to stay on opposite sides so we don't drop plaster on each other."

He handed the pry bar to me, gentle end first, and I grabbed it like I was shaking hands with it. The only way to describe its weight was substantial. The ends had been wrapped with rubbery black tape. It looked like a prop from a zombie film - I liked it right away.

It took five minutes of serious whacking to dislodge the lowest hanging, most delicate piece of ceiling. He didn't have another hammer so I used a rubber mallet, which didn't make the same terrible sound. It was satisfying work, watching platters of plaster fall and explode on the drop cloth. I swung the hammer until it felt normal to hold my arms above my head and strange to rest them at my sides. At one point a momentum took over, transforming my precise strikes into a wild, flailing attack. My hair became stringy with sweat and stuck to my mask. After finishing a particularly long row, I hit the crowbar one last time with a furious swing and sent a square of plaster crashing down on the opposite side of the room. At this, Corey dropped his pry bar, removed his safety goggles, and looked at me with something like awe. My only breaks consisted of quick walks out of the room to refuel on coffee, which I kept on the banister, covered with a paper plate to protect it from dust.

After we dislodged the largest pieces, the leftover bits of plaster had to be removed from between the strips of lathe. 'Plaque,' Corey called it, and it was like clearing snow from a driveway with a spoon. Individual pieces of lathe, and there were hundreds of them, had to be scraped of the smallest bits until the boards showed clean. But once I dedicated myself to finishing the job, time disappeared. Corey suggested I work from a corner outward, and just in that first corner alone I lost an hour. I took a flathead screwdriver down each lathe board, scraping away microns of plaster until each became like a map of an area I knew well. After I completed a board, I felt as though I had left part of myself up there tucked into the lathe where some future home refurbisher could dig me out. They would rip into the by-then ancient drywall, eager to replace it with some futuristic material, and there I'd be, a piece of me anyway, tumbling down from the attic.

Corey worked with a focus that made me look lazy and weak by comparison. In the hour of plaque-clearing, he had a pyramid-shaped area twice the size of mine cleared. I couldn't find a speck of white dust on that ceiling. He rarely tipped his head down from the ceiling. He never took breaks. But every hour his phone would buzz and he'd drop to the ground for pushups, counting each time the sweating tip of his nose tapped the floor. Afterwards he would leave and come back into the room as fast as I could blink, wearing a fresh white T-shirt. Responses to my questions came in two- and three-word bites, but they weren't clipped or gruff. He wasn't bothered by my talking because mentally he wasn't there; his mind was somewhere between the slats.

By the end of the job, we were caked in plaster. Granola-sized bits bonded to my scalp like lice. A fine coating powdered my arms. Thank god for the drop cloth, without which the floor would have been transformed into a pocked moonscape. I asked him about lunch, and he said "Nah, not for me. You can, though. Take anything you want from the freezer, I'm one ahead for the month." I didn't know what he meant, but he said it with such nonchalance that I felt stupid questioning it. He also said freezer, not fridge, and afterwards I understood why: the fridge contained one container of coffee and three bottles of hot sauce. By comparison, the freezer was a filing cabinet: six high and three deep with Tupperware. Each container carried a masking-tape-and-Sharpie label of a date and lunch/dinner. I grabbed lunch from last Tuesday and defrosted it in the microwave. That was what he meant by "one ahead." Apparently he hadn't eaten last Tuesday.

After lunch, I decided to give myself a tour of the house before heading back to work. The wreckage of the place was painterly in its detail. Pieces of ceiling had been removed due to water damage. The downstairs sitting rooms had nicotine-faded floral wallpaper, matched on the light and outlet covers and set against small patches of bright purple wallpaper. These second layers of wallpaper were exposed after Corey had removed electric heaters from underneath the windows. I scratched at the corner of a printed lilac and revealed the hint of a third level of wallpaper. In his house, you could literally peel back time.

Some of the baseboards, which were tall and beautiful and painted so many times that they resembled glazed donuts, had been removed and leaned against the wall with rusty nails facing outward. Corey didn't start one project at a time. At some point in the near past, he had started them all.

I walked the stairs, which were riddled with staple holes from carpeting that was now rolled into a furry pile in the hallway. At the top of the stairs, I stepped over a paint-caked rubber mallet and faced three doors set at angles like mirrors in a dressing room. Corey worked in one room, while the other was empty save an old couch. The center door was closed and locked. Its natural wood varnish and inlaid detail work stood out from the other, more traditional two-panel white doors. I guessed that it would lead me to the turret with rounded glass windows, the one I'd so admired from afar.

A quiet swear from Corey led me back into his room. He had cleaned the lathe boards such that you could see clear through to the attic. Now he was tugging at a trash can filled with a mere three inches of plaster, unable to move it. I took a tug, and the only thing that happened was the mouth of the plastic barrel stretched into an oval.

He exhaled. "You forget it's cement until you try to move it."

He picked out a few pieces so that there was only about an inch of plaster in the barrel. He pulled from the handle, and it moved, slowly.

"This is going to take all night," I said.

"Yep. Well, I better get started."

My arms felt like jelly, but I didn't want to stop.

Though I had beat the grime off myself earlier, the fluttering dust in the room had already floured me anew. I suddenly felt that I wanted to sweat again, and keep sweating until every granule of plaster had been mopped up.

"Let me help."

"You can go," he said. "I'll deal with it."

I pursed my lips. Something about the way he said it gave me the feeling that I was being dismissed. Normally I would have walked right home, but this time, I stopped short. A physical feeling of not wanting to leave overcame me.

"I don't want to go home, okay? I can't. Can I just finish the job with you?"

His eyes became alert, detecting that emotion had suddenly entered the room. Having discovered this, he was eager to remove it.

"Yeah, of course. Sure. Okay. Let's wait until the dust settles, though."

"Ha," I said, relieved. "Very funny."

"What?"

"'Dust settles,' it's a phrase."

"Oh. I meant it literally." He waved his hand across the dust, creating currents in the air. "There's all this dust." I slapped my palm against my forehead.

"Let's go outside."

We spent a moment in his back yard, Corey drinking water from a chipped mug and me drinking another cup of warm coffee. A Portuguese woman hung her upper body out of a third-story window next door and shouted, "You run the saw tonight?"

"Not late, no. I'm sorry."

"My husband, he cannot sleep through all the racketing."

Her nightgown billowed in the wind. I didn't know her name, but I had seen this woman from living in the neighborhood, and I knew that she didn't have a husband.

"I'm sorry. If I'm too loud, please let me know. Don't call the cops. No police."

"No no, no police," she said. "But no saw, no drill."

"Okay. Yes."

She ducked her head down and backed into her house, her loose bun of frayed hairs catching on the sash.

"She's a nice enough lady," he said. "But she's a liar. She doesn't have a husband. She lives alone in the whole building; the first and second floor apartments are empty."

"What is this?" I asked. There was a covered car in the driveway. From the exposed wheels, I could tell that it was a BMW.

"That," he said, removing a buzzing phone from his pocket. "That's from another life. Let's go back inside."

In the end, we only cleared half of the room that night. I put plaster into the barrels, two inches max, and Corey carried them down the stairs and onto the back of his truck. Fortunately, we had six trash barrels between us. After filling up his truck, we drove into Olneyville and emptied it into a dumpster behind a chicken restaurant. I offered to stand a watch, but he just looked at me, as if to ask, who's going to care, the guy working at the chicken restaurant? On the drive back I reached my arm, sore and throbbing, through the back window and held the stacked barrels. From my view out the back, Providence's seedier neighborhoods unspooled away from me, as if all of the rusted metal gates, bus shelters, and cracked asphalt had been rolled up on the back of Corey's truck. By the time we returned to his driveway it was well into night. He paused a beat between turning the car off and opening his door, and in that moment I thought I saw him smile. I'm still not sure if he really smiled or if I just saw what I wanted to see. Regardless, I took this as a signal and reached across the center console, grabbing his leg with a conspiratorial smirk.

"What are you doing?" he asked. Corey was suddenly very present in a way he hadn't been all day. I snapped back my hand.

"I thought..."

"Listen," he said. "I didn't mean to lead you on. I have more work to do. I don't have time...I'm sorry. I don't have time." He left his truck and walked back into the house as if pulled by a wire.

"Well, can I come over tomorrow?" I yelled, but he was already inside. I let waves of awkwardness wash over me. I realize now that I had grabbed Corey's leg on instinct, but it was a false instinct, a groove dug in over the summer months when a guy grabbing my leg had become as normal a way to end the night as curling up with a book.

Fortunately, I didn't have much time for pity because I was wiped out. Halfway through my shower, I was so tired that I sat down underneath the showerhead and watched the precise strings of water spray against my toes. Afterwards I toweled off, but just partially. Still wet, I trudged into the bedroom naked with my dirty clothes over my shoulder. While emptying my pockets onto my nightstand I came across my notebook, which I hadn't written in all day. For the briefest of moments, I considered what I should write. Then I sent it spinning across the room. My bed caught me like an open hand, and I fell into a dreamless, pulverizing sleep.

Chapter Nine

THE NEXT DAY I showed up at Corey's door, and he handed me a carpenter's square. He didn't bring up the night before. He didn't even look at me, really. Somewhere in the back room of his mind, Corey was queuing up projects: materials, tools, procedures. I walked into his house before the screen door shut and with that, I began my short career as his assistant, un-hired and un-asked for. It happened just like that.

I visited him nearly every night after work. I'd pull into my driveway around dusk, stopping with enough force to send books flying from the back seat into the center console. Inside my house, a packaging spree commenced, with all the day's book sales fanned out across the table. Packaging complete, I swept the long strings of foul-smelling tape and splinters of paper refuse from cut shipping labels into a trash can and immediately headed for the door. Before crossing the street, I'd toss the packages like footballs into my car's rolled down window. Then I'd be at Corey's door.

I helped him tile his downstairs bathroom. Corey handed me each tile, square and roughly the size of a dinner plate, which I dry-fit onto the bathroom floor. "Back your way out of the room, like a bank robber," he explained. "Full tiles first, then we'll go back and dry-fit the cut pieces." I marked the cut tiles with a grease pencil that I kept in my ear. Corey lined up the markings with the blade of his wet saw and sent the tile through it. Piece by piece, I covered the room in cream-colored tiles. Corey slopped down the mastic, fanned it out with a notched trowel, and put the tiles on loosely. Then I took over, holding each tile by its corners and gently pressing it downward like I was rocking it to sleep.

"Make sure every tile touches all of the spacers," he said. "Look back there. Wait, oh no." He jumped over my legs and stretched himself so that he could make a final adjustment. "That one was almost dry. Careful."

One night his doorbell rang, and when we opened the door, three small children greeted us under the porch light. One was dressed as President Obama, and the other two wore their pajamas. Neither of us knew it was Halloween. We didn't have costumes, but with all of our equipment and our mud-stained shirts, we may have fooled the children for zombies. I searched, but Corey's cabinets came up dry. It was the first time I'd seen him laugh. I came back in and shook my head.

"Nothing?" he asked.

"Not even hot sauce."

We sent them away and turned the porch light off. After that, he said something that gave me pause. Riffing on the Obama costume, I brought up some current event: probably the bailouts, and he very casually said, "I don't know anything about it." Then he gestured beyond his peeling walls. "That's all out there. It doesn't matter in here."

Corey never called for me, but when I showed up, he always let me in. When he hung drywall on a ceiling, the one we'd destroyed, I was there working the drywall hoist, spinning the crank with a sleeve pushed up. Not because he asked me to, or because he even wanted me to, but because I was there. With the drywall pinned against the ceiling, Corey set a dozen screws around the perimeter of the drywall. He had serious concerns about the strength of the lathe, and each time I lowered the hoist we shared a moment of silence as we willed the board to hold with our eyes. When he had me lie across the hoist, applying tape to the drywall joints, I asked, "Isn't this how Michelangelo painted the Sistine Chapel?" and waited for a chuckle or a witty response. And kept waiting.

At night, I'd walk home and fall into bed, the last bits of me draining out onto the mattress as I drifted off to sleep. One night, too tired even to shower, I collapsed into bed with mud in my hair and woke up on a pillow stained with brown splotches. Confronted with this mess the next night, I solved the problem by flipping the pillow over. I never dreamed during these deep sleeps, and I didn't want to. During October and November, I maybe wrote five entries in my notebook, and during one of them I had fallen asleep while writing. To give some perspective, from May through September I had filled roughly one moleskin a week. I found one quote of any substance in my notebook from that time. It read: *Corey will not do electrical work! Finally, something Corey will not do. He said "I'm not crazy. That stuff can kill you."*

That fall, on a rare outing from Corey's house, I saw

an art piece at the RISD museum titled "A Box with the Sound of its Own Making." Quite simply, it was a small pine box the size of a toaster with raw edges and a small brass clasp. From inside the box, a small sound device played a recording of the artist making the box. It immediately reminded me of Corey. I got the sense that it was the making that was important to Corey more than the end product itself. But for a long stretch of time I didn't know why, because I didn't know anything about him. I knew that I couldn't get him to leave the house, even to get dinner. I knew that he spent one day each month preparing food for the whole month, labeling each day and placing it in the freezer. I knew that when I made another awkward attempt to kiss his finely dusted neck, he pulled away, saying, "Do you know how much sanding we have left to do?" That's all I knew.

On rare nights when I didn't work with Corey, I sat out on my porch like I had each summer night. As the fall nights got colder, I bundled up to stay out past dark. My legs dangled over the porch railings, separated from the splintered wood by all color of leggings that were so popular then. I tried valiantly to catch up on work. Some nights I skimmed through my book inventory list, trying to determine which books were simply not going to sell and had to be liquidated. More than once I nodded off in the middle of work and woke up when my head hit my laptop. When my heavy head rose from the laptop I would be presented with the sight of Corey's house: the chipped blue paint, the molding fascia boards, all that gothic decay. Through one window or another, I could always see Corey shuttling through the space, doubling back, reaching his hands up like he was performing a one man play. I smiled each time, thinking that this sequence of events was a river, and that like a river it was always there for me now, available to dip my toe into.

Chapter Ten

I WORRY THAT I'm not giving a full picture of Corey. He had negative traits, which I think I've more than shown. Stubbornness. Apathy. Maybe even agoraphobia. But at the same time, he could be so kind, a kindness that he didn't need to conjure up because it was inherent in him. You could see it in the way he held a slab of pine baseboard and gently ran a calloused thumb down it, checking for straightness. Or the careful way that he handled his tools. Or that, when his phone told him to eat, he always brought my food without asking, wrapped with an extra napkin that he denied himself. When you talked to him, and he wasn't preoccupied, he stood so still to listen that his face became a stone mask. Deep down none of his shortcomings were intended to be vicious. Each time he was rude, his brain had simply deferred to the higher authority of his daily routine.

It was the routine running the show. At first, I accepted it, enjoying the brain-clearing, endorphin-releasing aspects of Corey's home improvement odyssey and accepting his rigid ways as a cost of doing business. But it didn't take long for me to start rubbing up against it, this routine that was like a thick wool coat, welcome in a chill but frighteningly itchy.

It started when I began sleeping at his house. Our first night together was chaste, a result of inertia rather than intent. I felt, or convinced myself, that I didn't have the energy even to walk across the street and collapse into my own bed, so instead I collapsed into his. When I asked, it felt strange, a girl asking for permission to sleep in a guy's bed. But he was practical-minded, and it just made sense. Despite the unseasonably warm air wafting in through windows, I wore a hooded sweatshirt to bed. Corey came in, shrugged off his shirt and removed his dark jeans. He sat on the edge of the bed and spun his legs around and into the comforter. I walked to the other side of the bed and tentatively dipped a foot in between the sheets, then followed with the other. Just like that, we were under the sheets together. "If I make noise or anything, just shove me," he said. I lay there, immediately reminded of how much heat another body generates. Over the first hour, I pulled off my hooded sweatshirt, peeled off my socks and shimmied out of my pants until finally I was Corey's equal in underwear and a T-shirt. I turned onto my side, the only way I can fall asleep, and tossed an arm over Corey's midsection. For a minute it lay there, dead as a fallen tree branch. But before I fell asleep, he took the arm and curled it in around him and nuzzled back into my body until my sweating knees made contact with the cool backs of his thighs.

After that night, I slept in my underwear, undressing and hiding in the sheets while Corey brushed his teeth. By the third night, I became self-conscious that he hadn't tried so much as a fake-accidental caress over my bra. Once, after he'd tucked in my arm, I tried to move my hand down seductively, or at least suggestively, but he had already fallen asleep. I tried the same move the next night knowing that he was awake, but I got rebuffed. He didn't say anything; he just bent my elbow and shifted my hand back up. That whole time I don't think he saw so much as a bare leg. I would have loved to show someone my leg. The work I'd done with Corey, and the ascetic lifestyle that accompanied it, had slimmed me down. I resembled my high school self, with energy to match.

When I woke up in the mornings, Corey was always already up. My eyes would open, daylight fumbling through the curtain-less windows, and Corey would be gone. The only traces he left behind were white T-shirts: the one he had slipped out of and left on the floor, the still-open drawer where he had selected that day's shirt, and the stacks of them, waiting in a laundry basket like fresh reams of paper.

The morning of our first fight, Corey brought me breakfast in bed. I was sitting against the headboard, reading a newspaper with my arms tucking the cream comforter over my breasts. Though I had the paper up, I couldn't concentrate, and I kept reading the same line over and over again. Ariel and I had just gone over Thanksgiving plans for the next week, and my head was spinning. Our family operates at a high level of dysfunction, but when the holidays come we sound the alarm and fall into a lockstep formation. The conversation had started out badly. She told me that Mom had already gotten to her house for an extended pre-Thanksgiving stay. This put me into a mild rage. "Why doesn't anyone tell me anything??" Then she asked that I check one of her unopened emails or untouched voicemails, which shut me right up. She had good news and bad news.

Good news: "I brought up the hospital and said we were going on Sunday. She didn't walk back into her room like she usually does. She just nodded. I don't know what that means, but maybe she'll come with us."

And the bad news: "She's with the girls right now, getting them ice cream. It's the first time she's left the house since she got here, and the third time she's left the guest room."

She asked me if I had planned on visiting Dad anytime soon and I said that I was, on Saturday. She wanted me to bring up Mom a lot in conversation to prime him for Sunday. "And also to take his temperature," she said. "See what the chances are he'll remember her. If that goes well, the next step is Thanksgiving."

"Okay," I said. "But it sucks that we have to try to make this perfect environment for her. I'm starting to sour on this idea that we have to convince her to visit her own husband."

"Well, you shouldn't, because it's the only way we'll have a chance at being a normal family."

Pretending to read the newspaper, I turned this over in my mind. *Our only chance at being a normal family.* It seemed absurd that our well-being should hinge on something so fragile. I felt her phrasing was flawed in two ways: that normal was an ideal state, and that we had a fighting chance of achieving it.

Corey came into the room, the bottom of his T-shirt bouncing along the elastic of his boxer briefs.

"Breakfast time," he said, underhand-tossing me a round Tupperware container with a screw-on lid. "Lots to do today."

"For you maybe. I've got book stuff until at least four." I scrutinized the Tupperware label. "Let's see. Week two, meal seven. Mmmmm."

He sat on the edge of the bed and dipped his spoon into the mixture of vegetables. "It's not bad." Then he got quieter than usual, and I could tell something was wrong. When I asked him what he had planned for the day he gave me clipped answers. "The usual." "Some floor stuff." Finally, I asked, "Is something wrong?"

"No, why?" He asked with mock surprise. He was so bad at hiding his mood.

"Come on - what's up?"

He considered his words. "I didn't, uh, see that newspaper last night. When did you bring it in?"

I lowered the newspaper and laid it open across my tented knees.

"It's yesterday's Projo. I had it in my bag. I like reading in bed when it's raining."

"I know that..." He was carefully forming his words now, with a big calloused thumb pressed against his temple. "I know I didn't say this to you, so it's no big deal, but I have a rule against newspapers and magazines in the house. I'm not holding it against you this time because you didn't know."

"Oh good."

I wasn't feeling very meek that morning, so I decided to say what was actually on my mind.

"I'm sorry, but that's insane. Is it an environmental

thing, like you're against paper waste?"

"No, you know I don't care about that."

"Well, that would have been the least insane answer. What is it then?"

But he wouldn't say. He hemmed and hawed. Then he redirected. "If you had a rule at your house, I would follow it, no questions asked." I could see him getting spun up.

"Corey, I don't have any weird rules in my house, and we never go there anyway. Just tell me." I flung my arms out in frustration. Talking with hand gestures runs in my family. Except that when I did this the comforter fell, unceremoniously springing my breasts from their cover. Corey jumped up immediately and turned around with vegetables still in his mouth. I'm sure that from Corey's perspective my breasts appeared to leer at him, pale and squinty, like two people walking out of a dark attic into the sun. I hadn't planned it - if I had, I would have tried to line them up better - but I decided that rather than be embarrassed, I would try to use the moment to my advantage.

"Corey, it's okay, they're just breasts."

"I know," he said to the door. "It's no big deal. I just didn't want to be rude. Forget about the paper. There's nothing wrong with a newspaper. I'm going to go start on the floors."

"Corey, turn around," I said politely.

"I don't..."

"Turn around," I said, this time forcefully.

He did, slowly.

"Sit on the bed for a minute. Just a minute."

He sat down on the far edge of the bed, looking at me but sort of not, the way a blind person looks at you.

"I think that I can skip my book work today and work on the house all day with you. That would probably put you ahead for the week, right? You didn't have me on the schedule today."

"I didn't. I did not."

"If I do that, will you answer a few questions for me?"

"With you helping, we can finish the floors before lunch. But it depends on the questions."

"No. It can't depend. It has to be all or nothing."

He finally made firm eye contact. "Okay."

He faced me cross-legged. The lazy rain outside lent a slow rhythm to our conversation. One of Corey's gutters had ruptured above his bedroom window, and the way the rain streamed down the window reminded me of cheesy rain effects in television shows.

"Are you going to cover up?" he asked.

"I don't think that I am."

"This is weird. We're facing each other like this is a game show."

"Why don't you have a job right now?"

"I'm unemployed. You could have asked that weeks ago."

"I did, you kept changing the subject to sandpaper grit. If you're unemployed, how can you spend so much money on this house?"

"I don't have to worry about money for a while."

"Why not?"

"I have some money saved. I made a lot."

"Why do you even have an opinion about newspapers?"

His phone buzzed and I braced myself for push-ups, but instead of dropping down, he pressed the silencer and tossed his phone on the bed. He stood up and paced for a minute, then changed shirts from one white T to another, affecting no change to his look. I allowed this performance because I got the sense that he was building up to something rather than avoiding my question. Lastly, he put on a pair of pants, surgically, one leg at a time, then socks. Maybe he didn't want to confront me half-naked and without dignity.

"I decided," he started, "I made a choice a while ago that this" - he motioned around the room - "was all I could control. And that I wanted to focus with laser precision and make *this* the best it could be. And I didn't want to be confronted even by accident with any of the problems going on out there. I change aisles at Home Depot when I hear people talking about the auto bailouts. If I'm stuck in line at a grocery store, I turn the tabloid magazines backwards. I don't want to know - it doesn't concern me, Robin."

"Why not?"

"Because I'm good at this, and I wasn't very good out there. When I had every indication that I was doing well, I was actually the worst I've ever been. The what - I don't think that matters. It won't change anything. That's just where I'm at now."

"What was your job before you were unemployed?"

His phone buzzed again.

"I'll tell you sometime soon. I promise. Even with

you helping, we're going to get behind today. I'm sorry. I've got to get to work. You don't have to help, but you can. I'd like you to."

It was the first time he'd expressed any kind of need of me. Coming from Corey, it sounded like a declaration of love.

Chapter Eleven

THE WEEK BEFORE Thanksgiving a big storm hit us, with angular sheets of rain pounding the streets of Providence. Walking from the car to my dad's building, my face became wet and raw from raindrops that turned on a knife's edge between liquid and ice. In contrast to the block of asphalt I lived on, the fall storm had only made the lush grounds of the nursing home more beautiful. The grass had been allowed to grow long, and the wind played on the blades as on a single large instrument.

Easing through the automatic double doors, I peeked around the corner to the receptionist's desk, where a group of wheelchair-bound patients loitered in a loose circle. From there the front desk attendant could watch the troublemakers of the day. I signed in with the attendant and walked the halls, averting my eyes from individual rooms in order to keep my spirits up. I squeezed the tissue in my pocket, readying it for use.

When my dad's room turned up empty I took the opportunity to clean. It wasn't unusual for him to be gone; patients at Shady Brook were always being shuttled toward or away from food, or into showers or activity rooms. Even the nicer facilities - and Shady Brook was top-notch in Rhode Island - imposed a near-military structure on its patients' days that seemed more for the sanity of the staff than for the well-being of the patients.

I swept around the wheels of his bed, then fixed his clothes so that the hangers all faced in the same direction. While lining up his wing tips, I found my collage of Mom haphazardly stashed behind the shoe shelves. This happens often with dementia patients. On bad days my father takes objects from the wall and hides them, frightened at the foreign information they contain. Written notes are treated worse than pictures, lists of phone numbers worse still. I removed the collage from the closet and tried to flatten it out, pressing my forearm across a dozen of my mother's smiles.

The nurse, Joanie, brought Dad in as I tacked the collage square against the brick wall. He had on a brown suit that he'd worn during the later years of his career. It lacked the sharp creases down the arms, and the collar had lightened from wear, but he looked good in it. It made him look full, substantial. After Joanie settled him in his big green chair, she squeezed my shoulder and smiled warmly. My whole day basically hinged on that smile. Joanie, a large, kind Jamaican woman, was the type of nurse who could convey whole mental states through her glances if you paid close enough attention, and that day Joanie conveyed my father's lucidity with just a warm look and a squeeze on the shoulder. It immediately brought down my defenses.

"Lot of people in detention at the front desk," I remarked.

"Gets that way 'round the holidays," she said. "They

see everybody leavin' with their families. You think they don't know what's up, but they do. Every one-a them."

Early on in my dad's stay, Joanie had saved my sanity by teaching me that humor not only existed in a place like the dementia ward, it thrived, and that harnessing it was as important as dispensing medicine. My father had been stuck in a loop, asking, "How long did it take you to get here?" over and over again until it felt like a demented mantra created to torture me. Each time I'd answered accurately with as much politeness as I could muster, but at the same time, I felt my insides tearing at me. Over time, he'd repeated the question with the frequency of a pendulum coming to rest at its center. Finally, lost with frustration, I'd yelled, "You know where I come from!" He'd looked at me out of big, confused eyes, like a dog awaiting a smack. Then Joanie walked in.

"Oh hello. How long did it take you to get here?" he had asked her.

"Twenty-seven hours, sir."

"Oh, that's not bad," he'd replied. To him no journey, no matter how long or treacherous, was ever that bad.

"How 'bout you?"

"Gee, I don't know," he'd answered. "I guess I live here."

Then she looked at me, her raised eyebrow playing a rim shot on my father's unknowing punch line. I don't think I had laughed in weeks. Joanie bent over my father's bed and started chuckling as well. Then my father got a hearty laugh going, like if he laughed, he would be in on the joke. He sounded like my old dad, the one who used to crack himself up telling us some joke or doing his ninja moves in his briefs waiting for my mother to finish ironing his pants. After that day, I knew that I had some tools to use when my father got stuck in a loop.

Joanie wrote some numbers on a chart and said a friendly goodbye. As soon as she left, my father popped out from his chair and gave me a hug.

"Robin," he said. "I've missed you so. You've got to listen to this."

He practically skipped over to his crate of vinyl and began walking his fingers over the sleeves. In setting up his room, Ariel and I had made sure to place the crate of records on a shelf in direct view of his green chair. We set an old record player up next to it, the type with fake wood around the base, and hooked it up to speakers, though I don't think our father had figured how to use it. Dad didn't collect records, exactly, but the ones he had were such cherished possessions that when it came time to decorate his room, we knew the crate would pack a concentrated dose of home. Joanie told me that she had once caught him removing and replacing each platter from its white sleeve, over and over again, throughout the course of a day.

His fingers froze over a black cover, and he whipped it from the crate and tore the vinyl from the package, the white jacket falling like an onion peel to the ground. He scrutinized the label, spun the record between his palms and placed it on the player.

"Have you heard this lately? Do you even remember this? I've been thinking about it all day."

A rubbery bass line vibrated the ground under my feet, the notes running up and down the scale with a loose kind of determination. It was *Astral Weeks* by Van Morrison, my father's favorite album.

"Dad, come on, you played this once a week for fifteen years," I said.

I settled into one of the wooden guest chairs, which itself vibrated along with the music. The curtains, a burgundy red drapery, swayed under a forced air vent. It seemed as if I was the only object not attuned to Van's jazz ramblings.

"I can't believe you remember this," he said. "This... this music is just magic."

"I'm glad you're in such good spirits," I said, and I was, although I was always suspicious of these feelings with my father – gladness, joy, relief – knowing how sharply they could sour.

If I ventured in the slipstream, between the viaducts of your dreams.

"He didn't even know any of these musicians," he said, his curly head bobbing with the music. "He told them 'oh just play whatever.'"

It did sound as if Van was in a different world from the band. My primary memory of this album growing up was that I couldn't sing along to it. He repeated strange phrases over and over again, stressing different syllables each time, pressing meanings out of the words like water from a wet rag. Sometimes he would sing with the beat, sometimes he would go off into his own direction, raising the pitch and volume of his voice like it was just another instrument running through a solo.

"I was thinking about my grandparents the other day," I said. I considered this kind of comment a neutral opening gambit, a lucidity test of sorts.

"Oh yeah?" he asked, settling back into his chair. "You know, I still think of them every day. Do you remember the smells coming out your grandmother's kitchen on Sunday morning? No matter how early I would get over there on Sundays, your uncle had already shown up and eaten all the eggs."

I ticked off the facts in my head: he knows I'm Robin, he knows he has a brother, he knows his parents. I thought, *Today, Robin, your lucky number has come up. You are the winner of the day's lottery. Let the other families sit sullen while their parents and grandparents throw strange sentences onto the table. You'll be having a real conversation while others are awkwardly smiling into their oatmeal.*

But when life gives you a perfect day on the river, should you float with the current or should you swim across to explore the other side? What I mean to say is, as my father's lucidity became a scarce resource, I had to be more deliberate about its use. Do I enjoy the father I know, passively basking in his warm personality? Or do I treat his mind like a lockbox, containing valuable information, to which I have just now been given a key? Throughout a given day, two or three questions popped into my head about my family that could not be answered by anyone alive save my father. My notebook pulsed in my pocket.

"Do you know where Nona and Pop's parents came into the country?" I asked. On that day, I felt, for better or for worse, that it was a swim across the river kind of day. By this point I had pulled out my notebook and opened it up, ready to transcribe. The first blank pages were covered with sweat spots and sawdust from work at Corey's.

"Let's see," he said, "your great-grandfather came in through Ellis Island. That I know. His family was poor; they never saw money until they came to America. He told me that he came over without any buttons on his shirt because he lost them all playing cards on the ship."

"Now your great-grandmother. Let me think" - here he closed his eyes and rubbed his temples while I scribbled madly in my notebook to keep up - "She might have come in through Boston. I think that's right. Gosh, my mother must have told me about her a thousand times. But I think it's Boston. Don't get old, she used to tell me. I should've taken her advice."

We continued talking about my great-grandparents, punctuated occasionally by a shout from Van. I wrote as much down as I could but found it hard to keep up with my father. I got down the towns in Italy where each came from, some first names of relatives, a few last names going back generations. He spoke with such enthusiasm that more than once I had to reach across the table and dab spittle from his cheeks. Anything from the distant past my father could hone in on with laser-like precision. At one point he spun out a string of facts so articulate, and so clearly true, that it made my lip quiver.

"Something wrong, Robin?" he asked.

"No, I'm fine, Dad," I said, reaching for my tissue. After a certain point, it's the lucid days that make you cry.

"And the bakery," I said. "You, um, said you have stories from that."

"Oh, yeah, more than enough to fill a thimble."

"Do you have Grandma's whoopee pie recipe written down anywhere?" I asked.

He pressed his thumb to his temple. "Let me think… boxes. Filing cabinets. Closet."

My father has a visual memory, and anytime you ask him for something he takes you on a mental journey to find it. On the speakers, Van Morrison repeated a line over and over: *And I'm conquered in a car seat, and I'm looking straight at you, And I'm conquered in a car seat, not a thing that I can do, but my heart just beats faster, and my feet can't keep still.* Eventually, he had shouted, whispered, and whimpered the words so many times that they changed their shape in my head.

"No. I don't think I ever wrote it down," he said, pointing at his head. "Guess it's all up here."

Then he started to cry.

"Oh, Dad." I hugged him and put a hand into his jet-black hair. "Why are you crying?"

"I don't know," he answered. He walked his hand across the armrest of his chair and to the end table, looking desperate for a tactile distraction.

"Do you want my Jell-O?" he asked, separating me from his hair and gesturing to the Styrofoam tray on his night table.

"Dad."

Van shouted, *I think I'll go walking by the railroad, with my cherry, cherry wine.*

"Ah…" he said, his ears perking up, as if unaware that he had just shed tears. "That's my favorite part. You can hear him unraveling, and the bassist couldn't care less, he just keeps bobbing forward." Slowly, he pitter-pattered his hand across his knees, using each finger as a different part of a drum set.

"Do you want to get some real food, Dad?" I asked.
He nodded.
"Then put that Jell-O down."

I skated my cafeteria tray across the rails, piling on croissants and muffins, skipping the pile of bananas and small, waxed apples, scoffing at the yogurts on ice. We'd checked in just before breakfast service closed, and the cafeteria was nearly empty. I made two stacks of thick, doughy pancakes, one for my father and one twice as tall for me, with a sidecar of soft butter served with a melon scooper. I put onto my tray only that which was glazed with fat or glistening with syrup. I gingerly brought the sagging tray back to the table, passing a custodian breaking down a keyboard stand like he was the saddest roadie in the world.

Sitting down, I divvied the food up between us, being sure to place a few disallowed foods in front of him, the pancake stack but also a muffin and a doughnut, foods that would have sent Ariel screaming.

"Don't forget to save a seat for Ma," my father said as I sat down. He said it, as he always did, in the cadence of someone gently reminding you of something that could keep you from trouble. I slapped my forehead; not once had I mentioned our mother, as Ariel and I had agreed on.

"Are you looking forward to seeing her?"

"Well, I'm always seeing her," he said, "and I always

look forward to it."

While I paused, wondering how to follow up, he said, "She's my whole life."

It felt nice to hear these sentiments, but the feeling was curiously empty, the emotional equivalent of aspartame.

"So what about Thanksgiving?" I said, sticking to the script. "Are you excited about getting Ma and everyone together with the grandkids?"

"Oh yes. A beautiful idea."

Turning around to stretch, my eye fell on the only other family in the room. A woman, slumped in a wheelchair, was gone even for this place. The family sat attentively around her in a semi-circle, but the woman's face hung forward, unable to look anywhere but down at her plate of finely cut-up sausage and potatoes. A younger woman, perhaps her daughter, lifted forkful after forkful up to her, where they hit her closed mouth and fell ineffectually back down to the plate. They didn't have to fall very far. I couldn't help but think of the woman as a logical end point, one of the many to which my dad could end up. I fondled the balled tissue in my pocket. Were we moving together toward that moment? Or maybe we weren't moving at all; maybe we stay still while time moves over us like slides over a projector light. I made a mental note to write that down. Before I could use my tissue, I heard my father behind me turn in his chair and say, "Hey, Ma! Sit down, we saved you a seat. Look, Robin!"

My shoulders dropped. Without feeling my head turn, the scene at the table rotated around to meet me.

First, I saw my father's plate with his utensils tossed down. Then I saw my father's face, smiling out as if awaiting applause. Nothing about this scene could be good. It was too soon for my mother to visit, and if she came uninvited it could not be for any good reason.

But it wasn't my mother. My father's arm, long and thin in his suit, stretched across the back of the chair next to him and touched on a cotton candy puff of electric red hair. I took the whole scene in like it was a newspaper comic whose joke I didn't quite get.

"Robin, you've met Ma?"

It was the woman playing the keyboard. My father and she sat in front of me with my father's heaping stack of pancakes between them. It took a moment to register that my mother was not, in fact, at the nursing home, so quickly and powerfully had I prepared myself for the possibility.

"I don't believe we've met," I said, smiling between clenched teeth.

"Oh, nonsense. Of course you have," my father said. He put his hand on the rail of the woman's wheelchair and looked down at her.

"Bettie," the woman said. Her wheelchair set her back from the table so that when she reached out her papery hand to shake mine, I had to stand and bend across the table to reach it.

"I'm sorry," she said when her hand shook. "I'm quite nervous."

"Oh please," I said. "Don't be."

A moment of silence followed wherein each person took in this new information, or appeared to. I observed

Bettie close up. Whenever she wasn't using her thin arms, she rested them at her side with her palms down onto the wheelchair seat, as if at any moment she could catapult her frail body from the chair.

"So, Bettie..." I said, shaking my head for lack of things to say. Normally this would have been perceived as rude. A benefit of the dementia ward, small fruits but dearly appreciated, was the patients' inability to read body language. This freed guests from having to compose themselves as finely as they did in the wider world. At the dementia ward, I let my head shake, and my shoulders droop. There was also no need to finish a sentence. I stood up, busing my barely eaten food off my trays. At the front of the cafeteria, the roadie broke down the keyboard equipment while kitchen workers vigorously Saran-wrapped everything in sight. I shot a quick text to Ariel, something along the lines of "*Abort Sunday. I think Dad has a fucking girlfriend.*"

Then I watched them for a moment, their backs turned to me. His hand rested at the top of her wheelchair, and the way his fingers fluttered caused his silver wedding band to glint in the fluorescent light. Once, when his wandering through the streets of Massachusetts became dangerous, we tried to remove the wedding ring to save it from being lost. But his hands had so grown since his wedding day, and his knuckles had so swelled with arthritis that nothing short of a Sawzall would have removed it. So we left it on, supposing that there was no safer place on earth for it than between those two swollen knuckles. As it moved closer and farther to Bettie's hair by centimeters, as Bettie's shaking arms moved her body, I got the idea that if the two touched my head would explode.

Walking back to the table from the busing area, I heard them talking. With their backs still turned to me, I heard my father say something about Florida. The sound was muffled. I heard it as, "We'll never get to Florida at this rate," though it could have been some variation of these words. What it meant, I couldn't say. They quieted when I sat down, as if they had secrets to keep. I smiled at Bettie, trying to neutralize her nervousness with my own false serenity.

I broke the silence. "I really loved your keyboard playing the other day. Have you been playing here long?"

She looked around, then mussed her hair, her arms making a parentheses around her face.

"You've been playing a long time," my father interjected.

"Yes," she said as if she'd suddenly awakened. "As long as I can remember."

Thanksgiving

"Grab your hat / Get your coat,
The cellar door / is an open throat."
- The Mountain Goats

Chapter Twelve

JOHN CALLED ME from work to let me know that they too had met Bettie at brunch. I let the phone drop a bit when I heard this. Part of me had written off my encounter as an anomaly. All of the activity in the dementia ward can begin to appear, from a distance, like atoms knocking around without any rational pattern, and I had been eager to attribute my brunch with Dad and Bettie to just another unlikely collision. But from John's description, it was all the same: the keyboard playing, the silent sitting, the talk of Florida. "What's this Florida?" John asked to no one. "They mentioned it a few times. Like they're going buy a condo and become snowbirds."

"They're trying to be a normal couple," I guessed. "That's what old people talk about – going to Florida." I said this with a hand cupped over my cell phone to block the sounds of Corey rolling over and groaning into his pillow. The subject of Corey, needless to say, had not come up.

John said that Ariel had psyched herself up on the car ride there, unfurling onto John her disapproval of the relationship, "this affair" her father had been carrying on. She told him that she was going to talk to the nursing home to fix this because our father was paying too much of his dwindling fortune to be allowed to commit adultery. "She had the crazy eyes," John said. "The way she was pointing at me while she talked, she had to wind up to point that hard." But once she got there, she lost her nerve. "Bettie pulled up in the wheelchair next to your father, and Ariel's voice just caught in her throat," John said. "They were being sweet to each other. She didn't say a word for the rest of the brunch. She could only nod or shake her head when I asked if she wanted food. So go easy on her, okay? She's not all bad."

"And call her," he added. "Just talk about Thanksgiving. If she needs you to bring a bunch of stuff, bring it. You're coming, right?" As if I would go anywhere else.

By then Corey's and my lives had merged in all the usual ways. Toothbrushes. Shoes. The door to his house was a check valve: once objects entered they rarely left. I colonized a nightstand with a stack of books, a miniature version of the dusty towers that surrounded my bed across the street. A few paperbacks were tented over the alarm clock, a device that no longer served any purpose for me. Each night I would pull a book off the stack and flip to the dog-eared page, stealing a few minutes of reading before I collapsed. I never had fewer than three books going at once, using them the way a climber uses multiple carabiners to stay clipped onto the mountain. Finishing a book, for me, is a small death, and it's important to have a second one going to combat the feeling of loss when it ends.

The night John called, I kept rereading the same

paragraph of *Jane Eyre*, a nice argyle copy with worn edges, absorbing none of it, quickly realizing that Thanksgiving fully occupied my mind. During our conversation, John said something that made me laugh out loud. As we discussed my father and Thanksgiving, he said nonchalantly, "Well we'll just invite Bettie along with him. That should work out." For one beautiful moment, a whole scene flashed in front of me: my father arriving with his mistress in lipstick and pearls, my mother at first confused, then livid. The chaos of one hundred dysfunctional families released at once. Ariel's children running around the table legs, adding to an insanity to which they're completely oblivious. John wordlessly standing up from the table and leaving to shoot free throws in the back yard. Would my mother throw the turkey across the room? Would she pummel the woman living in sin with my father? Or would she draw inward, as she usually did, using her only real weapons - sarcasm and disappointment, which she would lob over the wall from a safe distance inside herself. In this flash of cacophony that I imagined, I wasn't trying to fix anything or appease anyone. I simply sat back and took it in, scribbling notes into a pad as if I were an outside journalist, not angry or embarrassed, just interested.

But despite my fantasies, bringing Bettie to dinner wasn't an option. Obviously. And I teared up at the thought of my father alone in his room, eating hospital turkey encased in a bubble of coagulated gravy.

No matter what we decided, I wouldn't know how it would affect him, if at all. Each time I visited I was getting a fresh father, wiped and rebooted, and our family memories, the thousand-strand tuft of Velcro fiber that held us together, could no longer be trusted to exist. My problems still unresolved, I gave my head a vigorous shake, wishing that thoughts could be dislodged the way cherry blossoms fall from a branch. I opened *Jane Eyre* back to the dog-ear, entered the scene of her wedding and immediately began nodding off into the book. I closed it again and placed it back with its brethren. Turning sideways on the mattress, I pulled my comforter up to my chin and fell asleep to the sound of Corey muttering nonsense to himself.

I wrapped a powder blue scarf around my neck and tucked it into my jacket. My father's nursing home appeared, at first in the distance on a hill, then closer, sometimes sideways to us, but always watching through a thick tangle of leafless trees. Loose screws rattled across Corey's truck bed. It was just a few days until Thanksgiving, and we pulled in during the last of an exodus. Carloads of families waited in line on the winding path, backstopped at a traffic light, looking like they had just picked their parents up from school. When we pulled into the parking spot, Corey continued sitting with his hands at ten and two, squinting into sunlight.

"Mind if I wait in the car?" he asked.

"Mind if I wait in the car at Home Depot?" There was a Home Depot near Shady Brook, walking distance but tastefully hidden by clever landscaping.

"I need a second person to help me with the green board. That's why you said you'd come."

"Huh. Looks like we're at an impasse."

"Fine."

We entered from the side entrance, Corey stomping flat-footed behind like a petulant child through the dining hall, where orderlies removed pans of mashed potatoes.

"How was it today?" I asked one woman.

"Bad. Holidays are always the worst. They know they're missing something important, but they're not sure what."

Then, walking the hallway to Dad's room we passed Joanie walking that nurse's walk, as fast as legs can move without breaking into a run. In the split second that our eyes made contact, she fixed my gaze and filled me with sympathy, as you would pour water into a tumbler. I immediately sped up, and Corey followed, sensing something had changed.

I rushed in to find my father sitting in his chair, his eyes welled with tears, the tears not falling yet but threatening to. Balled-up tissues littered his side table and spilled over onto the tile floor, where they made a puffy line to the trash can.

"Dad, what's wrong?" I asked. His jet-black hair sat lopsided on his head.

"Gee, I don't know," he said.

Corey walked over to a cardboard box whose paper contents had been exploded around the room. He picked up a piece of paper and waved it.

"All these papers are jumbled up," he said.

I texted Ariel: *"Dad's a mess. Did you or mom visit today?"*

"Dad, it's important that you think for a minute. Did someone visit today?"

He wormed deeper into his chair.

"Did Ariel and John visit today?"

Nothing.

"Mom? Did she visit today?"

"Sure," he said, his eyes lighting up a bit. 'Sure' was a conversational trick, meant to stop me from asking questions. It didn't mean anything.

"Who visited today?"

"Your Aunt Eileen." She had been dead for years.

"Did Mom visit today?"

"Sure," he said.

"Dad – did anyone visit today?"

"Well gee, I don't know."

I grabbed my father by the lapels of his coat and shook him, shouting, "Who visited today? Why can't you remember?"

When I did this, time seemed to slow down the way it does in the seconds before a car accident. I locked in on a moment where my father's head bobbed as if disconnected from his body and his hair swayed, reed-like. It is difficult, even now, to get this image out of my head.

Corey came in from the side, pulled me off him and set me carefully on the floor where I sat crying between bent legs. All of his memories were in there somewhere. He held the answers to my questions. But where the fuck *were* they?

Corey bent down in front of my father, who was

more shaken than before. Tears followed the wrinkles of his face.

"How are you doing today, sir?" Corey asked, and placed a hand on his knee.

My father looked straight at Corey.

"When are we going home?"

"You are home, sir. We brought you home." He gave my father a long, clear smile. When Corey smiled, his face became frictionless with angles.

"Oh, well, good," he said. "I wanted to go home."

Corey walked over to my father's vinyl, dropping the needle onto the album, still on the player. First a few big drops of bass, like someone testing bathwater with their toe. Then the steady shake of an egg filled with sand. Then a birdshot of guitar notes. *If I ventured in the slipstream, between the viaducts of your dreams...*

"Music is good, right? We like music."

My father just nodded. As I watched him recede from the edge, Corey made a signal to me with his hand and left the room quietly. I stayed between my bent legs, letting the full weight of my pity drain away before getting up to approach my father again. When I got up, I only half got up so that I would be at his level. I put a hand on my father's knee, and it stayed there, unnoticed over the music, for several minutes. Which is fine – it was more for me than him.

Corey came back in with a basket overflowing with warm laundry and placed it on my father's television tray, brushing off the Kleenex with his free arm. On instinct, I placed my arms deep into the basket and mixed the laundry, spreading the scent of dryer sheets. The different levels of warmth soothed me, even the occasional hot metal button or zipper.

"Now, we need you to fold as many of these as you can, okay?" Corey said to him. "Put them right on your side table."

"Well, okay," my father said and started removing socks from the laundry basket almost immediately, trying to match them up. When he didn't have a match, he would place the sock across the arm of his chair. I sat on his bed and watched him for a few minutes. Corey came over and quietly said, "I think he'll be good if you want to go."

"Do you think that's okay?"

"He'll be better without us at this point. Trust me."

As we walked out of Shady Brook, this time with Corey in front and me the petulant child stomping behind, a text came in from Ariel: *"No. Mom in room all day. We didn't visit."*

In the truck on the way home, I looked at Corey as if I had never seen him before. He kept his eyes on the road, pretending not to notice my stare.

I looked back down at my shadowed hands.

"I know what you're feeling," he said. "You're not turning into a monster. It'll pass."

"I keep picturing my father's head bobbing as I shake him."

"You won't do it again. Trust me."

"How did you know that laundry trick?"

"I've had to deal with it before."

It was pitch black. Ever since daylight savings, the darkness had crept up on us without consent. Corey took a turn, and a cone of light from a street lamp swept across the windshield.

"Your parents?"

"No - they died when I was young. I had an uncle I kept in touch with who I tried to take care of later on. He was bipolar. Maybe schizophrenic. A lot of things. Sometimes he was like your father was today."

"He still alive?"

Corey shrugged.

"Not sure. For your father, it's easier when you think of it like a problem to solve," he said. "You occupy the hands first, then you occupy the mind. What else is there?"

In the sweep of another street lamp, I thought I saw Corey crying, but it was just the shadows cast down from his brow, rain from the windshield, and the arcing streetlights.

"It's all in there somewhere," I said. "His memories aren't gone, they're just not accessible. That's what kills me."

"Let's go to my house. I want to show you something."

Corey put an arm across my back on the way up the porch steps. The inside of his house felt no warmer than the street, and I thought I could see my breath. Fall had already peaked, and the rest of November and early December would commence like a training-wheels version of winter.

With a gentlemanly arm, he led me upstairs and into the bedroom that we had demolished together. Corey had spackled the seams between the sheetrock and painted the ceiling a flat white. New baseboards hid dark tar spots in the corners. The room looked immaculate.

"You finished it."

"That's not what I wanted to show you. Did you notice the indent?"

Corey took me to a corner of the room and squatted down over a rounded-out divot in the wood flooring large enough to hold a bag of marbles.

"I'm so sorry about that."

I had made the divot during a midnight floor sanding session. When I'd arrived at his house that night, my head still swimming with thoughts of my father and Bettie, Corey had greeted me at the top of the stairs leaning on a drum sander, a chrome machine with smooth curves, like a vacuum cleaner outfitted for war. With my help, Corey had first removed the stained carpeting, then the multi-colored foam underlay which tore like cotton candy from between the carpet staples. When we'd pulled up all the staples, a tedious task that involved a flathead screwdriver and a pair of pliers, we treated ourselves by rolling up the carpet like a Swiss cake roll and sending it tumbling end over end out the window.

He'd rolled in the sander and demonstrated how to ease the spinning drum onto the floor without creating a chatter mark. The sander wanted to move forward, he'd said, and my job was to hold it back, just enough. If I let go, it would crash into the wall. Holding it in place was far worse. "Thirty seconds in one place and you'll bore a hole through the floor."

Corey's first pass turned the tarry boards to a raw, red amber. I ran my hands along the still-rough wood. The room smelled like a pine forest after a rainstorm. I vacuumed the dust and ran tack cloth along the floor while

Corey loaded a finer grit paper for the second pass, my first.

He instructed me to hold the worn wooden handle at arm's length with T-Rex arms, then he stood behind me, lacing his arms through mine. He flipped the metal switch and helped me ease down the spinning drum. Upon contact with the floor, the sander made a world ending shriek, the cloth dust-catcher inflated like a balloon, and clouds of deep red sawdust fountained into the air.

As we moved forward, he placed a hand on my back, straightening me out like creased paper. "Keep the arms stiff!" he yelled over the noise. The more I worked, the more connected I felt to the machine and the three of us moved in step like dance partners. I stopped short at the end of a row and Corey pressed against me. The vibrations ran across my arms and down my legs like electricity searching for a ground. I closed my eyes, just for a moment, and allowed myself to feel the vibrations. Only after vacuuming did we realize that I'd left the sander spinning for a few seconds too long, creating an indent that a barrel could rest comfortably in.

"It's one of the few things you can't patch," he said now, skating his hand down the curve. "It'll be here as long as the house will."

"I know - I screwed up."

"No. That's not why I'm showing you. I don't care about the indent. What I mean is, this house has a memory. After we're gone, this house will remember us and what we did to it. Feel it."

He took my hand in his, moving it carefully over the chatter marks.

"After we're gone, someone else will live here, and they'll remember us by the work that we've done. If they're real house lovers, they'll walk into this room, sit down the way we are right now, and read this indent the way a fortune-teller reads a palm. They might not know the whole story behind the indent, but they'll know."

In bed that night, I took off Corey's white T-shirt, still caked up with grime and salted sweat. Neither of us dared say something trite or cheerful. Instead, I laid him face down across the fluffed-up comforter and ran my fingernails up and down his back. For the first time, he didn't resist. There wasn't enough of this in the world for him. My hands moved in separate rhythms as across the strings of a harp. He lay mostly silent, except for when I rose up on my sharp nail ends and made semi-circles underneath his shoulder blades, to which he would let out long slow groans. I went back to the spot, again and again, delighted at how easily I could make him shudder.

Before we fell asleep, we had sex for the first time. It was difficult, but eventually, our bodies found each other between the layers of cold sheets. After getting lost in it a while, I came back to reality, unfinished but still enjoying myself. I finally came on the bottom when I focused on a chain that was swinging from Corey's neck. It was a simple chain with small silver ringlets and a horn at the end, and it moved slowly, rhythmically. I focused on the chain until the edges of my vision blurred and there was nothing else but the chain and what I was feeling, and finally the finish was coaxed out of me. Corey didn't finish, but it didn't seem to matter. It just felt nice to have an excuse to create some heat. We disengaged at the same time and spooned to sleep. The inside fold where our bodies pressed together radiated a living, pulsing warmth, while the outer edges fought off a bitter cold.

Chapter Thirteen

THE TUESDAY BEFORE Thanksgiving, I indulged myself in something outrageous by Corey's standards. I took a bath.

With green board hung around the downstairs tub and the tile still sheathed in dusty boxes, I clocked out for the night and went upstairs. When I first started coming to Corey's, his upstairs bathroom had resembled the other rooms of his house: disassembled and dust coated, unusable. The first time I walked in, I didn't even notice the tub. But once we started working on the downstairs bathroom, we needed to make the other useable. During the clean-up I tugged on a drop-cloth, revealing a heavy clawfoot tub with copper feet. It had a sheen that both absorbed light and reflected it outward. "Corey, this tub," I said at the time, unable to finish my sentence. After that, I spent a little time here and there, making the room serviceable for a bath.

I dropped *The New York Times* on the sink, bulging at the fold, and turned the squeaky chrome knobs. Once the bathwater threw off steam, I twisted the rubber stopper into the drain and watched the tub fill while I stood over it, naked and expectant. That enormous piece of ceramic, glazed and buffed to a shine, filled with steaming water. The moment I dipped my arm into the scalding water the itching sensation from the green board dust disappeared. Kicking off my second sock, I put one leg into the tub then the other. When my ankles became acclimated to the sting of the hot water, I slipped down the side of the tub like an egg yolk into a bowl. Soapy water crested at the broad lip of the tub, lapping suds out onto the floor. I removed the paper from the sink one section at a time, folding and refolding it so that I could read without getting the paper wet.

Corey walked in holding a cracked coffee mug, a red towel wrapped around his waist. Seeing the paper, he raised his eyebrows but didn't say anything. Reading *The New York Times* in the bathtub was a combination of two things that Corey hated: outside information and a body at rest. At the time, I guess I felt we'd passed into a new phase in our relationship. Surely the Corey that helped me with my father wouldn't yell at me for reading the paper, I told myself.

The steamy water had me feeling chatty. "You know, I've been thinking. Why can't I just take my dad and Bettie out somewhere for Thanksgiving? That way he gets out of the nursing home, and I can avoid a family apocalypse at Ariel's house."

"Lots of restaurants are open on Thanksgiving."

"I think I'm going to do that. What do you think?"

"Yeah," Corey shrugged and began shaving by the light of the mirror. I went back to the paper, making origami out of each section as I read. A picture caught my eye. In its background, the three smokestacks of the

Narragansett Electric company loomed.

"Hey the *Times* has an article about Providence," I said after skimming it. "It's about the tent city down by the Point Street Bridge."

"I don't wanna know," he said, matter-of-factly. It had become more of a game to us now than an occasion to fight, something to josh each other with, like the way John and I were when I became a vegetarian my senior year of high school. One night I got him laughing telling him random useless facts. "Corey, I know you don't want to know, but this sandpiper situation at Second Beach is serious." "Does your media blackout include stories about Zimbabwe currency manipulation?" Stuff like that.

Corey shaved with his face pressed in close to the mirror. We had done a reasonable job cleaning up the bathroom, but some boards and drop cloths remained, and the round, exposed bulbs set around the mirror threw a dirty light onto the black bead-board walls.

"It's one of those recession-across-the-country type of pieces. Did you know they have a mayor? Fascinating. There's a lot of good going on down there. This is a random connection, but I think part of the reason I'm not good with my dad is that I've never done anything to help anybody. I grew up pretty privileged."

"I grew up in houses like this," Corey said.

"I think I'd like to be helpful. There are all kinds of organizations going over there to help out. I think I'm going to stop in after Thanksgiving."

Corey walked around the tub. He began working shampoo into my scalp with his fingernails, pulling out bits of dust from the green board. It sent chills down my neck.

"When I was eleven or so," Corey said, "I helped my grandfather make a cement base for his porch. It was just him and me. He was an old-world Italian guy; I was a ten-year-old kid. He made the whole wooden structure around the porch, then we mixed cement in this small mixer, right out of the dry bags. He poured batches of the stuff into the mold and there I was at ten years old, running a trowel over it to smooth it out."

He set his fingernails at the top of my forehead and ran them down my scalp.

"We did all that stuff together. I hadn't thought about any of it in years. Then when I lost my job, all those memories began seeping back in. I would see a big sweaty guy in his front yard working in a white T-shirt and my eyes would well up. He used to kill wasps on his porch with one bare hand. That's the kind of guy he was."

He finished by pressing his thumbs into the notch between my head and neck. The spot felt like a button to erase all memory. He walked back to the sink and began slowly rinsing the viscous shampoo off his hands with unusual concentration.

"I sold mortgages for a while," he said, finally. "Bad ones. That was the job I had. I made a bunch of money."

He continued to prod at his face in the mirror, clipping at tiny hairs with a concentration usually reserved for his finish carpentry.

I unscrewed the rubber stopper in the tub, with a plan to go over and comfort him if he would allow it. I felt that the admission was a kind of breakthrough for him, and I wanted to be supportive. Corey sighed and grabbed the meat of the newspaper, discarding one section at a time searching for the article. When he got to it, he glanced at the photo above the fold, then the article, then the photo again. He scrutinized it with a blank face like he was doing long division in his head. The picture showed the 'mayor,' a grizzled-looking man with a tobacco-stained beard, sitting in front of his tent, his pipe and a plastic flamingo for company as the sun set behind him over the Woonasquatucket river. He looked straight at the camera, his expression ghostly and blank, like the photos of civil war soldiers in camp.

"Would you want to come to tent city with me?" I asked. "We could go after Thanksgiving weekend. We could really help people."

He didn't answer the question. When the last of the gurgling bath water broke the silence, I stood up in the tub, naked save the archipelago of suds along my body.

"What do you think?" I asked. "Corey?"

Corey squinted, his eyes becoming small and hard. He continued looking down at the picture, holding the newspaper so that it sort of crumpled around his hand.

"Corey?"

When his phone buzzed, he dropped down parallel with the tub and began doing silent push-ups.

"Corey, don't ignore me."

He continued long past his usual twenty-five. He went to thirty, then forty, then fifty, until sweat dripped from his nose and he had to rest in a trapezoid position between each push-up.

While I watched this dumb spectacle, I toweled off my legs and looped them into my underwear and pants. I put my filthy T-shirt back on while Corey stood facing me, newly baptized in sweat.

"Are you going to answer me?"

"No," he said. "I'm not."

He said it in the calm tone of someone who was not calm.

"Well, that's bullshit. I'm leaving."

Corey's face changed, looking either pained or angry, and a quality of it scared me. He reached at me with his hand, and I spun away.

"Robin…"

"Don't touch me!"

Pushing past him, I slipped on a pool of soapy water and sent the full weight of my body crashing onto my right hand. The suddenness of the pain made me wince out loud. Corey tried to help, but I shook him off and stood up as quickly as my body would allow.

"Is your hand okay?" Corey yelled from the bathroom, sounding genuinely concerned.

Without answering, I stormed away. As I turned around the banister and down the stairs, Corey's shaving bag spun out of the bathroom and broke like a piñata against the far wall.

The street was freezing cold, but I moved in my own warm bubble of seething anger. Before I knew it, I was back up in my bedroom sitting among my stacks of books, my hair still dribbling bath water that merged downstream with salty tears.

My front door couldn't even lock. Anyone with a screwdriver had full access to my house, and no one knew this more than Corey. Downstairs, I lined up a row of chairs in front of the door, using my good hand, so that the end of the line rested against the bottom step of the staircase. I wasn't sure if it would hold, but I didn't have the energy to test it. I stood a short watch up in my room, staring out across at the down-turned shades of the turret as if I could open them by focusing. At first, no light issued from behind the shades. After a few minutes, a floodlight came on, illuminating the side of the house. Corey exited the side door. Slowly, as if inside his own dream, he pulled the gray tarp off his BMW. He stepped inside, backed out, and crawled down the street and out of sight.

Chapter Fourteen

WHEN THANKSGIVING MORNING came, I didn't need the sun to wake me up. My throbbing hand did the job. The pain came with such force that I expected my sheets to rise and fall with each pulse of blood. I slid my hand from the comforter and examined it in the overcast light. The two middle knuckles were still swollen, the creases of the skin filled in. I'd spent Wednesday icing it, reading, and spying on Corey - who hadn't returned home since our fight - from between the slit of my bedroom curtains. I also got in touch with Shady Brook about getting my father out for a date with Bettie.

I removed my hand from the comforter. The air's ability to ice my sore hand made me question the temperature of the apartment. I reached down behind the bed and put a hand on an ice-cold baseboard. Out in the hallway, standing wrapped in my duvet cover, I read the thermostat: 51 degrees.

Try as I might, I could not reignite the furnace pilot. The process required two hands: one to press a small red ignition button and another to turn a knob, increasing gas flow. Each time I tried to turn the cracked knob with my bad hand, sharp pains shot up my arm. Half-frozen by the breeze coming in through the cellar windows, and feeling defeated, I called my landlord and left a voicemail on his phone, as useful an action as putting a note in a bottle and throwing it into the ocean.

I briefly considered calling Corey. Only briefly.

After that I spent a short morning lying on the couch feeling sorry for myself, my hand elevated to manage the pain. I felt as if I were playing dead in a childhood game of capture the flag. Occasionally, I sat up to check for Corey across the street and, when he was nowhere to be found, to feel bad for myself. I felt that I was at an inflection point. Based on our fight, there was reason to think that Corey and I, whatever we had been, were over. The problem with inflection points is that in the moment their direction is unclear. My hands no longer shook when a pen and notebook weren't nearby. Without Corey, would this compulsion grow back, along with all the other problems of summer? Would I pick up new, different problems? I pondered this as I watched my breath rise from the couch.

At noon, I vacated my frozen house and headed for Ariel's. Realizing I was arriving empty-handed, and knowing my mother's feelings about such, I stopped at the only open convenience store I could find and stocked up on boxes of Devil Dogs to arrange on a tray. Each Thanksgiving, my father had made bite-size whoopie pies from scratch, filling and all, and presented them to the family on a complex scaffold of deviled egg trays. I considered the Devil Dogs as close as I could get, a sad but unmistakable tribute to our absent father.

I walked up the driveway to Ariel's house with the tray under one arm and my puffed, bandaged hand hanging like a flipper at my side. Sometimes it's possible to forecast with accuracy which *you* is going to show up to a family gathering. Will it be interesting, life-of-the-party Robin who expounds on the latest book she's read? Or shy, acquiescent Robin, content to sit in the corner smiling dumbly until her cheeks hurt? That day I could feel stoic, pre-occupied Robin poking her head out, the Robin that asks for questions to be repeated, staring off while a reservoir of feelings sloshes beneath the surface. I hated this Robin, this adolescent redux, but I could no more prevent her from showing up than I could force gabby Robin to materialize.

Before I got to the steps the inner door swung open and little Maddy stood behind the storm door, face pressed against the lower pane of glass. She grabbed the end of her pink skirt, pulled it up to her chest and started hopping back and forth. By the time I got to the storm door she had fogged up the lower pane with her stuttering breath and she wiped away a patch to look at me mischievously.

I opened the door with my elbow and looked down at her. "Well hello, girlie," I said. The blast of hot air rushing from the door flushed my cheeks. The heat must have been set at 75 degrees.

"Hiiiliili," she said, her voice trailing off. She spun around again and let go of her skirt.

I knelt down and whispered in her ear, "Am I late?

Did we eat yet?" and she shook her head conspiratorially. It's amazing how emotionally astute children can be. I think that we're born with the entirety of our emotional intelligence, and over time it cleaves away in thin slices each time we suffer an awkward moment.

"Here, take these into the kitchen so I can get my shoes," I said, trying to hand her the tray of Devil Dogs. She put her arms at her side and shook her head.

"What happened to your hand?" she asked

"I just hurt it. It's fine. Where is everybody?"

She began rapping on the shiny plastic porch rails.

"They're at the *table*," she said as if nothing could be so obvious. Since she wouldn't take it, I had to put the tray down to take off my shoes, but when I did, the family dog, a small, freakishly hairless thing, whipped down the hall and shoved his nose into the foil. I shook him away. Maddy grabbed the dog and held it in front of her. And with that, she ran down the hallway. I followed behind her as she zigzagged from the dark of the hallway into the open stadium of the great room.

"Hi guys," I said, standing before a seated audience, feigning a fatigued, apologetic facial expression. I took the tray of pastries to the countertop of the conjoined kitchen and placed it next to a tilting stack of paper containers with "Dee Ann's Catering" stenciled across their sides.

The family sat in two parallel rows on either side of a glistening oak dining room table. Food was piled high and cast across the epoxied wood: sweet mashed potatoes, inky red beet slices mixed with chopped apples, casserole dishes topped with browned crusts and tufts of shoestring onions, all overflowing prominently from solid white, modern dishware.

At one end of the table, John's parents conversed quietly. They were a perfectly nice couple that I saw exactly once each year. Ariel and John sat at the other end. The children sat in special chairs, acting as a temperate climate between the poles, and in the red hot, melty equator of the table two empty seats faced each other, reserved for my mother and me.

I hugged my sister and took my seat. Heat from sunlight streaming through the open windows mixed with hot air from the vent at my feet. My face felt cottony with heat. My brain crackled. Ariel's solid, high-backed oak chairs dwarfed me.

"Where's Mom?" I asked, ensconced in my chair.

"She went to her room for a few minutes," John said. "I guess we should get her."

"You guys didn't have to wait for me," I said. "I wish you'd just eaten."

"You're not late," John said. "Certain people thought we should get a jump on things."

"Don't worry," Ariel said. "Mom wouldn't start dinner without you." Ariel was always on her best behavior in front of John's parents. When I had hugged her, I took in a thin cloud of perfume, some kind of citrusy watermelon smell, not real watermelon but how the world decided watermelon candy should taste. She looked beautiful, too, out of her velour sweatpants, lumpy sweatshirt and loose ponytail, which was the outfit fashionable for mothers at that time, a kind of reverse status war to prove how undedicated they were to their own lives. I had seen all this when I went to the girls' play dates.

By now Maddy and Emma had gotten up and run over to the television on the other side of the room and had begun watching a cartoon on mute. John raised his hand, as if about to say something to them, but instead adjusted his glasses and rubbed the top of his shaved head.

"Do you want to get them back over here?" Ariel asked. "I have to get Mom. And grab the turkey from the oven."

"I think they're fine," John said.

"John."

He raised his hand to speak, then put it down yet again and went over to the children. He has a sense of humor about the parts of my sister that drive me crazy.

But Ariel didn't have to go upstairs, because as we spoke, our mother appeared hunched over the railing that overlooks the first floor like a balcony. She looked down at us, not saying anything.

"Mom, dinner's ready," Ariel said.

"Okay, okay," she said. "I'm coming."

The whole scene cut a wide swath across the great room: the shiny stone kitchen, the loose group of adults at the table, the girls in the living room glued to cartoons, and my mother lurking at the balcony, watching it all. For all of Ariel's dislike of small houses, all the action was right here in this room, the fishbowl that the family subjected themselves to. As the other rooms in their McMansion filled with sewing machines, vases, old clothes, and knickknacks, the accumulation growing the way a koi fish grows in proportion to its pond, Ariel closed and sealed their doors. The last time I slept over I had to sleep on a couch; none of the guest beds were cleared.

I stood up and gave my mother a dramatic hug when she returned to the table, one that she took with her arms straight down.

"Careful, I'm sick," she warned, but I hugged through her resistance, giving her a squeeze with my good arm before releasing and sitting down (hugs are to my mother like medicine to children). Her large pink sweatshirt, embroidered with sequins, betrayed her true size. Through the hug I could feel she that was rail-thin, her hair like straw.

"I was worried," she said. "You should have called."

She spoke quietly, as if her voice had trouble breaking the surface of her body. From across the room, John mouthed "early" and opened his eyes wide at me.

"Sorry, I know," I replied to her. "Work stuff."

"What happened to your arm?" she asked, lifting up the bandaging and examining it. "It's all swollen."

"Oh, I hurt it fixing something in the apartment," I lied.

"Doing what? The landlord should be fixing things."

"Sit. I'll tell you later. I'm sure everyone is starving."

As soon as she took her seat, she complained of a chill, and I switched seats with her, which worked out perfectly, as I was already dehydrated from sitting over the air vent. For all the inefficiencies of Corey's steam radiators, they at least kept the air moist. These air vents dried my lips and turned my contacts into a dry film over my eyes. My mother did not have this problem. There was no climate too dry or too warm for her. Her ability to be cold at any time of the year was famous within the family, almost a party trick.

While Ariel pulled the aluminum tub from the oven and removed the bulbous, sweating turkey, I cobbled together a story for the assembled about my hand, involving a dark basement and an unlit boiler. It was the story of my early morning except I lied and said that I tripped in a dark corner of the basement and fell on my hand. The best stories, if you want people to believe you, are ones that reinforce the stereotypes people already have of you. So I told a story about Robin the tomboy, way in over her head in some task better suited for a professional (or a boyfriend!).

"And that's what happened to my hand," I said, closing the matter.

"Uh huh," my mother said.

"Yep," I replied. "So, anyone else sprain anything lately?"

"I'm just wondering," my mother said, "why it's okay that the heat can go out in your apartment, and you've got to fix it yourself. What kind of a place is this?"

"Well, you visited, remember, Mom? So you know what kind of place it is. Hard to get ahold of the landlord on Thanksgiving. Plus it's hard to complain. I have two floors of a house to myself, and I only pay rent for one room."

"Oh, yeah?" Ariel chimed in from the kitchen as she carved up the fowl. "What are you doing with all that extra space?"

"I basically run my business out of there," I said.

"So is that the big house with the peeling paint?" my mother asked.

"If I moved I would have told you."

"How's business?" Harold asked. "Any big bestsellers?"

"It's pretty good," I said. "It pays the rent. But I don't really do bestsellers. Lots of older books, niche stuff. Genre."

"You know those Hudson News shops? They have them in all the airports. I read that publishers pay to put their books out front there. You think it's a meritocracy up there, and you're wrong."

"Yeah, I heard that, too." Harold and I shared an interest in books, though with him the conversation always tended toward everything but the books themselves.

"I thought all those right-wing political books must be so popular. Maybe they are, or maybe someone paid for them to be. You hear what I'm saying?"

"I definitely do."

Ariel brought the turkey down to the table with a gentle lean bitten from the Norman Rockwell painting. Josette said grace. While her wan voice competed with the television volume, I opened my eyes and snuck some looks at my mother sitting in Ariel's high-backed oak chair. Her hair was curly and unkempt as it had always been, but grayer on the ends. She had never put it in a bun or ponytail when we were growing up, and in so many of my childhood memories that effervescent hair lurks in the background. But beyond that still vivid hair, my mother appeared drawn. Frail. She held her shoulders up artificially high like she was ready at any moment for someone to sneak up behind and grab her.

I traced my eyes over the lines of her face, searching for emotion. My days of expecting a satisfying catharsis from her were long over, but I expected to see something, some subtle emotion on her first holiday away from our dad. Her husband. But if she harbored sadness at being apart from him on Thanksgiving, she wasn't showing it. Maybe she was storing it up in her shoulders, creating new, densely knotted muscle.

Josette said Amen, which I mouthed but didn't speak, and we began eating. I had to hand it to Dee Ann. She knew how to cook someone's Thanksgiving dinner for them. I ate a pile of stuffing mixed through with pepperoni bits, then a mound of mashed potatoes filled with a makeshift gorge of gravy. I ate like I hadn't had sustenance for days. Maddy, the older girl, cut my meat for me; I couldn't grip a steak knife with my bad hand. She enjoyed being able to help an adult and show that she was allowed to use a knife. Emma cried at this, demanding to be allowed her own utensils.

A scalloped potato dish passed me, moving from Harold to my mom. The starchy medallions floated in a neon yellow cheese, trapped under a layer of blistered sauce. I can recognize my mother's scalloped potatoes from across a room, which is about as close as I want to get to them. Powdered cheese, packaged, pre-sliced potatoes, and about three sticks of butter. Bake and serve.

"Mom, can you pass those back to me when you're done?" I asked.

"You don't like my potatoes," she said. "You never ate them."

"Well, you know, it's different when you're older."

"I remember when you were seven. You refused to eat them then. You would take the littlest nibble and make this big show of spitting it out."

I took a breath in to speak, then instead I just sighed. We continued to eat along with the rhythms of the television. There was small talk about the economy, the housing crisis, bailouts. I discussed some of the home improvement projects I had worked on, saying that I had helped out a friend, leaving Corey out of the conversation altogether. John, having talked a good bit during the economy conversation, felt, as many gainfully employed people do during a recession, that he was an expert and could provide the final word on the universe.

"So, Robin," John said.

"Yeah?"

"You feel like learning a bunch about home improvement is the most valuable use of your time?" The way he asked made me know I was being set up for something.

"I don't know – I'm enjoying it."

"I sounded like a dad there – I'm sorry about that," John said. "It's just something I feel strongly about, from a theoretical standpoint."

"Home improvement?"

"This obsession people have with becoming home experts. Decorators, plumbers, electricians. This fear that leads people to try to master it all for no reason."

"No reason?" I said. "My whole life I've lived among this stuff and I never asked or cared how any of it worked. There's value in understanding how the world works."

"My coworker, who by the way makes over six

figures," John said, mouthing the words slowly like he was removing potatoes from his mouth, "decided that plumbers charge too much and that he would go out and replace his own toilet. So he does, reads about it online, puts it on there however it goes on, turns the water on and everything works just fine. Flushes, fills."

"I wonder where this is going," I said.

"He's ecstatic. Mentions it five times a day. Well, one day about a month later he's sitting in his living room and he starts to see an off-color watermark, sort of oblong and like a coffee ring stain. So obviously there's a small leak happening. He says 'well, it was worth a try' and he shuts the water off down in the basement, tells his wife 'honey, bathroom's off limits until a plumber comes. Hey we tried.' No kids to tell, they're DINKs which makes this even more unbelievable."

"I don't know what that means."

"Double Income No Kids. Anyway, the following Monday – because you can never just get a plumber to your house, can you? - he's making his coffee in the kitchen and he hears some kind of soft sound, like pebbles falling. Just as he walks into the living room to investigate, the ceiling collapses in front of him and the upstairs toilet tumbles down a bit and gets wedged in the ceiling hole. So the toilet is stuck in the ceiling, half poking into the first floor, and there's a thin stream of cold water hitting their plasma TV that they had just bought. It turned out he had turned off the hot water feed to the upstairs, and the leak got worse all weekend and weakened the subfloor. The whole thing cost him around $10K to fix. He's got the money, but still."

He finished his story with a flourish, waving his hands out across the table like a DJ slowly spinning two vinyl platters.

"So my question is," he asked, "where is the value in that?"

I thought about it for a bit as John waited for a response with a smug sort of smile on his face. In responding, I felt that I was defending the reputation of Corey, a man that John had never met.

"You can find an anecdote for anything," I said. "I'm sure that has happened to people who call plumbers. Shit happens."

"Literally," John said.

"Robin, watch your language!" my mother said.

"But also," I said, "who has a floor that collapses in one weekend? What kind of house is he living in?"

"A brand new one, a lot like our house," he said.

"I spilled a bit of water in the bathroom earlier, you might want to keep a plumber's number handy."

"I do keep a plumber's number. A good one. That's what I'm saying. There will always be plumbers, and they will always be better than you and me at plumbing. For me to hack around on a pipe with some kind of wrench..."

"It's a pipe wrench," Harold chimed in from the couch.

"Now you're all just ganging up on me," John said. "For me to try to even use a, a pipe wrench, is the most inefficient use of my time. I'd be better off learning to salsa dance."

"No, you wouldn't," Ariel said.

"So John, jokes aside. If you're not going to learn to

use the wrench, what are you doing with your time?"

"Do my job, the thing that I'm good at, as well as I possibly can. Get as good at my job, learn as much about my job as I possibly can. Stay late, read trade journals on my own time. Make as much money doing my job as I possibly can. Take every opportunity provided to me. Then, when my toilet breaks in my house – which I bought, by the way, from money I got doing my job – I'll hire a plumber and pay a fair rate to have my toilet fixed. And if everything works according to plan, he'll have the same level of expertise at his job. He won't be spending nights studying up on financial products. He'll do his job – quickly, skillfully, and when he leaves, I'll have the good fortune of my ceiling not collapsing.

"And maybe," he added, "if I still have time on my hands, maybe get an advanced degree, something I always wanted to do but didn't have the time for."

"Are you saying I should spend this free time getting a degree?" I stared him down intensely from across the table. He held his hands out, carefully framing his words.

"No. I absolutely did not mean that. I was speaking strictly for myself."

"Sorry. I'm sorry," I said. "I know. It's just a touchy subject for me."

My mom, who had scarcely moved since she had finished eating, suddenly roused.

"He's right, you know," she said. "You had such potential."

This comment did not lead to a cathartic, teeth-gnashing scene, at least it didn't this time. It's a conversation my mother and I had had a dozen times before, with various levels of fallout, and I am adept at dealing with it. In the past, it has led to the kinds of overwrought, emotional scenes that I wouldn't write down even if they had happened at the Thanksgiving table because they are so cliché and melodramatic. Instead, I adopted a kind of upbeat, singsong cadence, as if speaking about inconsequential and unimportant facts.

"Well, you know, Mom, someone had to stay and help Dad when he was escaping without pants and pouring hot coffee into the silverware drawer."

Slowly, in a way intended not to disturb the air around her, my mother stood up, pushed her chair in, and walked wordlessly upstairs and back into her room. Normally Ariel would have blamed me for chasing our mother away, but it was a sign of Ariel's frustration with her that she sent me a sympathetic face across the room.

By now John and I were alone at the dinner table. I hadn't even noticed the migration to the television. The children lay on their stomachs at Harold and Josette's feet, everyone directed toward an episode of a home buying, selling or fixing up show.

I helped Ariel with the dishes, then sat in a big puffy chair by the television, draped with an afghan my mother had brought with her. I recognized it from growing up. It had these big, generous holes, and I used to lie under it with her as a girl when we would watch television on the couch. I would poke my fingers through the tiny holes and curl them over so that I became attached to it. Then when she tried to get up, the whole thing became tangled, and she had to stay with me. I took a corner of the blanket that had been hanging off the side of the chair, and I poked my middle and ring fingers through two of the holes. At a certain point, I dozed off, my fingers still laced through the afghan's holes.

I awoke to Ariel's grandfather clock striking four o'clock. I had told the hospital that I would pick up my father between three and five. I kissed the girls goodbye, which they barely noticed, being in the midst of a grand dollhouse reorganization. I passed Harold, who by now had passed out in one of the living room chairs, crop full and red-faced. Ariel saw my expression and followed me out to the foyer and finally came outside with me once I was bundled up.

"Not staying for the whoopie pies?" she asked.

"They're just Devil Dogs. I don't know how to make the real ones. I never asked Dad to teach me, and now it's lost."

I had to hand it to Ariel, she knew how to hug.

"You're visiting Dad?" Ariel asked as she stroked down my hair and pulled my flyaways out of her face. I nodded. "You think you're up for it?"

"I have to," I said. "It doesn't matter how I'm feeling."

"I know," Ariel said. "We're going tomorrow. I'm guessing Mom will just stay home; I honestly haven't brought it up yet."

"How much worse do you think she is?" I asked. "I mean really. Since last time she came."

"A little worse. She's fading, really. It's like she's here but she's not."

"Every time I'm about to feel bad for her she's such a bitch." I laughed through the tears when I said it, and Ariel laughed, too.

"Speaking of that," I said, "you're being a lot less bitchy than usual."

"You're making me blush."

"You know what I think it is?" Ariel said. "I think we're at our worst with each other when we're both happy, and everything is going fine. And this is the exact opposite of that."

I gave Ariel a hug goodbye and walked down the gentle grade of her smooth black driveway. One of my feet was on the asphalt, and the other brushed across thick green grass. As my car warmed up, I looked toward Ariel's house. The myriad peaks and dormers elbowed each other out of the way like children fighting for attention. Every line straight. Each angle sharp and severe. Inside the house, I could see slices of the great room through the large bay window. Ariel, back inside, picked up the tray of devil dogs and walked out of sight. She reappeared in the other visible slice, by the television, handing out dessert to the girls. My mother's chair was empty. I sat in the car for a few more minutes, not watching anything, not thinking of anything in particular, just enjoying the warm air on my shoes, feeling the vibrations of the car, and breathing.

Chapter Fifteen

THE SUN WENT down as I drove to Shady Brook, but residual light illuminated the deep woods surrounding the nursing home grounds and tinted the squat buildings with a picture book orange light. Residents sat bundled in chairs, slippered feet on the grass, welcoming an intrusion of color into their world. I stepped out of my car on unsteady legs and felt the wind bite at my bad hand.

Joanie, standing behind the reception desk, put down the phone. Her group of wheelchair-bound malefactors idled to the side of the desk.

"You're late, missy," Joanie said. "I almost changed your father back into his pee-jays."

"I know, I'm sorry," I said. "My dad is the easiest one to deal with sometimes."

She nodded to say she understood. "Gave me a devil of a time yesterday night, though," she said. "Did him some time here with the welcome committee."

It was a shoddy looking group, with old women wearing white dress slips and men in bathrobes. One woman, too large for her wheelchair, turned to another woman and said, apropos of nothing, "I just wait until they're on video. The movies are too expensive now" and the other woman waved her hand in response, too disgusted to speak.

"You've got a lot of problem children tonight," I said to Joanie.

She looked at me over the tops of her glasses. "You tellin' me."

Most of the rooms were empty, sparing me my usual brief, lonely glances. The televisions, extending out on their plastic arms, lacked their usual discordant chirps. I found my father sitting in a chair next to his bed looking off to nowhere in particular. Joanie had dressed him in a nice green sweater with a collared shirt underneath and dark grey khakis that lent him the dignified air of a professor. He looked up at me nervously. I hoped that he knew why I was there, and what day it was.

"Did you bring the flowers?" he asked, tapping his hands on his knees.

"What?" I asked.

"The flowers, for Bettie. Three petunias, three roses, one big sunflower." He said the flowers again in the same order: petunias, roses, sunflower. He started to tear at one eye.

"Dad. Why are you crying?" I looked deeply at his eyes, the way that a parent looks at a teenager's eyes for signs of drug use. I was searching for lucidity or lack thereof. It was important to know whether he was actually sad about the flowers or because his mind had become scrambled.

"Oh, I don't know."

His lip quivered, and I let it, waiting for his next thought to form.

"It's just, I told Bettie I would bring her flowers. Three petunias, three roses, one big sunflower."

I smiled at him warmly. "We can fix this, Dad."

I stepped out and checked down the hallway for nurses, but most of them were standing around the reception area on the far side of the building. Cheap vases of flowers sat on small end tables between every few doors. I grabbed a few flowers by the upper stem and lifted them from the vase, water still dripping onto the carpet when I went back into Dad's room with them. They were small and white, nothing fancy. Maybe paper lilies.

"Well, it's not your roses and your sunflowers, but I think she'll like these." I wiped the bottoms of the stems against my jeans to dry them. "Here, hold them in your hand like you're about to give them to Bettie. Not bad, Dad. Handsome."

"Well," he said, convincing himself. "I think Bettie will like these just fine." He took them from me and held them outstretched with an eye closed, like he was lining up a pool shot, saying, "Yes. These will do juuusst fine."

"Now, where's Bettie's room? I'm going to go have a moment, lady to lady."

He vaguely gestured down the hall. Before I left, I noticed his bare toes poking out from his dress pants. I found a pair of decent black dress shoes in the closet leaning up against a box of adult diapers. The shoes slipped on easily, my father's legs lifted up child-like in the chair. I didn't waste any time, pulling the small waxed laces hard to keep them tight to his feet. As I stood up, I gave his khakis a quick pull, nonchalantly checking the waistline to make sure Joanie had put on his diapers.

Corey was right: it's easier if you think about it as a series of problems to be solved. A sink of dirty dishes. A crack in the plaster. A few movements of the hands.

I found Bettie sitting in a purple Queen Anne chair in a darkened room. I entered tepidly and raised the dimmers, revealing an unbuttoned housedress and a lipstick line as jumpy as a polygraph. Bettie greeted me with squinted eyes. She had been asleep.

"Good evening, Bettie, how are you tonight?" I asked, using my best teacher voice.

"Where are we going?" she asked.

"Nowhere if you don't want to," I said. "But would you like to get dinner with your boyfriend, Terry?"

"Who are you?" she asked.

"I'm Terry's daughter, Robin."

"Oh, Terry. Terry, Terry."

Bettie's room had the same dimensions as my father's, but it had a real house's sense of interior design. The bed, with a dust ruffle and chocolate comforter, barely looked like a gurney. Every type of glittery greeting card covered the elongated windowsill. I forgot for a moment that I was in a hospital.

"These are some nice cards," I said as I passed a brush through her candy-colored mop of hair. I tried brushing it down, but my brush caught regularly and I worried that her hair would begin to fall out if I brushed it too hard. She sat in her chair like a little girl receiving a haircut, arms crossed over her legs. She told a few stories, sometimes sounding like she was talking to a daughter, other times like she was talking to a nurse.

Something familiar on the windowsill caught my

eye, like when you pick your name out of a dense page of words, and I began inspecting the cards. Most of them were small and tent-folded, covered in different patterns of violet flowers and muted blue teddy bears. There were cards for every occasion: a handful of get-well-soon cards, a girl's birthday, a boy's, anniversary, a Christmas card, a few more generic holiday cards, even a Hanukkah card with a glittery menorah. Every single one of them signed by my father.

"You've got quite the admirer, Bettie."

"Well gee, I guess so."

Walking out, I had her take my arm, and I said, "Okay lady, let's get you to the prom," to which she said, "Okay" in her same unaware singsong. We caught up with my dad, who was doddering around in the hall. He didn't have the flowers on him and it didn't come up again.

"Well hello, young man," Bettie said to my father. She seemed to straighten up in his presence. For his part, he just said "Bettie!" with genuine surprise and gave her arm a light squeeze.

Getting them out of the building proved as difficult as getting them ready. Our walk down the hallway toward the reception desk moved at a crawl. My father, one of the youngest patients in the ward, still had the ability to walk freely. Bettie was another story. Still hanging onto my arm, she managed a good step every few seconds or so. In retrospect, I probably should have gotten her a wheelchair. After a minute or so of progress down the hallway, it actually looked as if the exit was farther away.

The desk, when we finally reached it, was unmanned not counting the wagon circle of wheelchairs from the welcoming committee. They were a particularly difficult gauntlet to get past. They asked Dad and Bettie where they were going, for how long, what they were doing, etc. Dad and Bettie gave as many different answers as there were questions asked. Several questions were restated and answered differently. The welcoming committee was enrapt. Leaving the grounds is for Shady Brook patients what sexual experiences are for high schoolers: salacious gossip full of half-truths and embellishments.

After packing them into the back seat, I chauffeured them off campus. Driving between the double statues at the foot of the hill, Bettie exclaimed several times, "Look at all the trees!" to which my father replied, "Oh yeah."

It felt good to be the one showing them all the trees. Tonight I was their jail-breaker. Their savior? That might be too strong. But I was important. Their brains buzzed with outside stimulus, their eyes looked like the overlarge eyes of cartoon children. Every new object shown through the viewfinder of the car window shocked and delighted them. I felt several stabs of optimism, an occupational hazard for those caring for loved ones suffering from dementia.

"There sure are a lot of trees out here."

"All types of trees," my father replied.

I looked in the rearview mirror. Bettie and my dad's hands rested at their sides, just a few feet apart on the center seat. We left the woods and turned onto the main roads, and streetlights flashed across the car every few seconds like the turning of pages. Each time the light passed out of the car, I found myself hoping that when it returned their hands would be intertwined. That those hands, if they were to overlap by just one finger, would wipe away the whole terrible summer, this whole miserable day, and that when I reminisced years later, I wouldn't think about his dementia, or Corey and his emotional baggage. All I would remember about Thanksgiving is that I took my father on a date with his mistress and that it made him happy.

We got to the Chinese restaurant in no time. I parked in a handicapped spot and opened the back doors of the car with a flourish, like my Accord was a limo. I locked my father's and Bettie's arms gently and guided them under the awning into the soft blue light of the restaurant. My father looked up at me, smiling ear to ear. I smiled back.

Then things started going terribly wrong.

It was a nice, clean restaurant with dim lighting and dark blue carpets. A woman in a corner booth, rolling silverware into scarlet napkins, rose to greet us.

"Look at all these tables," Bettie said to her.

The woman ushered us to a booth under a painting of a clear blue mountain, left and returned with water in tall glasses filled with ice. My father grabbed the straw and looked cockeyed at it. "They've put something on my straw," he said, scrutinizing the tight spiral of the decorative straw topper. I pulled it off and brought the glass up to him. He took a long, powerful draw. Again he asked, "What did they do to that straw?"

"It was just paper, Dad," I replied.

"Is this new?" He looked at Bettie for concurrence, but her head was raised up, panning around the restaurant. Her eyes reminded me of a friend's eyes from high school the morning he came up to me in the hall, grabbed my shirt and said, "I took LSD."

Bettie looked back down and across at me. "Have you got my keys?"

"You don't have keys, Bettie."

"As long as someone's got my keys."

This became a mantra throughout the meal. As I drummed my fingers on the table waiting for menus, Bettie asked some variation of the key question a half dozen times. Working the same strategy that I used when my father got 'stuck in a loop,' I altered my response until I hit on one that most quickly appeased her.

"Does anyone have my keys?" Bettie asked.

I lifted my keys from the table and jingled them. "Got 'em right here."

"Oh, good! I thought I wouldn't be able to get back into my house."

In these situations, it was possible to predict almost to the second when the next question would come. Sixteen taps on the table with my fingers and she asked again, "Have you got my keys?"

The waitress handed us menus. My father looked like he'd been handed a scroll of hieroglyphics. Bettie put it straight back down on the table. I ordered three diet colas, unsure about everyone's sugar intake situations and afraid of a mix-up. My father fixated himself on a far table where two small Chinese children, sons of the owner, colored and watched cartoons.

"What are those kids doing?" my father asked with genuine interest.

"They're coloring," I replied.

"What are they doing alone at a restaurant?" he

asked. "They should have parents."

"That's how kids are these days," Bettie added.

"Do you know what you're going to get?" I asked.

"For what?"

"For food. What food you want to eat. It's on your menu. See, there's chicken, beef, shrimp." I was taking his finger and putting it on the different menu items. "Usually, you get General Tso's chicken. And I know you like crab rangoon."

"Are we almost ready to go home?" he asked.

"Let's eat first, okay, Dad?"

"Okay. Sure," he said.

Bettie was feeling at her pockets.

"Does anyone have my keys?"

Jingle. "Right here."

"So," I said. "How did you guys meet?"

Now we would get to the real meat of the night, I thought at the time. I still harbored a delusion that I, like a professional matchmaker, would draw them out with questions, creating a facsimile of a real date.

"Who?" Bettie asked.

"You, Bettie," I said. "And my dad. Terry." I pointed at him.

"What are all these things?" my father said, throwing the menu back down on the table. "I can't read all this funny talk."

"Dad, the menus are in English." He had raised his voice a bit and was looking around as if to ask the youngsters and the waitresses, the only other people in the restaurant, if this was all some kind of joke. Bettie's lower lip was quivering, her mind elsewhere. She had straight wrinkles at the outer edges of her mouth that connected down with her chin, making her mouth look like the mouth of a ventriloquist's doll. As she stared ahead, her jaw chattered separately from her body. If there was a ventriloquist controlling her, he was desperately working to hold her still. I wondered then what it felt like to be Bettie, and whether she recognized the exact point when her muscles, formerly at her command, slowly came to be controlled by a slow-witted puppeteer.

A water glass tipped over with a crash and a handful of ice skated across the table and into my lap.

"Dad!" I said, standing quickly. His oversized menu had been cast aside in disgust. Neither of them reacted to the blob of water spreading across the glass tabletop. Fortunately, the waitress came in quickly with cloth napkins to help me mop the water. Before the woman left the table, my father looked at me and asked, "Why didn't she clean the table before we sat down?"

"I feel like we've always known each other," Bettie said, answering my question from ten minutes ago.

Suddenly the incredible responsibility of watching two dementia patients came into sharp focus. I immediately pivoted into survival mode: get this dinner over with and get everyone home. With the waitress still at the table, I ordered a smattering of menu items, rattling off the numbers like a lotto drawing: 12, 15, 32. I barely looked at the words. To think that moments earlier I had been eager to hear Dad and Bettie order their own food with dignity.

As the waitress jetted away with sopping napkins, my cell phone vibrated inside my purse. I fished it out, still wriggling and buzzing. I didn't recognize the number.

"Hello."

"Robin?"

"This is."

"This is Joanie. I'm so sorry to interrupt your time with your father." Her tone of voice was serious, her accent wrangled into something that sounded formal.

"What's up?"

"Well, I wouldn't normally bodder you during an off-site visit. We're unable to find a patient that lives on the same hallway as your dad and we're calling everyone who's been in tonight. Name of Bettie, short woman with bright red hair."

Bright red hair. I was looking across the table at a mountain of it. Just a simple misunderstanding, I told myself. Stay calm.

"Oh, I'm sorry, Joanie," I said in a voice as soft as margarine. "I have Bettie with me. I must have forgotten to sign her out, too."

There was a pause on the line.

"I hope you're jokin' wit me," she said.

"We're at a restaurant just up the street. I thought it would be nice to take them out."

"Bettie's family gonna come in twenty minutes, Robin," Joanie said.

"I thought I told you on the phone yesterday...and she said she knew about this."

"And you listened to her?! Where's your head at, girl? You pull a woman out of here, and you're not a guardian, you kidnap her. Maybe her family laugh about it, maybe they call the police. Either way, someone get fired." I heard some commotion like the phone had been taken off her ear.

"Joanie? Are you still there? I'm soooo so sorry. I didn't know the policy."

"Plus...PLUS! She needs a fist fulla pills at ten o'clock. Were you gonna give her pills? You know how to use her epi-pen if she has an allergic reaction?? Does she have her epi-pen?"

I saw the waitress emerge from the kitchen with a tray of food and walk slowly toward us.

"No food! Don't bring that here," I yelled with the phone on my shoulder. "Joanie? I'll get her back, right away, I promise."

"..."

"Joanie? I'm leaving now."

"Come around the damn side! I'll give you FIVE minutes."

"Okay, Joanie?" but she had hung up.

The waitress was still walking toward us, confused. I stood up and physically blocked her from placing the food on our table. I kept saying "Emergency. Emergency." I told her "no food. Sorry." I don't know if she fully understood, but I put a twenty onto the table just to be safe.

"Let's go, guys, we have to go. Dad, get up."

"Have you got my keys?" Bettie asked.

"Forget about your fucking keys!" I yelled. "You don't have keys!"

"Well, I...I'm glad someone has them."

"I don't have them," I said, leaning down eye to eye with her. "We lost them. No one has your keys."

"Well...I, I don't know, how...then..."

I tried to pull Bettie up as gently as possible by the arm, but she said, "No! Nnnno! Stop! Hurts!" loud enough that I became embarrassed and stopped. Bettie stood up, slowly, on her own. I could see that her eyes were wet with tears not released. I slipped her jacket onto her. She pulled a balled-up tissue from her pocket and rubbed at the coarse wrinkles around her eyes. I took her arm and walked her slowly out of the blue light of the restaurant, my father trailing absentmindedly, looking at the blue mountains and golden dragons on the wall like a professor at an art museum. The door swung closed behind us. We left a trail of napkins, pulled-out chairs, melting ice, and wet menus behind us.

Outside, Bettie asked again, with some distress, "Has anyone got my keys?"

By now I'd calmed somewhat. I pulled my car keys out of my coat pocket and jingled them in front of her. "Right here," I said.

"Good," she said. "I'm glad someone's got them."

I drove too fast back to the nursing home, swearing under my breath at my stupidity. My naivety. The flipping pages of light flashed on the back seat, this time as fast as a strobe light. It illuminated their curled hands, but this time, I saw them for what they were: lifeless objects that would not overlap. And if they did touch, it wouldn't have meant anything. Unable to look at them anymore, I pushed the rear view away.

At some point during the ride my father poked his head up front and said, "Boy, I am hungry. We should have *eaten* at that place."

Chapter Sixteen

"I'M STILL QUITE hungry," my father said.

"Well, Dad. I think we deserve some drive-thru."

When I had pulled around to the side of my father's building, Joanie appeared silhouetted at the door, arms crossed and a wheelchair at her side. She ran to the car, yanked Bettie out of the back seat and wheeled her away wordlessly before I could even blubber an apology.

It began to rain, then mist, and a vague, wet cloudiness existed up ahead on the road like something you were chasing. My father slumped back in his seat, either asleep or far off in a hedge maze corner of his mind. At Wendy's I ordered a large number of nuggets and some burgers, taking grim delight in feeling down enough not to guilt myself about junk food. In my neighborhood, puddles kicked up rainwater and the car shook as if on uneven hydraulics. I pulled into my driveway and cut the engine. Across the street, Corey's house was pitch dark. My dad needed assistance navigating the muddy patch of grass between the car and door.

"Where are we going?" he asked, huddling against the wind.

"We need to kill some time. So we're just going to

hang out here, okay?"

I turned my screwdriver. The door popped ajar, and cold air wafted across the threshold. The furnace hadn't fixed itself, and if anything the interior of the house felt colder than the outside air, a rare feat in Rhode Island.

I sat my father down in a chair at the kitchen table, keeping his coat on and putting a blanket over his lap. I opened the grease-spotted cardboard containers, dumped the remaining nuggets into the bag and handed it to my father. Smelling the bag, he sat straight up, grabbed it and ate the nuggets greedily. My teeth chattered as I put a tea kettle over the blue gas flame. The gurgling of the kettle almost masked the animal sounds of my father eating. I faced toward the kettle, focusing on its curves, not wanting to turn around and look at my dad. I'm not sure I'd ever felt so low.

Out of nowhere, my father yelled, "Bring me that dog!"

"What are you talking about?" I sighed. I still didn't want to look over at him.

"I know that dog!"

"Oh god, Dad," I said. I couldn't take any more.

I heard him shuffling around in his seat, scraping the chair legs against the floor. Finally, I turned around. He pointed eagerly toward the countertop area. And he was right. There was, in fact, a small ceramic dog on my countertop, straddling a miter cut next to the microwave. I picked up the statue, a Boston Terrier with patches of white and black fur, about the size of an open hand. An eye was missing, and there were chips all along its torso. I had taken it with me from apartment to apartment, but it had been years since I had really looked at it.

Touching the dog triggered a memory: I'm a little girl, not an infant really but still young, maybe six, waiting for an afternoon television show to come on. I hear the furnace kick on downstairs and rush over to the wall-mounted vent to sit cross-legged and let the warm air stream over me. I've arranged the chipped dog, along with some other knickknacks, in a semi-circle on the floor.

I placed it on the kitchen table in front of my dad and bused away his paper bags.

"This dog," my father said. He ran a finger across its back slowly and down its tail. He did it over and over again in a petting motion. When he looked up, I noticed a depth in his eyes. "I know why this dog is broken."

"I've taken this everywhere I've ever lived," I said. "I probably dropped it."

"But I know why it's really broken," he said.

"Why?" I asked, readying myself for a tall tale.

"This was my brother Richard's," he said, holding it up in his hands. "A woman in our neighborhood gave him this when he was born. One day he was playing with the dog – he must have been six or so, and I told him, do you know where we got that dog? And he said, 'Greta gave it to me.' So then I said, I know, but do you know where she got it?, and then I leaned in close and under my breath I said, this used to be her real dog."

"He didn't buy it at first. He said, 'it's not alive stupid', and I said, yeah, but it used to be. It was her dog. I used to pull branches from the mulberry tree and play fetch with him. Its name is Toby. Greta loved Toby so much that when he died, she couldn't bear to bury him. So she preserved him."

"'So it's a statue of the dog?' he asked. I told him no, the statue *is* the dog. She had him dipped in liquid stone. People do it all the time. So he got real quiet, and he said, 'that can't be true.' But when I pushed the statue real close to his face, I'll never forget it, he ran right out of the room, hollering to the rafters."

My father laughed until his eyes became slits.

"So, a week later," he continued, "I found out – oh god, it's so funny to think of it - I'm in the bathroom and I hear this loud banging sound coming up the laundry chute. I went downstairs, and when I turned the corner into the workshop I saw my brother on his hands and knees behind the water heater. He had a ball peen hammer and he was tapping away at the statue with these little, careful taps. When he saw me he didn't jump. He just said, 'shhhhhhhhh - don't tell Mom.' He was trying to free Toby."

"Did he get caught?" I asked.

"Did he…? Let me think. He did! And here's why: he cut his hand on the ceramic chips, and he lied about it. They found his blood by the water heater."

He laughed harder now until it became a full guffaw. Tears ran down his face. Tears of laughter that slowly turned to real tears, the way hot water turns cold in a shower. The tears that accompanied a real, true memory. I gave him a big hug from behind as he supported his head with his hands. His thick black curls smelled like hospital, but I didn't mind. I inhaled deeply. During the entire story, I hadn't felt the notebook urge once. I knew that I wouldn't need to write it down, because as long as my lucid mind endured, I would never forget it.

Chapter Seventeen

"DAD, ARE YOU still cold?"

I thought I saw his breath, but it could have been a trick played by the cross-lights of the lamps.

I had brought him into the living room, sat him down on my slip-covered couch and pinned him down in layers of heavy blankets. My living room, a largely unused space, had a simple glass coffee table and a clutch of tall floor lamps, bent like reeds from being moved so many times.

"Am I what?"

But his shaking hands, one wedged under his leg, answered my question.

"Stay right there," I said.

"Are we going home?"

I stumbled down the basement stairs. Enough light trickled in from the basement windows to reveal a narrow path to the furnace. No basement amasses clutter quite like a college rental's. Mattresses and cat-scratched box springs lined the walls. A number of window-mounted fans leaned in an uneasy tower against a Jell-O-smeared cooler, and the far corner could only be called a bike graveyard. It all smelled like dust and grass clippings and bicycle chain grease.

Squatting down by the furnace with a cell phone as my lamp, I continued the ritual I had started that morning. Using the crude instructions on the side of the furnace, I opened the panel, turned the red knob and simultaneously pressed the ignite button with the wide end of my cell phone. This time, the clicks resolved into a small cone of deep blue flame. The freshly lit pilot light cast blue onto my hands. I let it stabilize, sucking on nearby oxygen until it grew plump. Then I turned the dial again to the right and the whole area lit up as the pilot gorged on gas.

Almost immediately, hot water crackled up the pipes toward my apartment. I closed the panel and stood up. From my spot among the rubble of former keg parties, I had a clean line of sight through the basement window to Corey's house. There was a light on in his turret room, and despite the drawn shades I thought I sensed a commotion taking place. Vague shadows paced from side to side and up, as if hands were being raised dramatically. At one point the shades themselves flapped. One whipped upward and flapped around on its spindle, but was pulled down again before I could glimpse the interior.

Upstairs, my father had fallen asleep. His head drifted down to his chest under the weight of itself, then bobbed back up like a buoy in choppy seas. I sat in the bay window, my eyes fixed on the shadow play across the street. I convinced myself a dozen times to go investigate, and talked myself out of it a dozen more. I checked my watch: we still had an hour to kill, far too long to sit and ponder. It would have driven me insane. So I tucked in the blankets around my father, dimmed the floor lamps, and stepped out into the night while he was still in a fitful, metronomic sleep.

Corey's front door clicked at the first jiggle of the handle and yawned open, silent on oiled hinges. I'd come into Corey's house on my own dozens of times, but this felt different because our fight had broken all the contracts between us. Light from the foyer reached partway across the threshold, illuminating the spatial seal of the house, which I broke with a scuffed yellow rain boot.

A clock struck ten o'clock, and each dong of the timepiece echoed around me into the empty corners of the house. I timed my steps to keep rhythm with them. Ten steps delivered me to the kitchen, ever a work in progress, where the clock hung, its round brass pendulum swinging freely.

Dusty cream-colored sheets hung vertically over every cabinet and cupboard, and power tools smeared with drywall mud rested sideways on the kitchen table. Quietly, I moved a reciprocating power saw to reveal a single slice of paper. Scribbled shapes and numbers clustered in the top corner of the paper. I tried to read them, but a muffled crash upstairs sent me spinning around. The thud shook the hanging sconce over the kitchen table, stretching and shrinking the shadows of the tools. I waited, motionless until the shadows stopped swinging. I wiped my hands nervously on my jeans, leaving white hand prints. My rational mind told me to calm down, that it was just Corey doing his usual home improvement dance. Nonetheless, when I tried to swallow, I found that I had not a single drop of saliva left.

I knew from experience that some of Corey's stair treads creaked so severely as to be cartoonish. So I grabbed the brass pendulum of the clock and held it in place. Next, I moved the minute hand back to before ten o'clock. Then I gently pushed the pendulum back into orbit and snuck over to the first step.

I pushed my hair away from my face. My bangs felt like they'd been brushed with olive oil. I closed my eyes, quieting my inner nerves. I heard no words, only dull scrapes of shoes on a wood floor and a light rustling of paper. With my body frozen, the air settled and a thick, peaty scent flared in my nostrils, like a cigar rolled in wet dirt and drizzled with whiskey. Words floated through my head, as they often did in moments of quiet, words I had heard in my father's room as he bobbed lucidly to his favorite album:

Well I may go crazy,
Before that mansion on the hill,
But my heart just beats faster,
and my feet can't keep still.

They were only in my head, but at the same time, I felt that I could really hear them. The words bobbed and stretched in Van's freeform delivery: yelled, whimpered.

I believe I'll go walking down the railroad, with my cherry,

cherry wine

The clock rang out in dull, metal dongs, like a church bell played through a tin can. Each one covered my footfalls over the creaky steps, which I took two at a time. I pressed my good hand against the wall for balance, and as I rose my hand touched on varying patches of colors, test paint that Corey and I had applied to the wall from small pods. As I stood silently at the top step, my mind journeyed across the street to my father. I will never know for sure what chain of events he fell into as I crept up those stairs, but I can create a scenario, plausible enough, based on what I found later.

He sits slumped on the couch, continuing his fitful, metronomic sleep. He's clutching a small, rough-textured throw pillow, left behind by Karen, until something rustles him awake: maybe a passing group of kids on bikes, or a loud, souped-up Honda racing to the bars on Federal Hill. Or maybe the rough stitching of the throw pillow scratching at his face.

He wakes up confused. Or does he? He wakes up unaware of his surroundings, but isn't it always that way for him? He sits up dazed, the unfamiliar room enhancing the waking-dream quality of his condition. The couch is not his couch. The walls are not his walls if they are even walls at all.

Of course, at the nursing home he is vaguely aware of the bars on his cage, even if he cannot see them. But in my living room, looking sleepily at peeling slices of wallpaper, I'm sure that he had not even a toe's purchase on his environment. Like an animal whose cage door has suddenly come ajar, he is suspicious. He sits straight up, the couch cover bunched up and creased around him. Then he stands and makes an instinctual, stumbling move toward the kitchen. That would explain where I found the pillow. But when he does this, the loose bunch of jersey cloth at the bottom of the couch cover catches his foot. He shakes his leg, puzzling at its tether. With a final tug, his foot dislodges and, free from its resistance, swings forward madly, sending his face, along with his sleep-creased hair, clanging across the coffee table.

After this, I imagine the house is eerily silent. He stays prostrate, for how long I'm not sure, his face at painful rest on the table. A hairline crack makes a glacial journey from the center of the glass outward. After a time, he rises up slowly, his surroundings even less clear than before. With all of the lights on in the house, the bay window acts as a mirror displaying his bruised forehead. He can't see out the window and across the street where I am, at that moment, climbing Corey's stairs in step with a clock. Nothing in the world exists for him outside of that room. He steps slowly into the kitchen. The unstuck wallpaper, the peeling paint, the curled-up corners of the vinyl floors must have all reinforced the idea of a dream world tearing itself apart.

In the kitchen, he spies a small trinket - a ceramic dog. He picks it up and turns it over in his hand, rubbing his thumb across its dull ceramic fur. Its lifeless eye brings absolutely nothing to mind. Nonetheless, it sparks something in him. He places the dog in his sweater pocket where it juts out precariously. Seeing a door ahead, he stalks down the hallway, turns the knob, and enters the night. Were he to have stood absolutely silent, he could have heard Corey's clock clanging as I climbed the stairs. As he stumbles directionless across the cobblestones, the dog peers out from his pocket, an accomplice to his escape.

And still, I stood at the top of the stairs. No more audible rustling or shuffling issued from the turret room. It was so quiet that a dull tone crept in, like a hearing test in school. I stood inches away from the turret door, brow rested above the keyhole. Shadows moved on the visible stair, but nothing else moved. The peaty, wet tobacco smell wafted at me, stronger than before. Air rippled across my arm hair.

I cupped my hand over the keyhole and watched the pattern of light play on my palm. I could have, at that moment, walked down the stairs and out the door. I could have called Corey the next day, met with him, talked out whatever the hell had happened between us. Or I could have just avoided him, dropping him from my life, and looked for a new apartment.

I could have. But that's not what I did. Instead, I took a breath and turned the doorknob. The mechanism clicked, and the slab of oak creaked open. The stairs doglegged to the left and into the small loft of the room. I took a few steps in, scraping my shins on the stairs, my head ducked.

"And who might this be?" The voice was of an older man, weary and impatient.

"Corey?" I asked, shaky. "Is Corey up there?"

"Not that I'm aware."

"It's okay," I said. "I'm Robin, a friend of Corey's. I'm not here for trouble."

"Well, I'd hope not," his voice rasped. "I don't

usually keep office hours. But by all means, come up."

Ascending the dogleg, the room traveled down to meet my vision. I took a step into the middle of the silo. The man sat facing away, hunched over a desk whose corners touched the wall in two spots like a segment of a circle. Shelves, darkly stained, curved around the walls and rose up close to the ceiling.

The man didn't turn. He remained hunched over the desk, running a hand through greasy patches of white hair. Minutes passed. My fears of this strange man coalesced, then slowly ebbed away, replaced over time by awkwardness, then frustration. Unsure what to do, I righted a tipped-over chair and sat in it. The chair must have at one point held a stack of papers, because dozens of them were strewn haphazardly around the chair.

After several more minutes, I finally broke the silence.

"Do you know where Corey is?" I asked.

"Did you say your name was Robin?" he asked to the wall.

"Yes."

"Well, Robin," he said, "it's not my intention to speak for any other man. I am in this room, working now. Beyond that, I am utterly useless to you."

He ran his hands through his hair and turned his head, though not far enough to reveal his face. "I'm not sure where he is."

I saw the raw stub of a cigar, like a loose bag of leaves, packed into the side of his mouth. When I breathed in, I coughed, overwhelmed by the acrid smell.

"Can I ask who you are?"

"You may," he said. His shoulders rose and fell slowly as if he were letting out a sigh.

I paused, waiting for him to answer. Finally realizing his game, I asked again: "Who are you?"

"I," he said, drawing out the word with grizzle. "Who am I? It's a fair question. I am a humble servant. I am bearing a burden that I did not seek, but which I hope I can endure." He shuffled his cigar to the opposite side of his mouth, away from where I was sitting.

This didn't come close to answering my question, and he knew it. I became impatient, which showed in my voice.

"Well, then how do you know Corey? What are you doing here?"

"Robin, I've just tonight had an argument with myself, the fallout of which you are sitting amongst. I am in no mood for cross-examination."

Frustrated beyond words, I put my head down, resting it, along with the weight of the whole day in my waiting hands. I didn't cry, but I sort of whimpered, with soft sounds only a dog could hear easily.

"I just…want to know what's going on."

"Okay. Okay. My goodness," he said. "Let's not bring emotions into this."

The man swiveled his chair around, and I connected with eyes three shades lighter than teal. I stared into them, their own personal oceans, and I felt instantly transfixed. They were intelligent and watery, a welcome resting place on an otherwise haggard face. The man scratched at his tobacco-stained beard and moved the mulchy stump of cigar to the other side of his mouth. I let a wave of recognition pass through me. It was the mayor of tent city.

"I saw you in the paper," I said.

"I hope not on the police blotter."

"No, you're the mayor."

"A burden I neither sought nor refused. But you're right. Every publicly staked tent in Providence is under my jurisdiction. This puts my standing just below that of a third shift security guard, lest you think the power has gone to my head..." he trailed off, waving a hand.

By then he had turned partway back to the desk, where he scribbled into a notebook as he spoke with me.

"I think it's great what's happening over there."

"Then you'll be quite disappointed when state comes bearing the gift of a wrecking ball."

"What's your name?"

"Seril. Former factory foreman, naval officer, convict. Former." He rubbed his temples. "This conversation is wearying to me. Don't take that personally. Would you like a glass of grain alcohol with punch?"

"Um."

"You'll like it. It burns, but it's a cleansing burn." He poured the clear liquid into a cup, mixed in the electric red juice, and handed it to me. I took a sip and felt a bubble of pure heat travel down my throat.

"I thought that article would be trouble, we nearly threw the reporter in the river, but in some ways I am grateful. Grateful enough to thank God, that rascal, because it reunited me with Corey."

"How do you know Corey?"

"Corey. Dear Corey. Corey saved a man's life, and that man was me."

He looked off for a second, fingering the cigar in its glass ashtray. I noticed a thin film of dirt on his face, so deeply ground into his skin that it produced an artificial tan. It was hard to pull away from Seril's eyes long enough to notice the rest of his skin. His eyebrows resembled feeble brush growing between rocks near the ocean. But those eyes. In another far-off time and place, clans of warriors would have charged to their slaughter on command from those eyes.

"Though it is a cliché I will say: at one point in time, he was like my son, and I his father."

"Shit," I said. "My father."

He raised his eyebrows.

"I have to go check on my father."

"Well, that is none of my business. You are more than welcome in tent city, Robin. Stop by anytime. My tent is the big white one, though I no more own it than the President owns the White House."

I gulped down the last sip of grain and retreated down the dogleg of the turret. As I did so I yelled, "I might."

"Do," he replied.

Jogging down the stairs to the foyer, I didn't have time to soak in the oddity of what had just happened because thoughts of Seril were immediately replaced by worry for my father. Making the connection that seeing Seril in the newspaper had sent Corey over the edge in the bathroom, that all came later. Just then I could see my apartment through the rounded window in the front door, and my alarm turned to a warm calm, thinking that I would be coming home to my father asleep on the couch. I thought about how nice it would be to keep him overnight, to wake up in the same house with him again. To spread the newspapers over the table and put his paper plate of eggs right on top of it like he used to do, rolling it all up like a carpet after he finished.

What a beautiful, unfeasible thought, and how quickly it turned to panic when from the middle of the street I could clearly see a vacant couch and magazines fanned across the floor. I threw open the door to find a throw pillow greeting me from the ground. My mind conjured up blood, broken bones, incontinence. But beyond the magazines, the pillows, and a hairline crack across the green coffee table glass, there was no evidence of my father's visit. I rushed through the house, tapping the walls as I checked each room, my breath growing heavier in my lungs with each upturned space.

I sped through the house again, knocking my shins against the stair treads. The grain alcohol had created a hollow warmth inside my chest, a foreign body that wanted escape. I burst out the back door, but my sad, square yard was empty save the rainwater emptying down from the gutter spouts. I looked up. For the first time, the stars seemed just as far away as they really were. In a shudder-inducing thought, I considered that for a great many people, my sister included, news that I had lost my father might not be a surprise, but a call they had been waiting for, a logical extension of our doomed trip to see the snowy owl.

And I had another quiet thought: If he dies, I will be the one that killed him.

I opened my phone, pressed 91 and stopped with my thumb over the 1. I hit cancel and sent Corey a text: *Dad's missing, was at my house, I need you.* Then I bent over with my arms in the air and vomited the whole miserable day out onto the cement steps.

Inside the doorway, I had started to curl up and cry on the ground when my phone pulsed out from my pocket. Message from Corey: *I'll be right there.*

The time on my phone read 12:05. Thanksgiving was over.

I decided to run across the street, re-enter Corey's house and plead for help from Seril, but before I left my sidewalk I spotted a small lump of ceramic on the ground, halfway between my house and my neighbor's. It was Toby, the little chipped dog. The front door of the three-family house was cracked open, and I rushed in without a thought. I must have touched every third step in that narrow, spiraling staircase. Both of the bottom two apartment doors were locked, but the third, its landing decorated meticulously with vases of fake flowers, yielded to my shaking hand.

It was the Portuguese woman, the one whose husband didn't exist. She stood over an olive-green stove, taller than it by a head, stirring a large pot of soup. Dizzying brown and yellow wallpaper patterns made the kitchen appear even smaller than it was. At the opposite side of the room, my father sat at a dark wooden table, upright and attentive.

I stopped at the door frame. Neither of them noticed or acknowledged that I had entered the room. The woman, hidden in a floral housedress, hummed a song in Portuguese. Her hair was held up in a loose bun with dozens of bobby pins. My father did not look injured or distressed. He looked around vaguely, his eyes wide open, his hands carefully tucked under his legs. The woman scooped some soup into a bowl and brought it over to him. She didn't speak, but she smiled as she placed the bowl in front of him. She smiled the way married couples smile at each other. A smile that doesn't have to say everything, because it is just one smile, and there are lifetimes yet.

He took a bite of the soup, filled with all of the things he should not be eating: salted greens and rich, fatty sausage. Potatoes and littlenecks. It might have been the best thing I've ever smelled. He looked positively overjoyed, and she sat next to him, watching him take bite after bite. Neither had noticed me, and the apartment was still silent when I heard stomping up the stairs. I looked over. Suddenly and without warning, Corey was standing at my side.

Before Winter

"I must drag my body through the muck and mire,

Gather branches for its funeral pyre,

Twigs I would rather twist into nests,

Or whittle wooden wings and fly."

-Brown Bird

Chapter Eighteen

ON THE COLDEST days, swans still glide down the Woonasquatucket at sunrise. They move in closely clustered pairs from under the Point Street Bridge. A little ways up, the river runs under the Providence Place Mall, but I'm not sure if the swans go that far. My father once explained to me how these birds can bob like buoys all day in near-frozen water without freezing. It had something to do with the circulation of blood through their legs. On a few occasions my father compared me to a swan – as a birder, he was lousy with bird comparisons. He said that my personality reminded him of a swan's in the way that its still beauty hid a relentless paddling under the surface.

But boy could he see the kicking on the drive back to the hospital that night. When the Portuguese woman noticed our presence, she ran at us in an attack posture, yelling, "You get away!" Corey, on site for less than a minute, tried to block the woman with a bear hug, but she got me on the back with her ladle. The whole drive to the hospital I could feel the broth running down my back.

I don't remember much about the rest of the trip except little details, the things you attach onto when you're distressed: that the hallway lights in the nursing home seemed almost comically bright, that the paper turkeys, brown streamers and other Thanksgiving decorations had already been pulled down and that we slid in just before absolute, no shit curfew. The detention area held one wheelchair patient who woke up just in time to see a man and a woman in a soup-stained shirt wheel a patient down the hallway. I walked backwards in front of my father, unbuttoning his shirt to speed up the process of putting him to bed. The hallway lights reflected in his black eyes. "Is it bright in here or what?" he asked. It was the first thing he'd said in an hour.

I knew that the next time I visited, our disastrous night together wouldn't come up, and unlike the snowy owl incident, there weren't any physical remnants to implicate us. One of the benefits of a father suffering from dementia is that your lesser mistakes wash away like a sand castle in the tide. I kept looking for a silver lining, and that's the best I could come up with.

Corey and I didn't talk on the ride home. I turned the radio off, and we drove in silence. When the car became too hot, I turned off the air vents and a second, deeper silence set in that exposed the fraudulence of the first. I let out an occasional sniffle, aftershocks of a hysterical crying jag. I watched Corey in the flashes of the streetlights that illuminated the car. He kept his eyes forward, his hands on the wheel. I wondered whether another sound I hadn't noticed yet would go quiet, then another, like we were excavating down to pure silence.

Corey cut the car engine in his driveway. He put his hands back on the wheel, right at ten and two, as if he were going to keep driving. I thought that maybe he was working himself up to say something. It is difficult to describe the imbalance of information between us then. A lifetime existed between our fight in the bathtub and that moment. I looked at Corey sitting dumbly, like a child pretending to drive. He looked over at me just for a moment, hands still on the wheel, then looked ahead. Paint splotches laced the backs of his hands like tattoos. He could have been thinking of anything.

I thought he was waiting me out, hoping I'd leave, but instead he broke the silence.

"I finally got those shutoff valves," he said. "And the right solder. We can replace the feed lines to those toilets whenever."

"Oh." It was all I could say at first. He rested his hands at his side, looking a bit more comfortable with the state of the conversation. I looked forward to where our headlights exposed the raw edges of his rotting porch stairs.

"Actually," I continued, "I think I'm going to take some time off from home improvement."

He looked at me, confused. I think I was scared to say what I was going to say. I pictured the shower bag he threw in a rage and how it exploded against the wall like it was an egg.

"I'm going to volunteer at the tent city." I flinched, waiting for an explosive reaction, but Corey just put his hands back on the steering wheel. Then he picked at one hand with the other, removing bits of paint.

"Well. That's your choice."

"I know."

"I'm looking forward to it." I continued, "There are

some good people there, I'm finding."

I was giving him an opening, which he didn't take.

"I'm sure there are."

"Hey, thank you for tonight, Corey. Everything aside, it was really helpful to have you there."

"Are you sleeping over?"

I tried to glean his posture from the windshield reflection, not wanting to look straight at him. His shoulders slouched, appearing chastened.

"I'm not sure. Is there anything else you want to tell me while we're talking?"

He gathered himself up a bit and raised his posture to something approximating confidence. He said, "No, why? Is there something I should be telling you?"

That was enough for me. I opened the truck door, scooted out and shut it hard as I could. He opened the window.

"Robin, wait.."

"I met Seril, Corey. I met him in your house. Where you wanted me to sleep over. Jesus."

He didn't say anything right away, and I wasn't going to stand waiting. I stomped across the street back toward my house, fishing around in my purse for my screwdriver. Corey's headlights stayed on as long as I was awake, which wasn't long.

When I finally got to bed that night, I slipped into the dreamless sleep of drugged hospital patients, fully clothed under a thick down comforter. When my eyes opened next, it could have been the morning, or it could have been several days later. I felt the cold mattress next to me, then remembered that Corey hadn't slept over. I rolled over and fell into a second, more fitful sleep, with terror dreams of nude bodies with flamingo heads and regrets etched into unevenly canted roof lines.

At one point in my dreams, I entered an empty room lit a deep, raw blue with a solid row of unframed windows across the room's far side. What looked at first like shadows were missing floorboards, the empty spaces leading down to an unseeable place. The only way to avoid them was to wait for the slow, sweeping spotlight that passed through the windows. Each time the light hit head on, I was nearly blinded, making for slow passage, and I was still making my way across the blue expanse when I woke up for good, roused by a beam of sunlight through the shades.

The lit dust particles blew around the room like snow, and the towers of books were just becoming visible around me. I worried that I may have slept through the entire weekend, but it was early afternoon on Black Friday, a cold, bright Providence day. I wrapped myself in a blanket and pulled the curtains open to a game of street hockey, the boys looking like stuffed dodos in their winter coats. At one point their orange ball ricocheted off a cobblestone and bounced onto Corey's porch. The turret above him stood hidden from the world with its shades drawn. His truck was still in the driveway, but his BMW was gone, its cover held down with rocks and whipping in the wind. My phone buzzed on the table, and I picked it up. Corey had sent me a text in the night. It read: *he was my uncle*.

Chapter Nineteen

AFTER HANDLING SOME book business, I visited my mother at Ariel's. I'd sold dozens of books over Thanksgiving week, a new record, but one which I hadn't kept up with among all the chaos. I cringed thinking of the bad feedback imminent on eBay and Amazon. After logging my sales, I printed a stack of invoices and gathered books from Karen's room. My filing system strained from lack of upkeep, and it took forever to gather all the right books. As I scratched each from my ledger pad with a dull pencil, I prodded at my phone's touchscreen, keeping Corey's text alive on the table. I didn't respond at first. I made the connection between this text and the night we drove back from the nursing home when Corey had helped so perfectly with my father that I had seen him for the first time. He mentioned a family member then, and now I knew he must have meant Seril.

After emptying a trunkful of boxes at the post office, I hit the highway. The world was returning to bed after huddling together in the cold for Black Friday sales. From the highway, streams of shoppers issued from Best Buy, giant boxes resting askew in their carts. I thought about the text more as I drove. For a mere four words, it gave me a lot to think about. Why did he use the past tense? The guy wasn't dead, and I felt no one deserved a present tense more than Seril. I exited the highway, whipped through McMansion lane and steered into an empty driveway. Ariel had taken the girls to the Warren Audubon and John had checked into the office for a few hours, leaving the house quiet except for the echo of television and a light rustling of laundry.

A good visit with my mother can best be described as uneventful, and this one fit the bill. We passed a few pleasant hours together in her guest room, folding clothes and watching television. She worked from a rocking chair, not being a believer in watching television in bed. As interior design gurus chittered away on the screen, she folded one tiny shirt after another, putting an impressive amount of care into each fold, caressing the finished product before adding it to a stack. She breathed entirely through her nose; her mouth never opened unless she needed to rip loose a string from a shirt. I matched socks, rolling and tossing them among the frilly pillows on the bed.

The only sour note that afternoon came when I brought up Dad. She asked what I had planned for the rest of the weekend, and I said that I had to bring some decorations to the nursing home. I didn't even say Dad, just nursing home. Maybe that was why she didn't walk out, like usual; instead, she just changed the channel and picked up one of Maddy's tutus from the laundry basket. She couldn't figure out how to fold it crisply, its frills anathema to her exacting specifications. Finally, she rolled it up and threw it limply back into the basket. She rubbed her temple.

"I cannot go to that place." She ran her hand through her curls, rough as hay. "I cannot."

She'd said it before, and given her track record, she meant it. In the past I fought her, I cried, I yelled. But that day I looked at her statement like a puzzle box to be solved.

"You know, Mom, he doesn't have to be at the nursing home. We could take him out. Then you wouldn't have to go there."

She didn't answer, but she didn't look puckered either.

"Do you take him out of that place?" she asked. "Has he been out of there for even a day?"

"They get taken out all the time."

"Who's they?"

"The patients. Dad."

"Does he go out with other people? Do they get to choose? Can they go out together?"

She fixed a stare on me. When my mother gets into fact-finding mode, she is frightening. Her questions come rapid-fire, and then she quiets down and stares at you, expecting you to squirm. Needless to say, I got away with nothing as a teenager.

"That's not what I meant, Mom. Just they. The patients can leave. I've taken Dad out a bunch of times. I could bring him here if everyone wanted."

She continued looking at me for an awkward amount of time. I didn't flinch, or at least I don't think I did. I kept my eyes forward on the television. Eventually, she picked up an article of clothing, turned away, and went back to folding. It took a while for the air to warm back up in the room, but it did, when I made fun of someone's shirt on the show we were watching, and she snorted laughing.

Aided by the show, we began talking about home improvement. I sidled up to her recliner and showed some grainy photos of Corey's house on my phone and tried to hide my amazed face as she not only complimented the sanded floors and new faucet hardware but actually asked to see more. Once, while pointing at something she touched the phone's screen by accident and jumped back in shock when the photo zoomed. I asked her if the phone gave her an electric shock, but she just laughed and held her hand against the neckline of her housedress.

It had been my intention to turn our conversation about my father into a payoff. To set a date and bring him to Ariel's. But in the moment, laughing with my mother, I couldn't make the words come. They existed in the yesterday, dark-tinged and ominous. Now a cold sun was shining through the windows of the great room, revealing not one fingerprint on all the steel appliances. A trunkful of books I had sold, products of my ingenuity, were traveling by truck and plane to postal vectors across the country. And my mother was laughing. I looked out the bedroom to the hallway. Shimmering rainbow streaks of floor cleaner shrank and evaporated before my eyes. This was one of the moments you stayed in.

Chapter Twenty

I APPROACHED TENT city with a fake Christmas tree hanging out the back of my trunk and the usual thumping of books replaced by the gentle rattle of ornament boxes. I'd left my driveway with a plan to visit my father, but a compulsion sent me in the opposite direction. I rolled off the highway into the pot-holed Jewelry District, pulling U-turns past plating factories and pizza shops, finally finding the erector-set bridge on Point Street. Across the river dozens of tents in every shade of blue, grey, and maroon dotted the crescent of land between the river's shore and the highway overpass. In the far back, a large white tent loomed over the others. I thought that this must be how armies traveled in ancient times.

To my surprise, the city had a design. The tents faced each other in rows, planted tight as crops. The land had been parceled out as by a city planner. Residents had dug small moats around each tent to route rainwater down to the river. From the curbside, the distinctions between neighborhoods came into sharper focus. The first wave of tents near the road, beat to hell, hid a cluster of large, clean nylon tents, farthest from the river and fully sheltered by the highway overpass. Some of the lesser tents flapped in the wind, but most stood solid as a house. Men and women in sweatshirts and old Starter jackets sat outside their tents in plastic chairs, smoking. By the river, a woman with long hair hung pairs of jeans on a clothesline wound between wooden poles. Another woman brought a basket of clothes down to the river while at the same time two men stood downriver urinating into the lazy black waterway.

I got out of my car and looked backward down Wickenden Street. I couldn't believe it: through the portal of the overpass shone some of the oldest, most expensive houses in Providence.

I walked down the main thoroughfare, sneaking thin-sliced views into the smaller tents. I saw shelves with knickknacks. Green desk lamps. DVD collections. Even Xboxes. Sometimes a pair of eyes stared out from inside the tent, half shadowed. People outside sat in lawn chairs. Some stared at me, others said a friendly hello no differently than if they'd been sitting on their stoop. Two black boys passed me, half-pushing, half-riding a shopping cart rattling with green glass. As they pushed it back down the path, people came out of their tents and threw small plastic bags of trash onto it. I expected filth and barrel fires and instead I found barbecue grills and Coleman tents.

One of Seril's helpers, a man I later met named Lenny, was spraying down the wedding tent with a hose. The slick nylon was blinding in the mid-morning sun, and the spray rainbowed out into the air before dissipating in the cold wind. The man stopped spraying and waved as if he knew me. Before entering, I looked sideways through the flap. The tent was quiet, and I couldn't see anyone besides Seril, sitting behind a large metal desk dwarfed by giant maps. I started to turn.

"Is that you, Robin? Come in. Don't peer like a child through the staircase spindles."

I ducked my head in and walked down a spotless carpet toward him, marveling at the support beams, big as telephone poles, that ran up to the spacious ceiling. It was one of those fancy tents that they set up at Newport mansions for special events. White Christmas lights strung up the poles lent the room a soft focus. In the corner, two women in sweatshirts raked an apron of grass.

"Want some coffee?" he asked.

I picked up a coffee pot on his desk, sloshed it around, sniffed and winced.

"Always the dregs at this hour," he said. "You should get up earlier and watch the place come to life."

It wasn't the coffee.

"Little early to be drinking," I said.

"Isn't it, though?"

"Mind if I make more?" I asked, and he waved a hand absent-mindedly.

I poured the coffee out onto the ground, rinsed the pot with a jug of spring water and put more coffee on. When the alcohol hit the ground, Seril crossed himself, ran a hand through his greasy hair, and turned back to a giant map of Providence that dwarfed his desk.

"Have a seat," he said. "I know how cold it is out there; I've been."

Compared to the outside, the tent felt tropical. Space heaters faced in every direction. I put the jug of water down, waiting as the coffee maker gurgled, and he immediately moved the jug to the ground and lined up some pens. "Everything in its place," he said.

He picked up a marker and began marking the map. His eyebrows moved along with his arm motions, and occasionally he would take a step back and look at the whole map, rub at the dirt on his face, and swear under his breath.

"Robin, I know we don't know each other well, but Corey is quite fond of you, and I think you've been good for him."

"He has a strange way of showing it."

He smiled. His bottom row of teeth looked like dominoes falling.

"Ahh. That," he said and sat down at the table across from me. "That is a perfect segue. What I was about to ask you is: how do you suppose I know he likes you?"

"He told you?"

"No. He exactly did not tell me. That's how I know."

We continued talking. The first cup of coffee erased my headache. The second left me shaky. It was strong stuff. During the second cup, Seril began laying into me with flattery, and I'm ashamed now to say that I ate it up.

"I was, at least, able to get out of Corey what you did for a living," he said. "It's quite impressive. Having your own business, in an economy where…well, you know." He gestured outside to the rows of tents.

"Thanks," I said. "It wasn't planned. I worked at bookstores for a while, and I spent half my time shipping out. Then I read an article about scanning software for checking prices, and I thought I'd give it a try."

"That's very interesting. Have you ever thought about being a writer?"

"Always." No one had ever asked me that before, but I thought of it so often.

"Why aren't you?"

"I've never finished anything."

"A writer is simply one who writes. So by that definition, you are one, whether or not you finish a book."

"It's so difficult that I wish I hated writing," I said, leaning over my coffee. "I wish my compulsion was for stamp collecting."

"Well, there's a reason I brought it up. There are two things I need help with that I think you're uniquely qualified for if you're interested in helping."

I had come specifically to offer my services, but now I hesitated to speak. With flair, Seril stood, then dropped back into his chair and spun it so that we sat face to face.

"Robin, is this about Corey?"

"No."

"I'm certain that it is. He and I have had our troubles, and he's probably had all manner of things to say about me. I don't blame him for being wary. But at this moment, all of this is bigger than our petty squabbles. It's important work."

He stopped to pack a dip into his lower lip.

"He's just concerned about me, I think," I said, not sure if it was true but wanting it to be. "He doesn't think a place like this is safe."

"Robin. This place is not perfect. There was almost a knife fight last week. But it's safer than it has a right to be."

He spit into a coke can.

"That said, the moment this place no longer needs to exist, I want it to just…what's the word?"

"Recede?"

"Yes, exactly! Recede. We have a wordsmith. Recede slowly, and then all at once. And be gone. But right now, there are no spots left in the shelters, and it's an unfortunate fact, but tent city needs to exist. Corey can wish it isn't so, but it won't change facts on the ground."

A man in an army coat peeked his head through the flap, but Seril waved him away.

"Not now. So Robin, assuming we are all on the same page, hear me out. While this place exists, it's important that I get a sense of morale, of what is bothering people. Improvements, issues, dangers. You know what I mean. The easiest way to get this would be to ask, or to observe. But when I observe, as mayor, it changes the outcome; I'm sure you've heard of that principle."

"What I need is for someone to observe for me. Thoughts. Opinions. Concerns. No names, this isn't some Big Brother operation. I need someone with a quick pen and a tuned ear. Now here would be the good part. All that information: complaints, tales of woe, hopes. Dreams. That could be used, if not now then sometime in the future. I think it would make a hell of a book, to be honest, and it may lend some significance to what happened down here, this little community underneath a rusting overpass. Nonfiction, or you could even spice it up a bit and make it fiction."

I didn't say it aloud, but my hand had practically itched for my notebook from the moment I got out of my car. In my head I had been jotting down just the kinds of notes Seril was suggesting. Tent city was a rich meal for my compulsions. But I didn't want to tip my hand right away.

"I'll think about it and let you know soon. I promise."

He reached out, touched my shoulder tenderly, and looked straight at me with clouding eyes.

"I hope that you will. Now excuse me."

He stood up, marker in hand. I watched him a while as he connected houses with lines, shaded in streets. The map was dense with information. Along the side, Seril had written out a legend in different colors that was nearly unreadable. Two quotes graced the top of the chalkboard where the map had been taped. One said: *By concord little things grow great*. The other, underlined violently, said: *A Shelter for Persons in Distress*. It was either the most sophisticated map I'd ever seen, or it was utter nonsense.

I drove onto the highway from a road that ran perpendicular from tent city, arranged so that the road resembled the stem and tent city its spoiled flower. At a stop light, I adjusted the rearview mirror and watched a woman hobble back to her tent, lift her infant child up and pull it to her sweatshirt. A gruff man on a mountain bike coasted down the main thoroughfare with a box under his arm. He skidded to a stop, reached into the box and began tossing cans of Narragansett to the men in chairs. The traffic light turned green, and I pulled away. As the tents became smaller in the distance, the city took on the look of a patchwork sail made of burgundy, gray and blue tarpaulin, stitched together with twine, laid across a sloping expanse of grassland, billowing in the New

England wind. The tents disappeared completely as I merged onto I-195 and away from the city, the sharp turn of the onramp sending ornaments jangling across my car floor. I felt a real sense of purpose, and I couldn't help but smile.

Chapter Twenty-One

WINTER CAME ON a bit like the low-rent ornaments I hung on my father's wire brush Christmas tree: a signifier of the thing rather than the thing itself. It hadn't snowed, and most days I could walk outside with just a short-sleeved shirt and a scarf. My hand had healed by early December; still, on the colder days a soreness radiated from between the knuckles. I felt it most as I threw taped-up packages into the postal drop. As books sold, my stocks grew so low that I could walk freely with arms swinging through every room in the house. One day, leaving Violet's room, I ran my fingers across a long row of spiral-bound notebooks, former dumping ground for my compulsive thoughts. I lingered over the last in the row, thought a moment, then pulled it out to leaf through the fresh blank sheets. The last entry was stamped early October. I placed the notebook in my backpack along with a government made gel pen (I'm very particular, almost fetishistic about my pens) and headed toward tent city.

That notebook followed me all over tent city. I scribbled into it madly while residents waited in line for chicken dinner, trying to outdo each other with stories of woe. It nosed nervously into tents with me and rested on my lap as I shared a cramped cup of tea with cheery middle-aged moms, a beer with strung-out teenagers, and once, an ambulance with a drug addict named Mitchell. One warm morning I discreetly followed a hunchback man, his beard halfway to the ground, as he walked the city pouring buckets of water to check the integrity of the city's moats. He worked fast, and took a certain pride in his job, or so I thought until I saw Seril pass him a flask. This happened in the postal tent, which is tucked between two highway pylons like a crumb in the binding of an open book. Each week, through back-channel connections too byzantine to understand, a postal truck sped by, throwing out a twine-tied bundle of letters. I noted, with a double underline, that an enterprising tent city dweller had strung a sign onto the tent flap that cheekily read: "HOUSE OF UNPAID BILLS."

My notebook travelled so far and became so dense with writing that it bowed in the center and sweated from the inside out. Finally, I holstered it in Violet's room and opened a fresh spiral, marking the date and weather on the inside cover. By the time I'd filled my third notebook the next week, Seril had ordered Lenny to set me up with a ceremonial tent outfitted with the amenities befitting someone of my importance: a sleeping bag, a shelf filled with notebooks, and a hot pot, normally contraband due to its risk of electrical fire. In spending my days around tent city, I had become a regular: a person who could tell an aid worker which tents needed clean needles, and newsmen which residents they were allowed to interview. Without realizing it, I had become enmeshed in the city in exactly the way Corey didn't want.

Depending on the day, I came home energized, or defeated, or both. I ended more than one day curled like a hedgehog into my comforter. But I also had spans, days in a row, of coming home and writing my congressmen about homeless policy, tuned up on righteous anger. This new passion existed uneasily with my job, and even less easily with my familial relations. I still got all of the books I sold out the door, but visits to my dad dropped off a cliff in early December. One night, after staying up late writing by the fire, I actually slept in tent city. I hung my clothes in the middle of the domed tent and slipped into the flannel sleeping bag. At first, I lay in bed, reading my notebook by the green desk lamp, unable to sleep among all the cacophony. But eventually it quieted down and felt no different than camping. When I put my notebook away, I noticed that on top of the shelf, Seril had left a triangle of paper for me with words written in a small, delicate hand. It read: *The librarian of a small town was once also its historian. And in recording the town's history, the librarian endowed the townspeople's lives with meaning. And in granting their lives meaning, set them free.*

One night, as I sat cross-legged in bed copying over lines in my notebook, Corey showed up at the door looking like a lost dog. Sometimes when interviewing city residents I wrote so fast that I could barely read my own writing, and when this happened I always tried to rewrite while the words still lived in my memory, because is there anything as sad as coming across an old note from yourself and not knowing what it means? I looked down at my front door from the bay window, and Corey looked up. Maybe it was the angle, but Corey looked small in stature from up in my room. Diminished. I sighed, but to be honest, I had been waiting for the moment. I told myself after our fight that I would wait for him to make the first move, that I needed to wait for him. He looked up again, as if looking into a security camera, and jangled his keys. I held up a screwdriver and tapped its milky blue handle against the window.

We drove to Prospect Park and sat at the base of the Roger Williams statue with our feet dangling over the sheer cliff face. Conversation came slowly, our words carefully considered. From up on College Hill it looked as if we could kick out and make contact with the minor skyscrapers downtown. I commented on Corey's white T-shirt, more spotless than usual, and he admitted that he hadn't so much as hammered in a finishing nail since our argument. It was unthinkable to me.

"What have you been doing?" I asked.

"Watching a lot of television. Trying to cook better food…cook any food. Thinking."

"You don't have a television."

"I got one off Craigslist."

I leaned against the base of the stone leg, surveying Corey the way Roger Williams now surveyed his land. Over even this short period of time Corey had become softer, his arms less sinewy. What I didn't realize until later is that Corey, an ascetic monk of home improvement, was beginning to integrate himself back into the real world. Real food. Television. Being outside with me in a public park. He looked more healthy, but if I have to be honest, also less compelling. The animating spark that kept Corey in ceaseless motion - those first days of watching him carry load after load of refuse to his curb past dark came to mind - was, if not disappearing, then at least waning, and I wondered what would fill the void left by it.

"Want to hear something funny?" I said. "This isn't Roger Williams. I mean, no one knows what he looks like exactly. This is just a generic revolutionary era guy."

"Seril teach you that?"

I didn't respond, instead taking an unusually long sip of my soda.

"Sorry."

"He did actually."

"He knows his Rhode Island history," Corey said. "Ever since I was a kid."

"Why did you say he *was* your uncle?"

"Two reasons, I guess. He's my dad's brother, and my dad's dead, so I feel like it's optional at this point."

"I don't think it works that way."

"Well, there's a second reason. I basically disowned him. I reached out to him a while back when he was having some trouble. I tried to help him, and when he started to get better, he ran off on me. I thought he was dead."

"I'm sorry." I put my hand on his leg. "It sounds like he had issues."

"You think? You've been down there, you haven't seen him acting strange?"

I told Corey that he seemed no stranger than I'd expect from a mayor of a tent city.

"He's a little...grandiose, I guess. But he seems to mean well."

"Well, I was with him when he was catatonic. The

hospital had him so drugged that he remembered less than your father when we went to see him. I signed him out of there. It was two springs ago, I think. Maybe three. He stayed with me for a while in my apartment, then moved with me to my house now. One day I woke up, got dressed for work and brought a cup of coffee up into the turret where he was staying, and he was gone. Clothes. Bedsheets. He had this World War II poster of a diesel-powered submarine, and he took it off the wall. From that day until I saw him in *The New York Times*, I figured he was dead."

"He's family - don't you think he's worth another chance?"

A couple strolled behind us, arm-in-arm, and Corey leaned in, lowering his voice.

"Well, I'm letting him stay in his old room when he needs it. That's enough for now. I'm worried about his motives."

The couple, college-aged and in thick flannel, jumped the low fence and stood by Roger Williams's other leg and looked down to the grass a few stories below.

"Whoa," the girl said and held the boy tighter. "I got chills. Sorry to interrupt - nice night."

The boy said, "So this guy, what'd he, he invented Rhode Island?"

"Sort of," Corey said. "But this isn't him, I guess. No one knows what he looks like."

I smirked at Corey.

"Whoa," the girl said. Then the boy raised his hands up and yelled, his voice echoing out across the city.

"HISTORY IS A LIE!!"

Chapter Twenty-Two

AFTER THAT NIGHT, a mild, shambling kind of order returned to our lives. We were back together, spending nights tapping in crown molding then collapsing onto the floor at night to fall asleep to whatever television show I could call up on my laptop. Often he would outlast me, and I would fall asleep to the light cacophony of home improvement. Sometimes we slept in his bed but more often than not we drifted off to sleep curled up on his living room floor, surrounded by cheap cups and a patchwork of blankets. If I awoke in the middle of the night with a sore arm from sleeping on hard wood, I'd gently nudge him off me and spend the rest of the night above him, unfurled on the couch. We thought nothing of going two days without a shower. The only difference now was that when I woke up in the morning, Corey was still asleep next to me. We woke up together. Seril stopped by to shower or to work in the turret, but whether by chance or by design, we never ran into each other. I only knew he'd come by if I saw silt deposits around the shower drain.

Our physical reunion proved harder to rekindle. Corey was game; more than once he even stopped in the middle of a project, which would have been sacrilege a month ago, and tried to put a hand under my shirt. In every case, I was the limiting factor. I found myself concentrating when I kissed him, and Corey finally told me, "it feels like I'm kissing a table leg." I just couldn't get there. Every time we got into a horizontal position, I would test myself, but each time I went to the well I came up dry. We even tried to watch porn, setting the laptop on the end of the bed and clicking from one three-minute video to another. But we ended up spending most of the time dissecting the sets, trashing the vanilla McMansions, the tacky pools, the cream carpets freshly parqueted by vacuum. "Are these sets?" he asked. "They're probably whoever owns the porn company's," I replied. Someone once said that porn tries to be about sex, but instead, it's usually about power; I think it might actually be about home furnishing. The houses played into the fantasy; they were as joylessly beautiful as the blonde actress's flesh. Corey shut the laptop lid, and we kept the conversation going for what felt like a long time trying to get to the bottom of it, happy for the distraction.

Why the sudden coolness toward Corey? I couldn't say at the time, but there was a certain distance, self-created, that I found myself pushing against, which, since I was pushing against myself, was like trying to lift a chair while sitting in it. I kept in the back of my mind the memory of the night we brought my father back to Shady Brook. Corey had asked me if I was going to sleep over but he hadn't told me about Seril. For some reason, it still bothered me. Was he going to wait until Seril and I bumped into each other in the middle of the night, groping around in the dark to find the bathroom?

As degrees fell from the thermometer, Providence did its best to dress up for Christmas, coming off like someone late for a party who finds their suit crumpled in the corner, smooths it out as best they can and heads out into the night. Half of the storefronts on Westminster were empty, and men stalked under Christmas lights, which were run like streetcar cables, begging for change. One guy with a braid and thin lips, who I'd seen many times at tent city, told me that he'd just gotten out of jail the day before and needed some help to turn his life around. Inured to it, and knowing he wasn't violent, I said, "Again?" He smiled at me. "Seriously, though, if you're hungry, go to tent city and get some food."

"I already been there today. Once a day's the rule. Those college boys brought a feast."

He was referring to a group of Brown University kids who'd started collecting goods and bringing them down regularly.

"If you're hungry again, tell Seril Robin sent you," I said, and ducked into a craft store, looking for a cheery totem for my mother.

RISD kids were helping too, in their own way, right on Westminster. In an attempt to fight the desolation, RISD students had installed art into window displays of empty storefronts. These students, who would leave Providence and go on to design Nike ads and work on Pixar movies were for a short time filling window displays with neon bursts of their own youthful hope. The site of drab, bearded men holding Tim Horton cups out in front of sprawling creatures made of green plaster and pink glitter showcased, to me, everything that was beautiful and tragic about the city.

Looking at one of these storefronts, my face cast with the blue glow of an alien world, I received a tap on the shoulder. When I turned around, James Freezer was smiling nervously at me, holding his top hat at his side.

"You haven't been on my tour," he said. He already seemed more mature, and his curls were brushed away from his face. His Harry Potter glasses made him look studious now instead of like Harry Potter.

"You still have that fucking top hat."

"I come down this street now for daytime tours and work up to Benefit. Lovecraft used to go to a library up there. It winds down after Halloween though."

"Are you stalking me now? I thought I was supposed to be the stalker."

"Hey, I'm sorry I said that. If that's why you left me in the middle of the night, then we're even. You didn't even get breakfast."

I took his hat from him.

"Jesus, you could actually fit a rabbit inside this thing - so you were going to make me breakfast? Easy-mac?"

"No. We get guest passes for the dining hall."

"The perks."

A man across the street stopped his loping stride and

seemed to squint across the street.

"Ms. Robin - that you?"

It looked like someone I'd interviewed, but the name didn't come to me.

"Hey, there - tent city?"

"Yes yes. Sir, you've got one of the good ones right there - yes you do!" he said, and continued down the street.

"I gave that guy a dollar last week," James said. "Friend?"

"He lives in that tent city out by exit 2 by the river."

"Oh, one of my friends does some work down there. You don't..."

"Don't...what?"

"..."

"No, Jesus. James, do I look homeless?"

"Actually, you look great. I almost didn't recognize you. Not that...you know."

His cheeks went red, then turned back to peach as if by force of will. A good lesson to take from this is that single-minded obsession, when it leads to missed meals and relentless manual labor, is at least good on muscle tone.

"Thank you." I took the compliment without laughing it away. "I help at the city sometimes. I'm sort of their archivist."

He grabbed onto his hat, but I didn't fully give it up.

"Hey - I need my prop."

"You're stronger than I remember."

He looked at me, suddenly very seriously.

"Come back to my room with me."

"You're walking in the opposite direction. Do you have plans?"

"It doesn't matter. Just come."

I thought about it. I could feel my body tugging forward, could imagine it walking back up Westminster, over the river and up to James's dorm, tumbling into the dark void of his room.

"No. Sorry, I have plans tonight."

"Can I at least get your number?"

"No." It felt strange to say the word again. "Sorry."

His smile dropped.

"But I'm at tent city a lot. Go with your friend and ask for me. I might be there."

I let go of the top hat, and his arm shot back. We said goodbyes and headed opposite ways. After watching him turn and disappear into a restaurant, I found my car and wound my way back to Corey's. I turned the music up in my car and opened the windows despite the cold. When I got up the stairs, Corey had just flipped the switch on an industrial vacuum, and the ceiling lights flickered. I ascended the stairs under crackling lights, followed the sound to his bedroom, yanked the cord from the outlet and threw Corey against the wall.

Chapter Twenty-Three

I'M GOING TO transcribe a phone call I received mid-morning the next day while I was still half asleep and tranquilized by sex. I rolled naked under Corey's comforter, trying to find the phone through the feel of its vibrations against my body. When I stretched, my hand tapped against a warm coffee cup that Corey had left on the night stand. I exhaled and rubbed one leg against the other. Finally, after an eternity, I found the phone pulsating at the small of my back.

While the conversation happened, I'd say I was about forty-percent awake; only afterwards did I jump out of bed and scramble for a scrap of paper to write on. Later on, I transposed that scrap into my tent city notebook and am now placing it at permanent rest in this account. It's likely that something was lost in the transfer. For such an important conversation, it's frustrating that I'll never have an exact record of the exchange, and that over time this one, with all its flaws, will through sheer force of time become the truth.

"Good morning, am I speaking with Robin?"

"Yeah."

"This is Denise calling from Shady Brook. How are

you this morning?"

"Is my father all right?"

"Oh yes, I don't mean to alarm you. Your father is absolutely fine. I'm calling to inform you of a relationship that your father is currently engaged in."

"This is Bettie, right?"

"Yes, that's right - Mrs. Chapman."

"Are you calling to tell on my dad for having an affair?"

"Under the circumstances, ma'am, I don't think we'd use that word."

Corey came up from behind and tussled my hair, but I shoved his hand away. He started pacing through the bedroom pulling up shades, letting piercing light into the room.

"Then why are you calling me about this?" I asked, covering my eyes. "He's an adult."

"As you know, at Shady Brook we strive for a delicate balance between the wishes of the family and the freedom of our patients. We're just calling you to tell you that your father and Mrs. Chapman have formalized their relationship."

The word hung in the air.

"Formalized?"

"Yes, stated their relationship formally."

"Like, consummated?"

"Oh, Robin, no. That's not what we mean. Our patients are strictly supervised. This is a paperwork exercise in many ways. We have a rule that when patients state that they are in a relationship, we notify the immediate family for cognizance."

"Cognizance," I said.

"We're sorry to have to tell you this. It can be difficult to picture our parents with other people."

"Or with each other," I muttered.

"What?"

"Nothing. What comes next?"

"This is it. We just like our families to be aware of it, and aware that we have counseling services if you find them necessary."

"I know you guys are expensive, but shit."

"Do you have any other questions today?"

"No. Thanks for telling me, I guess."

"Have a good day. Goodbye."

"Wait, did you say 'immediate family'?"

But the call had ended. My mind immediately traveled an hour north to a cushy suburb in Massachusetts, and a landline ringing, and a woman with grey, frizzy hair shuffling slowly toward the phone, and all her fine china rattling behind glass.

The conversation between Ariel and me is easier to transcribe accurately because it took place over text message.

Me: *Did you get the call from Shady Brook?*

Ariel: *Yes.*

Me: *Mom?*

Ariel: *MOM.*

Chapter Twenty-Four

THE NEWS OF my father's senescent affair didn't explode immediately upon impact. Instead, it trickled out as a kind of nuclear radiation. We couldn't see it and everything seemed fine. Only later, when a woman gave birth to a baby with three arms, were we forced to recognize the problem. Calls to our mother went unanswered - our voicemails unreturned. She planned to stay with Ariel for the weeks surrounding Christmas, same as Thanksgiving, and we kept that in our heads as a worst-case scenario. Pushing the reality of our father's affair onto our mother while sitting around a Christmas tree: I couldn't imagine a better holiday.

Meanwhile, Corey had finally embarked on the white whale of house projects: re-doing his kitchen. The night that we ceremoniously pulled away the drop cloths, the raw surfaces and stripped wood resembled a patient mid-surgery. To even place one's hands inside the construction zone was to risk danger. He'd removed sections of the yellow countertop and thin chips of Formica, like jaundiced razor blades, mixed into the silverware drawers and scattered across the remaining countertop. By the time Corey finished, his hands looked like they'd lost a fight with a cat.

Over a long weekend, we removed the whole countertop and replaced it with another, nicer Formica countertop that resembled marble, with a backsplash built in. Corey let me cut the hole for the sink. He traced a rectangle onto the surface in marker, drilled four pilot holes, then handed me the jigsaw. I placed its thin blade into the first hole and rested the plastic feet onto the countertop, waiting while a buzz ran through my body. It dawned on me then that there are two types of home improvement tasks: those that can be easily redone, and those that are final. Though it should have been nerve-racking, I never felt more in the moment, alive even, than when I was about to perform a job that could not be undone. All my thoughts dropped away. I stared with laser focus at the jagged edge of the jigsaw blade, squared my shoulders and pulled the trigger. My focus stayed on the blade as it made a tentative journey around the countertop. Sawdust obscured my fine marker line. An inch away from the blade my vision became blurry, two inches away may as well have been pitch dark. The searing sound of metal on wood only seemed to get louder when I concentrated on it, and I let the sound colonize me. Corey lay underneath the countertop, which was propped up on sawhorses, and held the inner piece for the last cut - he didn't want its hanging weight to crack the Formica. When I finished, Corey gently let the slab slide down and away like a trap door so that I was looking down through the sink hole at his sawdusted face. He wiped the dust from his goggles and looked back up at me.

"There are so many things I'd like to tell you," he

said.

"Like what?" I asked.

He considered his words. I thought that he might be on the verge of saying something important.

"You look hot with a saw," he said.

By the middle of December, I had sat through enough tent city meetings to feel like a beat reporter for a small-town newspaper. With some discipline, I could probably wrangle my material from that period - five notebooks and counting - into something approaching a definitive history of the place. This near constant presence gave me the equivalent of a third ear for information, and in what I was hearing, I began to get suspicious that Seril had a grand plan in the works. I had no direct proof, but now when I entered Seril's tent, I had to wait by the door while his cronies "staged" it for me. When I did get in, I often found his big chalkboard had been turned to the wall, his formerly disarrayed papers neatly stacked and covered with a cover sheet that read 'Classified.' During meetings, one of his inner circle would respond to a proposal by saying something like, "How would that align with the thing..?" and Seril, with only his eyes, would shut the guy up. I didn't run into James at tent city, but according to Seril he had come twice and asked about me. "A little pipsqueak was squeaking your name," is how he put it.

"Did you talk to him?" I asked.

"The day a pipsqueak like that gets into my tent," he said, and left for more important business.

And then, out of the blue, James began texting me. I didn't know how he got my number, but I suspected Nizme. At first, I ignored him. Then I moved to short, unspecific responses until a conversation began that seemed to have no beginning, no end, and no point except to continue. I missed the text bubble in high school and never went to college, so I'd never been courted in that way. Many of the exchanges went like this:

James: *[random fact about his day]*

Me: *you're boring me to tears*

James: *what ru going to do about it? ;)*

I tried to tell myself I was annoyed by this. In reality, it felt like I was carrying a living secret around in my pocket. And it had another side effect. On nights when I pulled the phone out a lot, Corey paid more attention to me. He asked whom I was talking to (I always lied). Then he started acting strangely: he'd ask what parts of the project I wanted to do, instead of telling me. Sometimes he asked if I wanted to go out afterwards (I usually declined). This would have appeared, on its face, to be what I wanted to accomplish. But when I finally got Corey's attention, I found it distasteful. It flew in the face of what I understood Corey to be. With each query from him, with each earnest consideration of my opinion, a little bit of the mystique of Corey chipped away. When I went to bed with him on those nights, he took extra care with me, treating my body like something worth taking time with. I kept my eyes open through it in the dark. I didn't think about James exactly. Instead, lying under Corey, I thought about the idea of the living secret, the phone about to buzz on the nightstand, the thought of texting James in the darkness, still in the afterglow of sex with Corey. It was more than enough to get me there.

Chapter Twenty-Five

"TILE HAS GOT to be my favorite material," Corey said, shaking the box like he was offering me a corn chip. I took a small, shiny tile and held it up to the light. "It reminds me of having a big box of Legos as a kid and running my hands through it."

After we installed the countertop and the sink, Corey got right to work on the backsplash. He came home with a small pallet of two-inch tomato-red ceramics that had been pre-glued into one-foot by one-foot squares. He immediately put me to work with a box cutter, disassembling a few of the squares so that we would have spare tiles for finish work. When I asked how many spares we'd need, he took out a measuring tape and began muttering to himself.

"Let's see - height of the backsplash, in inches. Divide by two, roughly. Look for a remainder." Then to me: "A lot. We'll need a row of half tiles all along the top. We need to score and snap like, a hundred of them."

This took us well into the night. I placed tile sheets down over a layer of cardboard and traced my box cutter between the rows. Once they were separated, I tipped the cardboard, and the tiles slid into a plastic dish basin with the dull sound of money.

While I did this, Corey frosted the walls with mastic and secured sheets of tile to it.

"Hey, I think I saw your landlord the other day," he said.

"You know what he looks like?"

"No, but a guy pulled up in a blue truck and walked around the yard. He sort of looked like a landlord." While he spoke, he placed a piece of wood across the secured tiles and tapped it with a hammer, the mastic oozing out at the edges.

"That was probably him. Where was I?"

"You were out and about." That was his way of saying I was at tent city.

I laughed. "Maybe he just got my message about the furnace from Thanksgiving."

"Maybe."

Once he hammered in all the sheets, he began making half-tiles from the spare pieces in my basin. He scored lines on each tile with a diamond wheel, then placed it into a hand vice that resembled a curved pair of pliers. The score line appeared as a mere fingernail scratch against the tile, but when he squeezed the vice with one hand, the tile split cleanly in two and tumbled into a Tupperware container. I mopped up his dust with a dish sponge, but before I finished, my phone buzzed in my pocket. I ended up sitting in a chair at the kitchen table returning texts to James, my face lit by the glow of my phone.

"Who's that?" he asked.

"What?"

"On the phone."

"Oh - my sister."

James was visiting a friend in New Jersey, and he had sent me a pic of a Princeton bumper sticker with the artist Prince's face and '-ton' after it. *Nerd humor*, the message read.

"So how's the stuff with your family?" Corey asked.

"Oh, I don't really feel like getting into it. It's okay."

"Man," he said, snapping another tile, "this stuff is tedious."

A silence followed between us, with Corey's steam radiators whistling out of tune. Eventually I put my phone away and went into his area to watch him snap his last few tiles.

"Look at those smooth cuts. It seems crazy how perfect they are. They don't ever break wrong?"

"Very rarely."

"You've got a talent."

"It's not me. It's the tile." Corey reached in and grabbed a couple of tiles, running a finger carefully down their glass-sharp edges.

"That's why it's my favorite material. More than wood, or plaster or lathe. Definitely more than drywall board. It has this really shiny exterior. But then the inside is different: it's rough, but it's consistent. It's a perfectly uniform material, like glass. It's strong, but it just needs a little bit of pressure, and it breaks where it's weakest, even if that weak spot is just a tiny scratch."

He split the last tile and placed down his tools. His hands had taken on the shape of the curved pliers.

"I lied before - I don't think this is tedious. I could

tile all day."

My phone buzzed again, and Corey noticeably flinched. I checked the message - it was the same bumper sticker as before, but the camera had zoomed in closely on Prince's eyes. The message said *look at me, Robin*. I chuckled.

"Something funny?"

"My sister," I lied. "She's going stir crazy in that house."

"Hey, so I was thinking..." he said. This is how he'd tried to get me out with him the last few nights.

"You know, Corey, I don't really feel like going out."

"How'd you like to go to tent city tonight?"

I paused.

"With you?"

"Yeah. I figured it's worth seeing what Seril's up to."

"I don't know, Corey."

"This is what you wanted, isn't it?"

It was, but it felt like an idea past its sell-by date. I looked over. Ceramic powder dusted him, making him seem like an antique. Behind the layer of dust, he looked out at me with large eyes cartoonish with emotion. I understood his confusion; he'd expected cathartic excitement and instead got apathy. He held my gaze. The radiators bled out the last of their wet air.

"Fine," I said. "But clean up first."

Before we left, Corey finished the tiling. Using a butter knife, he spread mastic into the thin strip between the newly set tiles and the bottom of the cabinetry. Then he carefully placed each half-tile into the row, pressing it hard while performing minuscule corrections until the piece sat square with its brethren. I watched him from the kitchen table, holding two emotions inside of me at once. The wry smile on my face corresponded to the thin victory I felt at convincing him to enter tent city, something I had been hinting at for nearly a month. But under the table, where my hands shuffled and picked at their own cuticles, feelings from the previous nights were being replayed of an almost disgust at the capitulation I had so badly wanted.

Corey placed the final, odd-shaped slivers of ceramic around outlets and light switches, then placed a final, triangular piece on the side wall where the backsplash tapered down to a point, a piece that had taken a dozen tries to cut correctly.

"Finished."

When we pulled up to tent city, Corey let the car run for a minute with a hand placed on each heat vent, as if strengthening himself with warmth. I got out of the car and looked down the main thoroughfare. The tents, tightly zipped and lit from inside, resembled paper lanterns laid across a grassy field. New spotlights lit Seril's tent from the bottom up, lending it the creepy grandeur of a castle.

"I just need a minute," Corey said.

"It's sketchy to sit in your car out here. You'll look like a gawker."

Reluctantly, Corey exited his car. His height forced

him to crouch when getting into or out of his BMW, but this time, when he emerged from the car, he didn't fully unfurl himself. Instead, he looked permanently half-inflated, his shoulders slouched forward into a horseshoe. He looked nervous, and I think he wanted me to take his hand and lead him forward. But instead, I just said, "It's this way," and headed down the main walk, forcing him to catch up.

Several people appeared from around their tents and greeted me. I practically got mobbed, to tell you the truth. It had been a few days since I'd been to the city, and I underestimated the importance of my ear and my notebook as a pressure release valve. Nearly everyone I talked to had new wrongs to report, new reasons to feel pity and skepticism. Some stories sounded fabricated, but most others seemed all too real. Forms rejected for vague reasons. Shelter space refused. A thousand paper cuts of bureaucratic failure so incompetent that their victims were forced to create conspiracy theories because the banal truth was too depressing to comprehend. Their only salve seemed to be that they could tell me, and that I would listen and write. Standing outside this mob of people as they shouted their sadness - "there were ten spots in the shelter, but I was still refused!" "I hear they're going to start refusing tent city people at the hospitals" - Corey said nothing, but I saw the pained expression spread across his face, starting at his forehead and working down. Because he had hidden in his house while the entire economy slid into recession, he hadn't seen these sights on the street or heard these stories on the news, and had no antibodies against them. Members returned to their tents after saying their piece, and some of them looked at Corey, wondering who this man was with uncombed hair and a white T-shirt. Their eyes splashed against him like cold rain on bare flesh, and I saw him shudder.

In front of Seril's tent, Lenny nodded to me and peeled open the flap. The heat trickled out like a scent trail. Again Corey stood unmoving. The uplighting cast our shadows long and thin against the stretched tent fabric. I smelled stale tobacco. For reasons I didn't understand at the time, I didn't want to comfort Corey or help him ease into this. He had agreed to come to tent city and, in a way I'm not proud, of I relished the thought of this place and every other problem of the world that he had been ignoring hitting him full in the face. I gave him a stern look. He furrowed his brow, took a deep breath, and stepped onto the grass-flecked carpet. At the far end, Seril sat at his desk flanked by brushed steel cabinets.

When we got to Seril, he made a show of slowly standing from his desk and shaking Corey's hand, the deliberateness of it indicating its importance. He put out plastic cups pre-filled with liquor and topped them off with a splash of soda from a two-liter bottle.

"Sit. Sit," Seril said. "I have the best of news."

His desk, normally a tornado of paperwork, had been reorganized into neat stacks weighed down by rocks. One particularly large pile on his desk had the look of an official report and read *HousingWorksRI - Foreclosures*.

"I've just now at this desk had an epiphany. I figured out the problem with Rhode Island."

"One problem?" I asked.

"Lack of smallness." He chuckled and scratched his

beard. "It's so obvious to me now."

"Are you kidding? It's the smallest state."

"So it is." He looked off. I glanced over at Corey, who was sitting dumbly quiet, looking around the tent in disbelief.

"That's exactly right, but I meant people. It's important to feel insignificant sometimes. We don't have that in Rhode Island, it's too small. We don't have the mountains of the west that make men feel insignificant. No sweeping plains or deserts. Here, everyone feels significant."

"There is one thing, one I just now thought of - the ocean. But you can't just look at it from the shore, can you? You have to be out there in a boat. And that's the problem - who can afford that? Have you ever been out there? I mean way out. The average Rhode Islander needs that, I think. Needs to be brought out there like Pip and driven mad."

"You been drinking much?" I asked him.

"How devilish of you to ask me that," he said, and took a pull of his drink, holding it up first in mock-salute.

"You know what we have to make us feel small? It's unfortunate, but it's our domiciles. Our obscene McMansions. But the same trick doesn't work, because these monstrosities are made by man and only serve to inflate his ego. What do you think, Corey?"

Corey hadn't heard the question; he was still looking around stunned.

Lenny walked in. "Time for dinner for the third shifters." Seril wound up and tossed a ring of keys across at Lenny, who used them to open a brushed steel cabinet and remove handfuls of dry goods to serve by the grills.

"Corey," Seril said. "Would you like to help Lenny set up dinner? We're short-staffed, and I'm sure he would so appreciate it." Corey looked at me, and I shrugged to say, either way. He stood up and nodded, sort of sadly, and loped over to Lenny, who got to work putting boxes of cereal and jars of peanut butter into Corey's arms.

When Corey had left, Seril sat straight in his chair and narrowed his eyes at me.

"That pipsqueak was asking about you again."

"Okay."

"I'm very loyal to Corey, you know."

"He's just a friend."

"Robin, I have few friends, so, for now, I'll take your word for it."

Then, like an actor breaking character, his eyes widened to expose his full, cerulean pupils, his whole body relaxed into a slouch, and he started to laugh.

"What am I talking about? Robin, Robin. What a dump this place is, and how soon our sheltering overpass will be turned to rubble. It's important that I show you, as town historian, the succession plans I have in place."

I didn't know quite what he was talking about. He stood up, holding onto the chair and then the table as he walked to his oversized chalkboard. A turn of a crank revealed its opposite side where a large map of Providence had been glued to the board. Marked up, pinpricked, and traced with bits of yarn, the map looked like a late night cram session by a fifth-grader the night before a civics fair. It would have been comical if the map weren't so accurate, and the man standing before the map not so piercingly serious as he watched me take it in for the first time.

I looked closer. Some buildings were circled in red. Others had green X's on them. The spot we stood on, the crescent of land between the highway and the river, had been burned from the map, the singed edges obscuring South Water Street. My eyes hopped on the highway, took the Broadway exit, and turned down Knight Street. In our neighborhood a few spots had been marked around Corey's house, and maybe Corey's house itself, though I couldn't tell exactly. Seril smiled a mischievous smile at me. His open mouth contained just about every color but white.

"Welcome to tent city 2.0," he said.

I found Corey after dinner service, standing alone on the river bank looking up at the three smokestacks of the Narragansett Electric Company. At this time of night, everything existed in gray scale: the inky river flowing past, the unlit brick buildings across in the jewelry district, the hurricane barriers way downstream. Only the smokestacks, with their warning lights like blinking jewels, brought outside color. I half-expected Corey to reach up like Gatsby and try to grasp one of the lights with his bare hand.

"Hope they didn't work you too hard," I said.

He jumped.

"Robin? Sorry, I didn't know it was you," he said. "It gets so dark down here. Dinner was fine. Easy."

I heard a wet sucking sound and looked down.

Corey curled his toes into the spongy dirt.

"Where are your shoes? You must be freezing."

"My feet? Oh no, they're fine. When I walked down here, I knew I wanted to stand in the mud. I can't say why."

"Can we walk?"

I led Corey along the riverbank past the charcoal grills. A series of fires created small pockets of light where hands rubbed together and voices slurred over each other into a tight mesh of sound. The banks of tent city ran less than a quarter mile, so the walk up and back felt short.

"What are you thinking about?" I asked. He looked distracted, far off.

"I was thinking that you were right," he said. "Seril's done something good here. I feel ashamed that I've never come down to help."

"I was about to tell you that I thought you were right," I said. My meeting with Seril had left me shaken, unsure of every nice thing I'd ever said about him.

But Corey either didn't hear me or he ignored me.

"I have this same feeling in my gut as when the mortgage company I worked for collapsed. When that happened, I got the urge to fix my house. Not tinker - fix everything. Lose myself in it - forget about every bad mortgage I ever sold and what they might have done to people. I'm getting that same feeling now about this place."

"You're going to finish the house first, though, right? Wasn't that always the plan?"

Corey's face beamed now as if there was light inside it. He stopped walking, leaned in close and kissed me. All I could smell was the river water and grass clippings.

"So what did you and Seril talk about?" he asked, resuming our walk and ignoring the question.

"Um, he showed me his plan for tent city when this place gets shut down, which will probably be soon."

"Oh, yeah? That's exciting. What is it?"

I shook my head, trying to gather my thoughts. "It's...insane. He wants to spread everyone out across a bunch of abandoned factory buildings and houses. He has scouts, and he's been like, tracking good sites. He has this map that's all color coded like it's from that *Beautiful Mind* movie. He wants to use some places for housing, some for central storage of food, trash, etc. He basically wants to layer a shadow city on top of Providence."

"Wow. That sounds ambitious."

"It's unworkable, it's crazy. These abandoned places aren't really abandoned. Someone owns them."

"Well," he said. "Let's not judge it right off the bat."

I was so frustrated. We had suddenly appeared on opposite sides of an argument and hadn't even seen each other in passing.

"Are you serious?" It was like a single visit to tent city had delivered an electric shock to his system.

"I understand now," he said. He didn't explain further but said it again, smiling. "I understand."

Understand what? That helping people is good, not bad? That leaving your house to engage in the world is worthwhile, and not a revolving door of horrors? What was he trying to say? We ended our walk at the southern tip of tent city, near the Point Street bridge and away from any tents. He looked up again in contemplation at the three smokestacks, towering in the distance and blinking away low-flying planes.

"Maybe there are more important things than fixing my house."

A splash broke his reflection. Ankle deep in water and hidden by tall grasses, a middle-aged woman emerged at the edge of our sight. Corey looked down from the smokestacks and searched the water. Excitedly, he took my hand and walked with me toward her.

"Ma'am," he said. "Do you need any help? Are you okay?"

The woman looked up from her washboard. Moonlight caught on the corrugated metal and reflected outward like a mirror. Her sweatpants were rolled to her knees. She tossed a wet cloth into a bag of clothes sitting just out of reach on the bank. When we got closer, she placed her board down and pushed some hair out of her face with a jingle of a charm bracelet. Instantly, the light went out of Corey's face.

"We're okay," the woman said. "Considering."

Corey squeezed my hand and began to backpedal.

"Okay then," he said. "We have to be going. Have a good night."

When he said that, the woman's eyes flashed with recognition, but before she could speak a little girl appeared from behind her mother's legs and ran out, her feet splashing in a pair of blue crocs.

"Corey!" she said.

Corey stopped backpedaling and crouched down, red with embarrassment.

"Hi Isabelle," he said. "Have you been good?" She

nodded proudly.

"Remember the game, Iz," the woman said. "Too close to the tents is minus points."

Walking toward us, she unrolled her sweatpants and put her hair into a bun. She smiled, and her face made a round, joyful shape. She looked like a soccer mom that hadn't showered in a few days because that's likely exactly what she was.

"I recognized you," the woman said. "Just like she did. Too many hours in your waiting room reading Highlights."

"Stephanie?" he said, and she nodded.

"Corey, do you live here?" He didn't speak but instead shook his head and looked down and away.

"Well, we don't either, officially. They don't allow kids, but there's ways around it if you're careful."

I'll never forget her T-Shirt. It had a whimsical stick figure on it, and it read *Life is Good*.

"We'll be okay, though," she said, and then she looked intently at him. "And we don't blame anybody."

Isabelle ran around Corey in a circle and stopped at his leg, coming up to about his thigh. Her eyes were the same deep-well black as the water that had been moving concentrically from her mother's ankles.

"Corey, do you remember my fish?" she asked. He didn't respond because he looked frozen in time, a statue.

"Well...I don't have my fish anymore because he *died*. And we don't live in our house anymore, but we have a big, big van so we're actually very lucky."

Some of my biggest laughs at my nieces are when they, in obvious plagiarism of their mother, speak far in advance of their age. "Oh, these strawberry flavors are very in-ter-testing," Maddy once said while eating a plain strawberry. When I hear something like that, I can picture Ariel saying it, probably while eating a fancy dessert that John's boss had brought over. That's part of the magic of kids. But it cuts both ways, and that night I pictured Stephanie zipping up Isabelle's sleeping bag on the reclined car seat in their van, breath visible, saying, "You know, Iz, we're actually very lucky." And by the look on Corey's face, I think he pictured it, too.

Winter

"I think it is all a matter of love; the more you love a
memory the stronger and stranger it becomes."

- Vladimir Nabokov

Chapter Twenty-Six

COREY DIDN'T TALK on the ride home. He'd wandered to the car in a daze; I practically had to guide him to keep him from tripping over the nylon ropes staked out in front of the rows of tents. He kept his eyes closed and tipped his head back as if in prayer. When we walked into the house, a chalky smell hit my nose. I looked down; he hadn't put his shoes back on, and mud caked his feet, kissing the ends of his rolled-up jeans. I asked him if he had even brought his shoes back, but he just clumped past me and up to bed.

Two days later, a man showed up and handed Corey an envelope of cash and drove away in his BMW. Without missing a beat, Corey put the envelope under his arm and walked down the street in the direction of tent city.

As he spent more and more time helping Seril, his house, once a riot of construction sounds, became eerily silent. It felt unnatural to even be sitting inside it. After one particularly long day of looping to the post office and back, I took a bath in his glazed tub, but I found it impossible to relax among such mundane silence. When I slipped my head under the water and rose back up to the surface, I yearned to hear the scream of his circular saw.

More and more days stretched on like that, with Corey

gone at tent city and me wandering through a silent house. He would arrive back at the end of the night, tired but not sweating like before, and not in his white T-shirt. He'd take off his jacket and crumple into bed.

At the same time, I pulled back from tent city, still shaken from Seril's deranged 2.0 presentation. Without getting an okay from Corey, I decided to work on the house myself, filling it with my own sounds of construction. After shipping out the day's books, I would change into a bad pair of pants and one of Corey's shirts and tackle a room. Surprisingly, I found that we'd already finished a lot of the house once the grime and construction debris had been cleared away. Instead of worrying about the big jobs, I focused on finish work, on the type of details Corey could never settle on because he always wanted to jump to the next big demolition.

On my best day of work, I painted and nailed in new baseboards for the living room and kitchen, measuring and mitering each cut to handle the unique angles of a hundred-year-old house. I laid the long boards out on drop cloths and sanded each before coating them with high-gloss paint. Afterwards, I got down on my knees and looked down each board with a flashlight, looking for errant brush strokes.

At first, it felt wrong to be doing home improvement without Corey, like I should be getting permission for each job. What if I botched a cut and nailed the piece in, making my error permanent? As an answer, I told myself what Corey had taught me: that almost any house problem can be fixed with enough time and care. And if it can't be fixed, like the rounded divot in the upstairs wood floor, that would be okay too; the mistake would act as information, telling someone a hundred years from now who we were.

One night, Corey slept at tent city. He texted late at night, asking if it was okay if he crashed in my ceremonial tent. He wanted to get started helping at dawn. I texted back *sure*, probably the most ambiguous word in the language of relationships. I spent the rest of the night poking and prodding at my phone, exchanging inanities with James. At one point, he asked if he could come over. I thought about it for a while, but in the end, I said no - not tonight. Not yet.

Chapter Twenty-Seven

CHRISTMAS WAS RIGHT around the corner, and Ariel texted me to say that Mom was coming to stay at the house. She didn't mention our father, his mistress, or my mother's knowledge thereof. Instead of pressing her for information, I let myself enjoy my ignorance, certain that it would be temporary.

Sure enough, the next day I got a text from Ariel saying, *now would be a good time to come over,* followed by *NOW.* I was already in my car, and I jerked the wheel to divert myself onto I-95, a post office full of packages thumping around in the back of my car.

Outside, standing on the apron of Ariel's freshly cut grass, the world was serene. An early sun had melted the glittery frost on top of the cars while a few birds, the last in Rhode Island, chirped slowly from trees, unaware that they should be gone. All the yards on Ariel's street were laid out on top of an invisible grid: the neat rows of shrubs, the staked lanterns following the elbow curve of the walkways, mulch islands with thick black outlines. A boredom that so much of the world yearns for. I found John crouched in the middle of the yard inspecting the grass, wrapped in a winter parka.

"What are you doing?"

He held up a green color swatch.

"Checking the grass. We just cannot get it the right color. Come look."

"This is a thing?"

"We have guidelines, Robin, this isn't a slum. I really thought the Chemlawn people..." He lay down across the grass, stuck the color swatch in the ground and shined a flashlight on it. "Shit."

"And you're not just avoiding whatever's happening in the house?"

"Are you kidding? We're two shades of green away from being kicked out of the neighborhood association.'

'But yeah, I wouldn't go in there."

"Thanks for the heads up."

"Hey, when are you going to bring your guy over?"

Ignoring the question, I kicked frost crystals from my shoes and opened Ariel's front door. Immediately, I heard a low wail echoing through the house. No one came up to greet me. No little Maddy or Emma scampering up to hang at my legs. No cat. No dog. Only a low, mourning cry that came down the open staircase to fill the foyer. If Ariel hadn't called me over, I would have guessed the sound came from a nature program, a feature on the songs of dying whales. Sound didn't hide in Ariel's house; even in the middle of the great room, the cry was always right above me, droning into my ear.

The dining room table where we'd had Thanksgiving was heaped with bags and stacks of hastily dropped paperwork. Past that, Maddy and Emma played quietly in front of a television that was off for the first time since I could remember. They played with the enthusiasm of children who were told against their wishes to have fun, and I wasn't sure if they didn't notice me or if they simply didn't care. I patted them on their heads, and they looked up at me silently, their hands still deep into their pile of toys on the floor. Maddy had grown fast, but Emma still had that translucent, porcelain face, tinged with the color of a tulip petal where it starts to blend from white to red.

"Grandma's sad," Maddy said finally.

Upstairs, I cracked the bedroom door to find my mother lying across the length of the bed in one of her floral housedresses in low light, a damp rag over her eyes. Ariel, whose head was hung either in sleep or grief, looked up at the sound of the door opening. She held on to my mother's hand from a rocking chair. My mother's wails subsided a bit, now sounding more like the moans of someone with a chronic ailment, but otherwise, she didn't acknowledge that I had entered the room. I gave Ariel a big hug in her rocking chair and saw that she had been crying, too. Since the end of high school, I had seen Ariel cry exactly two times: once on her wedding day, and once when a contractor had accidentally hung the wrong wallpaper and she slept surrounded by neon green and pink flowers for two weeks. Nothing about Ariel crying was natural; the tears themselves looked out of place on her cheek. Her auburn hair, normally pulled back or bouncing around her neckline, pressed against her head like hair stuck to a shower stall.

Unsure who needed comfort the most, I sat down and put an arm around each of them, creating a familial circle of grief. It was hard to know how to react. Here were two people chiseled from the same stone mold, and they had shattered at the exact same time.

"Hi, Mom. It's me, Robin," I said. My eyes adjusted to the low light and after a time that felt long, but wasn't, she took my hand from her shoulder and held it. When I am sad and unoccupied, I tend to focus on small, concrete things. A button on my shirt will get an hour's attention, or else I'll live in the contours of a coin in the palm of my hand. That day I focused on the wallpaper border that made a Mobius Strip of roses around the room, tracing it with my eyes over and over. Like all well-hung wallpaper, it looked painted on and seamless. The chalky red tint of the roses matched one of the flowers on my mother's housedress. After looking at it for a long while, I noticed a major inaccuracy: the rose vines did not have thorns. The flowers on my mother's dress did not even have stems or buds. Nothing was in its proper context.

I leaned in close to my sister and she whispered to me, her chapped lips pressed against my ears, "She knows." At this, my mother's moan rose again and oscillated in pitch as she searched for a pain that felt correct. She rolled onto her side and bent her legs up to her chest. Mothers shouldn't be limber, I thought. They shouldn't be able to bend into vulnerable shapes. They should only be able to sit straight, stand up straight, and lie flat as a board. The rest is too difficult for a daughter to watch.

I rubbed my mother's arm gently, comforting myself as much as her. I focused on the papery callous around her elbow and the loose skin that bunched there from her upper arm. Everything about my mother's age could be gathered from that spot where her skin puckered at the elbow: that slow cutover in designation between mother and grandmother. I remember very little about my grandmother, but I remember similar housedresses. I wondered if my mother had balled-up tissues in the pockets of her dress. If there were bobby pins or other treasures tucked away in there.

"Robin, I was just telling Mom," Ariel said, loud enough for both of us to hear. "The hospital staff have been saying it for a while. It's very common, and it's healthy for him."

My mother's moaning stopped and she spoke through what felt like layers of gauze.

"An affair is common?" she asked, the damp cloth muffling her words. "An affair is healthy?"

"Mom," Ariel said, "I think, given the circumstances, with Dad's condition, that the *A* word doesn't really apply."

"So, because," Mom said, grasping for words that dribbled out slowly, "because of a, a condition, your father is allowed to have an affair, and it's not an affair? Like we aren't even married? I told Cheryl and she said, condition or not, that it would be grounds for a divorce if I wanted it."

"Let's just give it some time to sink in, Mom," Ariel said. "I don't think we should make any rash decisions now." I was happy to see Ariel provide a sane perspective. It hadn't always been that way.

"This isn't the first time, you know," my mother said. Ariel and I looked at each other.

"Mom, this isn't the time," I said.

"Everyone loves your father, but he hasn't been perfect. Good luck convincing anyone of that." She reached into her pocket and removed a tissue to blow her nose, lifting her facecloth in the process and revealing dark, tired eyes.

"My life hasn't been some perfect, happy thing."

Chapter Twenty-Eight

THE NEXT DAY, Ariel invited me back over to help wrap presents. Mom had taken the girls to see Santa Claus at the Providence Place Mall, which had become a yearly ritual through all the usual opaque pathways of family tradition. Ariel and John skipped it, with John saying, "If you've seen one fat stranger make your children cry, you've seen them all."

When I walked in the door, John was sitting at the dining room table with his head firmly in his hands, like his head was a cantaloupe that he was checking for ripeness. The papers that I had noticed sitting on the table the other day had been separated and fanned out. He lifted his head and looked at me through his fingers, then removed his hands and resumed sorting through the documents, making strike marks with a black pen.

"What are you working on?" I asked.

"Your mother," John said, sighing. "She brought all this. I'd been asking for months. Months."

My father had always been successful in business, and since we were old enough to understand what wealth was, we understood that our father had some of it, or at least enough that we could forget about it and move on to another topic. As we got older, he made it clear not to expect an inheritance, that they would be quite able to spend all of their money in their lifetimes. But that, on the brighter side, we would never have to worry about them. When they said this, I pictured them bleeding their money away on cruises around the world, buying a house in Florida with the rest of their friends in a strict, rule-happy gated community. Five-thousand-dollar-a-month nursing facilities never factored into these scenarios.

"I knew we should have just driven up there and taken all this by force."

Ariel came up from the basement with wrapping paper rolls under her arms.

"How bad is it?" she asked.

"Bad," he said. "You name it. Credit cards. Unpaid bills. A second mortgage I didn't know about."

The fact that Ariel and I had not gotten involved in our mother's finances earlier carried a hint of magical thinking held over from childhood, when parents were gods who could do no wrong. How could we have assumed, just because we didn't hear anything about it, that my mother had been handling her finances?

"Do you think some of this is from Dad's loopy phase?" I asked. This referred to a time before we had fully caught up with our father's condition, when Dad began to spend money with manic zeal. Just before we took his credit cards away. For weeks, boxes arrived at our mother's doorstep from the Home Shopping Network. Sometimes giant boxes appeared with multiple wrapped packages inside, gift wrapped with crisp, thin striped paper that tore away like tissue. Jewelry. Kitchen gadgets whose names we couldn't pronounce. Packaged meats from Italy. Tiny massage balls that you were supposed to spread out on the floor and lie across. After the months of deliveries, even my mother couldn't keep it quiet anymore. I still have his HSN platinum rewards card sitting somewhere in my purse; he had put my name down as a co-member with him.

"I think letting your mother ignore this is unwise," John said. "Her monthly obligations are way above what your father's pension and Social Security bring in."

"Do you think I'm going to get anything out of her?" Ariel said. "Do you think she is just going to explain her whole financial philosophy to me? Have you just met my mother?"

In the lull between John and Ariel's escalating conversation I heard the furnace click on with a gentle vibration. Hot air began circulating calmly through the house, a crisp, dry breeze that reddened my cheeks almost immediately. Maddy and Emma watched us from the corner, not even pretending to play anymore.

"What happens if she runs out of money?" I asked.

"I don't think we need to take it in that direction just yet," Ariel said.

"No, we absolutely do," John said. "It's complicated – I don't know exactly how it works. If your father doesn't have any money, the state would probably take the house and any assets, but he would get to go on Medicaid and he could stay in *a* nursing home, but not the castle he's in now. That's what happened to my grandmother. We need to get a lawyer on this. As is, your father's nursing home bills are going to drain her savings completely before long.

I thought your father was at least semi-wealthy.'

'I don't see a scenario where your mother gets to keep her house unless we get your father out of that facility." John's voice got quiet, his head back in his hands. "Oh God – she's going to have to move in with us. Otherwise she'll end up in that tent city I read about in the Projo."

I thought about this the whole drive home, my mind going back over our predicament. If John was right, the choice was stark: either my father stays in a home, or my mother stays in her house. The two appeared to be mutually exclusive. In my kinder moments, I tell myself that my mother was genuinely in over her head when my father lost his mind. At first, she kept up with the bills and health care statements with their patchwork of billing codes. Then one bill slipped through the cracks, then a second. She stopped opening the statements because they stressed her out, instead throwing them into a satchel in the closet.

That's when I'm feeling generous. In my more cynical moments, I can't help but think that my mother's financial ruin was a weapon she had been sharpening slowly, carefully choosing when to press its flinty tip into our flesh. My mother's intelligence was vast and well-hidden, and you underestimated it at your peril.

When I got back, I went into Corey's house and

stomped up the stairs. Every time I came back now I saw the house with fresh eyes. The living room where I'd installed the baseboard no longer hid beneath drop cloths. Without dust and grime, the wood floors shone reddish amber. The holes from old electrical boxes had been patched over. For the most part, the room looked complete. The only blemish on the house was a set of muddy shoe prints, which I followed up the stairs into Corey's bedroom. They were still wet, but he wasn't home. I checked the tower room and that was empty as well.

On the bed, which I'd carefully made that morning, Corey had left a stapled packet of paper with yellow sticky notes stuck on top. They read: 'Robin - Seril gets these reports from a friend. See page 12. You should move your books ASAP. - COREY.' The second one read: 'probably will sleep TC tonight.'

I held up the papers, which had those tear-away holes on the sides, and inspected them. They listed all of the houses in foreclosure in Rhode Island. Right in the middle of page twelve, circled twice in pen, I saw my house address. The house where I never saw the landlord, where there was no complaint when my roommates moved out and stopped paying. Where my single rent check was cashed each month without comment or complaint.

I didn't spend much time on self-pity. Instead, I sent out a text to James, then got on my computer and found a storage unit within the city limits. It would eat into my profits, but I consoled myself with the fact that I'd no longer be paying rent. I wondered if my landlord would call and complain when my next check didn't arrive as planned. That would be a funny conversation.

Across the street I did a quick inventory of my books with an open laptop balanced on my forearm. Stepping into each former roommate's space was like unsealing a tomb. My organizational system, which seemed so intuitive in the months before I met Corey, no longer made much sense to me. I ran my finger along a row of cookbooks in Violet's former room and watched dust fly into the air.

I stepped into my room and found it was no longer a room. It looked like a scale model of a city, with each tightly spaced stack of books resembling a skyscraper. I stepped sideways through the stacks and sat cross-legged in the center of my bed, which in its lack of height resembled the city's park. I looked out at the stacks of books and found that some were above my line of sight, obscuring the outer walls of the room. It hit me at that moment how much my business had grown, even in the depths of the recession. A wave of gratitude flowed through me that felt like a lightness in my chest.

James found me sitting in the center of my bed, leafing through old notebooks. He had brushed back his curls behind his ears, and since the last time I'd seen him he'd replaced his Harry Potter glasses with something more boxy. They sort of fixed his look, if that makes sense. His face was no longer a series of concentric circles.

"Let yourself in," I said.

"Sorry, I knocked a few times. Did you know your lock doesn't work? You could probably open it with a screwdriver."

"Did you bring your car?"

"A van, actually. It's a friend's for his band. And one of those wheelie things I borrowed from the school."

That's how James and I transferred all my books to a storage space, packing books into boxes and stacking them onto the dolly. He moved with a wiry energy, taking steps two at a time and jumping down from the van each time he unloaded a dolly. The temperature dropped as we worked until I could see my breath, though we were both hot as furnaces underneath our sweatshirts.

"You've got enough books for a bookstore," he said, slamming the van door shut. "You should open one."

"I'd love to, but the only reason I make any money is that I'm not a bookstore."

On the way back, I told him about my mom's finances and my foreclosure.

"You found out both of those things today?"

"Yeah. I'm waiting to see who else is getting kicked out of their house."

"I'm not sure what you mean."

"Doesn't bad news like this come in threes?"

"Actually, that's a perception bias. We learned about it in probability class. Like celebrities dying in threes? Celebrities are dying all the time. We chunk them together into threes to impose order on something senseless."

"Don't use your fucking intelligence on me today."

In response James smiled sheepishly and tugged on the strings of his hoodie. I smiled back, unable to pretend I was annoyed.

I brought James up to my now-empty room. Without the books, it was palatial - just a bed and nightstand in the center of a high-ceilinged room. Walking around disturbed the dust, which made starry-night patterns in the air. I looked out the bay window, across the street to Corey's house.

"What are you looking at?" James asked.

"Nothing." Corey must have stayed true to his note and slept at tent city. I sat down on the bed and took my sweatshirt off. The cool apartment air nipped at my skin, waking me up. Since I barely spent any time there, I'd kept my apartment at a cool fifty-eight degrees.

"Thanks for being there for me." I looked up at James and tapped the spot on the bed next to me.

We made out for a while before bed. I let him explore a little, but set some firm boundaries, which he respected. It felt nice to do that, like giving someone a tidy fenced-in yard to play in. For my part, I'd be really into it for a little while, then come back to reality. I'd never cheated on anyone before, and actually I wasn't sure if I was even cheating then. But the thought fluttered in my mind, and it was enough to keep me from really enjoying myself. At one point, James moved down to kiss my neck and I opened my eyes, checking over his curls to the bay window, scanning for signs of life across the street. I did this a few times, but no lights ever came on in Corey's house.

Chapter Twenty-Nine

THE NEXT MORNING I woke up slowly to the smell of coffee and the sight of dust clouds circulating around in a dull winter light. James loped through the door with a ceramic mug in each hand. In the daylight you could just make out rectangles where the books had been stacked the night before, the dust bunnies that had collected around each stack forming a grid that James disturbed as he walked toward me.

"I don't know if this'll be good," he said, resting a cup on the nightstand. "I never know how to use other people's coffeemakers."

"Thanks for being a gentleman last night."

"Of course."

We sat in bed drinking the coffee, which wasn't bad, marinating in the heat under the covers. He took a *New Yorker* off my nightstand and began looking through it, carefully folding back and creasing each page that he turned. He seemed nervous in the daylight, exposed. We'd first met in a dark warehouse and moved on to a pitch-dark dorm room. This was the first time we'd sat together in natural light. He looked at me only in quick glances, as if I were the sun. His nervousness made me feel dominant in the situation, which calmed me down. I got up and did a morning stretch, letting my camisole separate from my pajama pants, exposing my belly button.

"Do you have class today?"

"It's December twenty-first - finals are over. I'm getting a ride home for winter break tomorrow."

His eyes were cycling again, from his magazine to my body. I smiled and soaked it in.

"When are you coming back?"

"Late January - twenty-something. Want to get some brunch today?"

"Today's the last day to ship out books for Christmas. And I haven't bought a single present for anyone."

"Bummer."

After finishing the coffee, I saw him off with a chaste kiss and got to work, logging in and compiling my last sales of the season. Earlier that morning I'd decided I would avoid James for a few days to see how it made me feel, but once he said he'd be gone until the end of January I switched course, coolly mentioning that it would be fun to see him on his last night in Rhode Island.

I wasn't sure whether I should get Corey a Christmas present, and I was almost certain any gift-giving would be one-way. So, when I saw a tattered olive-green binding peeking out from a stack of home improvement books, I pulled it out, dusted it off, and put it in my bag. It was the Ansel's *Build Your Dream Home* book, the one I'd bought in a daze the first time I saw Corey up close. Even if I didn't give it to him, I figured I'd at least bring it home and add it to my personal collection. It wasn't going to sell.

Back at my apartment, I started packaging up books, then took a break to leaf through the Ansel's book. So many of the chapters and phrases I couldn't have even recognized a few months ago. Now I was fluent in the language of home ownership. The systems: plumbing, electricity, framing. Reading the yellowed pages brought me right back to the early days, and I felt a twinge of longing for when I worked alongside Corey, sweating in his white T-Shirt, when he was still a puzzle to be solved. In solving Corey, I'd drawn him back out into the real world. It's what I thought I wanted, but now I wished I'd left him alone, like a photographer in a nature program who doesn't intervene on the animal's behalf. Maybe if I hadn't, Corey would still be the mysterious stranger striking his pry bar with a hammer, sending sparks into the night.

I wrapped the Ansel's book and brought it over to Corey's house. Over there, I washed some dishes and tidied up from my last project of counter-setting finish nails with an awl and filling the holes with wood filler. I had the distinct feeling of suddenly living a different life. Just a few days ago I was living with Corey as if he and I were married. Now I was a captain's wife, keeping an empty house in order while my husband was away at sea, entertaining other men, unsure if I should feel guilt at fulfilling my womanly needs.

As if he could read my mind, Corey began texting me. When I felt the vibration of the phone in my pocket, I assumed it was James and was instantly disappointed to find out the truth. First, he asked, *Did you move out your books?* I ignored him, and he asked again: *Did you get my note?* This even though I hadn't seen him in days. I lied and told him I was busy doing Christmas shopping, then he asked: *Did you have someone over last night?* I started to reply, but instead I took a few angry breaths and turned my phone off.

I went out and rushed through Christmas shopping in a cloud of anger, throwing any book into my cart that even resembled a fitting Christmas gift. I was furious that Corey could even now reach out from afar and push my buttons so successfully. To paper over my feelings, I sent a stream of texts to James, some of which hinted obliquely at a parting 'gift' I would give him tonight. We agreed to meet up after dark; I'd pick him up and take him to a dive bar on Wickenden.

But by the time I picked James up, Corey had continued texting me throughout the day. His messages had become less coherent and more emotional. Some were unreadable and looked like the result of an animal scratching at a keypad. At a certain point I passed through anger and began to feel worried for him.

"Would you mind if we stopped by tent city just for a minute?" I asked James. "I just have to take care of one thing."

I didn't mention Corey. As far as James knew, I was still helping out around the city, setting up dinners and interviewing residents for an oral history.

"Okay. Will you be long?"

"No - not long."

I pulled up alongside the southern edge of the city, my car half-shadowed by the overpass. Before I got out, I leaned over and gave James an extended kiss.

"I won't be long - just stay in the car." I kissed him again, this time grabbing his collar with my hand and letting my fake pearl necklace swing out and back from my cleavage.

"Okay," he said, sounding hypnotized by the swaying pearls.

I stumbled along the outer edge of the city, avoiding rocks and mud patches in my flats. Seril's tent loomed ahead, up-lit and inflated by heat. I snaked around an empty blue and grey Coleman tent that had been set up adjacent to Seril's tent; the smaller tent snuggled against the giant wedding tent like a child into its mother. From my vantage point I could see Seril through two flaps, leaning back in his chair with a loosely packed cigar in his mouth. Corey sat off to the side, slumped but awake, tapping at his phone despondently.

The space heater nearest me clicked off and I could hear Seril talk. He was holding forth from his chair like a minister at a tent revival.

"We have no way to feel small in this smallest of states. That's our problem. Not like the mountains in Colorado, or the skies of Montana. Not like the sweeping plains, or the deserts. I've been there."

Seril drank heavily from his chipped mug until dark liquid began to run down his chin.

"We've heard all this," Corey said. He seemed more exasperated than usual, looking down into his own mug impatiently. The low-strung lights, sagging from post to post, lit Seril a dim yellow. The tent creaked against the wind.

"What was I talking about? Smallness, yes. It's

important to feel insignificant sometimes. We don't have that in Rhode Island, and everyone feels significant. You feel significant, don't you, Corey?"

"I'm not listening to this shit," Corey said. He stood up, steadying himself on a folding table. When he unfurled his full height, his eyes met mine and he seemed to sober up in real time.

"Chirp away, little bird," Seril said.

I turned to walk away and heard his footsteps follow. The ground outside had frozen already, and its radiant cold transferred quickly to the soles of my shoes. My watch read just past midnight, the time when most of the short-term homeless turned into bed, clicking a small padlock onto the zipper of their tent. Down at the river's edge, where the more chronically homeless slept, the night still raged around several large fires.

Corey caught up with me as I weaved through the late-night revelers. I stepped to the waterline; the Woonasquatucket at night showed an inky blackness that stole the moonlight rather than reflect it.

"Robin, stop. Wait up."

"What are you doing here, Corey?" I asked.

"What do you mean?" He was trying to talk like he hadn't been drinking.

"I don't care if you're drunk, stop acting like you're trying to get out of trouble. I was at that tent for a while, I heard Seril repeating that nonsense."

"Robin - I helped make this problem, and I have to help fix it."

"Were you listening in there? Your uncle is fucking crazy. You need to put him in an institution."

"I know. I know how it sounds. But he put all this together, and people still trust him over anything. They need him. And I can't abandon him right now. He's not usually this bad."

"How did you know I had someone over last night?"

"You did?"

"You didn't answer me."

A man approached me from the side. He had a puffy jacket and a thinly braided ponytail.

"Good evening. Sorry to bother you folks. I was released from prison just last week and I'm trying to live a better life. Could you spare a few dollars?"

"God Charlie, try it on someone else," I said.

"God bless," he replied, retreating back into the dark.

"Did you come home last night? If not, then how could you have known? Did someone tell you?"

He stopped walking toward me.

"My front door opens with a fucking screwdriver. Do you see how scary it is to think you're being watched?"

"Robin, I love you. I know I haven't been around, but I want us to be together. I just have to see this through."

"I need to be alone - don't follow me."

I threw up my hood and walked away with my hands tucked into my pockets. The wind on the water was mild but persistent and had no problem finding ways past my layers of clothing. Corey yelled out to me, but I kept walking. As I headed back toward my car, I passed the fires, catching a bit of their warmth with my head down to avoid attention.

A man sat cross-legged at the lip of the water talking quickly and quietly to himself. I couldn't hear the words, but the changing inflections suggested that he was answering his own questions. He rocked back and forth, adjusting his orange wool hat. My father, born at a different time or place, could have been this man if there wasn't a support system keeping him in a facility. I shuddered as a vision came of my father walking down the side of the highway, stumbling in a hole-ridden jacket. As he walks he is telling stories to himself, tall tales of which the kernel is some half-forgotten memory.

I could see from a way off that my car was empty. The inside light was on, and the door had been left ajar. I stomped back into the city, angry at James for getting out of the car. I weaved my way through the grid of tents, then walked around the back of Seril's tent and made for the waterline.

A commotion drew me toward the fires, where it sounded like an argument was brewing. Three men were standing around the fire and from my line of sight I could see arms flailing. Other men, beer-sopped and thirsty for conflict, shouted into the action. I crept back toward the scene, keeping on the outskirts of the area visible by firelight. Everything became obscured in such low light. I thought I saw two regulars locking arms, but after going in for a closer look I instead saw one regular and one younger man, smooth skinned, untouched by tent city. He was trying to disengage from the other man and in doing so made some very high-pitched noises.

"Get off me, get. OFF of me!!" the younger one screamed.

"Fight back, college boy," the man in the middle said, locking in the younger man's arm and squaring his hips.

The light of the fire reflected off of a pair of square-framed glasses.

"James!" I screamed.

The shouts echoed across the river. A few threw beer cans into the fray. I ran to the sidelines, waiting for someone to break up the fight, but it quickly became clear that no one was going to. All of the civility swept away after midnight, the voices of reason safely asleep. The man with the scraggly beard had James in a head lock. With a twist of his arm, his glasses fell off into the fire.

Another squeal from James. Then another. I couldn't believe no one was breaking it up. Finally, I ran into the fray, trying to separate the man from James. James's face flashed across a patch of light. The fire roared hot with fragrant cedar logs, warming the sand under my feet. I kept trying and failing to separate them. James looked at me with a face of the damned. Time slowed down, and I smelled the cedar as strongly as I have ever smelled anything in my life.

From outside the circle of light cast by the fire, Corey came running at full speed. Despite the cold, he had on his T-shirt, which was so blazingly white that it lit the darkness around him. He pushed me safely out of the way and locked his arms around the man's head. They jostled around the fire like crazed dance partners. James's head came free, and he spun away onto the ground. I ran over to him and put my hand across his cheek, wiping away his tears.

Corey and the man continued to struggle. Outside the light of the fire, up on a short hill, I saw Seril watching the fray stoically, his arms crossed. He could have stopped the fight with a wave of his hand, but he didn't. A group of bodies crashed into the scene, and Corey capsized in the crowd. I saw his arm bang down across one of the rocks ringing the fire. He tried to sit up but failed, moving slowly, as if sandbags had been dropped onto him.

James pulled on my arm and squealed, "Let's get the fuck out of here."

I looked back, but I couldn't see Corey in the crush of bodies.

"Robin?!"

"Yeah, okay. Let's go."

I took James's hand and we ran along the waterline, under the overpass to my car. As we drove away, I looked down across the row of fires. It looked more peaceful from afar, like nothing more than the friendly campsite it aspired to be. I scanned the darkness for the light of Corey's T-shirt, but aside from the red light of the fires I saw only dark.

Chapter Thirty

SUDDENLY, HAVING A door that opened with a screwdriver seemed like an irresponsible way to live. The thought dawned on me on the drive home from tent city, as if before that night, living without a lock and key were completely reasonable. James spent the ride home slowly petting the upholstery of the center console. He wasn't hurt, but he was shaken. He offered to have me sleep at his dorm, stuttering as he spoke. His room was protected by key card, roaming public safety vehicles, and a two-billion-dollar endowment fund, but the last thing I wanted was to enter a hive of teenagers for the night. Instead, I piled some chairs up in front of my door and we slept in my bed, or tried to. I mostly stared up at the plaster ceiling, listening for sound while I traced each crack to its endpoint.

The next morning, I got a text from an unknown number telling me that Corey was in the hospital. I replied back quickly but didn't get another response. By that time James had already left to pack up his dorm for break. I didn't know if I'd see him again before he left. It was hard to know what the rules were. We'd been through a lot over the past few days, but in so many ways we were still strangers to each other. When he went in for a parting kiss, I moved my head at the last second and he ended up planting his lips on the bridge of my nose.

I tried to force myself not rush to the hospital. I started wrapping up some presents and ran accounting on the last batch of holiday books I'd shipped out. I also opened Craigslist with the intent to search for a new apartment, but found I couldn't gather my thoughts enough to know what to type.

Now that the books, my professional lifeblood, had been moved out of the apartment, I was less concerned about foreclosure. Even if the house was repossessed and they changed the locks, I could probably get in there and get my stuff out - after all, I was an innocent party. And if I couldn't? I'd probably just head to Ariel's, have a pity party over losing my one good pair of pants, and then regroup. Spend a few nights with her and the girls until I found a new apartment. Until then, I was living for free. The truth was I had so many safety nets around me, something I'd learned to appreciate after embedding in tent city and hearing residents' tales of woe. I stopped working and headed to the hospital.

Corey's room had that plasticky smell of rubber gloves, a smell I associate with all hospitals. When I walked in, he was asleep and making a sort of half-snoring sound, his head slumped down and to the side. I sat awkwardly on a stool, removed a book from my bag and tried to read. My posture was board straight; even with everything I went through with my father, I still couldn't get comfortable in hospitals.

Finding that I couldn't read, I sat back and zoned out. My eyes kept scanning over Corey, to his stubble and the circles around his eyes. He looked so tired. A blanket was tucked around his stomach, and above that he was wearing one of those emasculating hospital gowns that almost seem like they were created on a dare. Tubes crisscrossed over him. One thick tube, filled with amber liquid, disappeared under his blanket on his left side, under his arm. A few times he moved as if he were waking up, only to shudder back into sleep.

A nurse came in and with swift hands started working underneath Corey's blanket. On a chart attached to a whiteboard, a smiley face and sad face asked, "How is your pain today?" and underneath someone had written a "7" in dry-erase marker.

"This may wake him up," the nurse said to no one in particular. She reached her hand deeper under the blanket and Corey moaned a little, slowly coming to.

"Sorry about that. How do you feel?" the woman said. He rubbed his eyes with one hand. She stood over him from the side of the bed, her upper body casting a shadow that blunted the fluorescent whiteness of the room. A small cross dangled from her chest, inches from his face like a hypnotist's watch.

"What day is it?" he asked.

The nurse stood tall and picked up a clipboard that hung from the side of the bed. Her brown hair kept tightly to the side of her face, giving her head a perfectly rounded silhouette. "You've just been here overnight."

"It feels like a week. I keep waking up and going back to sleep, and I'm having the strangest dreams."

"We had you on something to help with the pain. Restless sleep and vivid dreams can be side effects."

"I just dreamt I was underwater lying on a couch. I could breathe underwater, but these bubbles kept settling on me, making parts of me dry for a second, and it was this hot itchy pain."

"I've been moving you around to change the sheets. That might have been some of the pain. You had quite a fall."

"Is there something wrong with my arm?"

The nurse lifted the periwinkle sheet and stole a glance underneath.

"It's looking better," she said. "You burned it pretty badly. We strapped it down to prevent you from thrashing in your sleep and injuring it worse. It's important we keep it clean to stop infections. But you'll recover."

"Can I see it?"

She pulled back the sheet a few inches at a time, folding it with expert precision as she went, stopping at the waist's midline and tucking the ends tightly under the bed. I squinted my eyes, afraid to look, but Corey stared down with a stone expression on his face. Then I allowed my eyes to drift over briefly, skating across the area then coming back for a closer look. From the shoulder to the elbow appeared unblemished, but below the elbow joint his arm had been mummified by white cotton bandages. A vinyl strap secured his wrist snugly to the bed with a cloth wedged in between for comfort.

"If I remove these I'll have to repack them. And it's going to hurt. But I'll do it if you want."

"If you don't mind," he said.

I drew my eyes away as the nurse unmasked the wound. I checked the area again using my peripherals and saw jaundiced yellow and grey char. A closer look brought to mind a volcanic moonscape, gray and dead but at the same time bubbling with fertility. This was Corey's reward for re-entering the world.

I looked away, but Corey never took his eyes off his arm. He was exploring its landscape like it was a map of a new territory. His teeth and curling toes told me that he was experiencing real, dynamic pain, pain with peaks and valleys. Pain with its own time zone.

"My arm feels like it's beating - like it has its own heart," he said.

"It'll feel better once I repack it."

"What's your name?"

"I'm Mary. My shift is almost over so don't ask for me by name. One of the other nurses will help you."

"Mary, when you tuck in my sheets, can you tuck the top middle part into the neck of my shirt?"

"Sure."

"My dad used to do that for me. He called it 'the bib.'"

The second packing was not as tight, and Corey said that if he held it in the right position, he could get a soothing brush of air under the bandage by puffing up the sheet and letting it fall bellows-like back down onto his hospital gown. The puffs of air communed with his exposed flesh, feeding the surface the atmospheric fuel it needed.

"You know, I don't remember too much about the other night. It's all sort of fuzzy."

"You were very brave," I said. "You saved James. Not his life, probably. But you saved him from getting beat up."

"I was just being the voice of reason. I didn't even know he was with you."

"Has Seril called?"

"Don't call him that. His real name is Frank; Seril is some kind of Providence reference. He hasn't called me. I don't even know who brought me here, if they called an ambulance or just drove me to the hospital and dumped me at the emergency room like a bag of garbage."

A wave of pain must have passed over him because he looked to the side and winced.

"He's losing it again - just like the first time. I could see it in his eyes. I dug up this picture a few weeks ago and I actually had it in my pocket last night. Let me show you."

His jeans were folded on a table beside the bed. I reached in and pulled out a creased square of photo paper. It depicted a young boy, button cute with dimples, standing next to a snow pile in a poofy winter jacket. His face looked forward, but he held his arm awkwardly back, connected to a serious-looking man with dark glasses. Tall and reed thin, the man glanced to the side, taking part in the picture in body only. His five o'clock shadow traced a thick outline up his long face and connected with a navy hat with yellow oak leaves stitched into the curved brim. Next to him stood an identical-looking man dressed in a polo shirt with horizontal stripes.

"That's Frank," he said, pointing to the Navy hat. I picked up the photo and held it to my nose. The blue eyes were hidden, but the shape of his face, his bulbed nose, could not be denied. Subtract thirty years, grey hair, and a few layers of grime, and this was Seril. Frank. "And that's my father," he said, pointing to the other man.

"Oh my gosh, Corey."

"I probably never told you that they look exactly alike. They were three years apart, but past a certain age they could have been twins. He was a Navy guy, based out of Groton, and he would be gone on subs for four to six months at a stretch. You can imagine how cool that was to a little kid. He never had any kids himself, and I remember thinking he was a little weird, and strict in his thinking. It must have been pretty obvious if I could sense it as a little kid.

"You know, I started hearing about tent city last spring in Home Depot. For a six-month span, I was basically either at my house or in a Home Depot. People were talking about this place wistfully, like they wished they could live in a place like that rent-free. They were envying homeless people. I was still trying to avoid news at the time, but even I couldn't avoid it. And they kept talking about this mayor. Honest to God, Robin, at one point I thought to myself, that's the kind of crazy scheme my uncle would get involved in.

"And when I saw your paper, and went over there, for a minute it was like I was talking to my dad. When Frank is lucid, he's basically a carbon copy of him. But when he veers off course, like he's done before, it's like he's nobody. Nobody I know. But I never know how to handle the change and figure out when he's crossed a line. It's complicated."

"I understand completely." And I did understand. It was the same reason that the situation with my father was complicated. Because the landscape of their conditions was fluid and unpredictable. And because they were family.

Day in the hospital turned into cold, dull-streaked twilight, with frost encroaching on the window that looked down three floors onto a parking lot. I decided to stay until visiting hours ended. We shared a sad meal of roast beef and carrots, lightened by the gallows humor of taste testing and comparing the hospital Jell-O against that of the nursing home (Shady Brook won, by leaps). A news report played in the next room, at wall-rattling volumes, predicting light snow later in the week. I tried to tune it out, thumbing through my book. Corey read, too, which I had never seen him do, trying to find some narrative stream to slip into and take him past the tooth-scraping pain throbbing inside his arm.

When his pain ratcheted to a level that made him grip the hospital bed and try to lift himself into the air, I pressed the nurse button and before long a new full bag of amber syrup was hanging from the medicinal coat rack next to his bed. The nurse flipped a few switches and turned some knobs on the tentacled machine, playing it like an instrument. The beeping slowed and in its place lights began to fade in and out. They continued this pattern, the machine breathing light as the syrup disappeared into his arm. We didn't talk any more about James, or my apartment. Instead we just read, letting the silence of things unsaid settle in the room like a heavy gas.

Before I left I asked Corey if he needed anything. He had only one request.

"I have some shirts in storage in the attic, packed in vacuum bags. They're old work shirts from my mortgage job. Could you take them down and wash and dry them for me?"

"Sure. Why?"

"I think that when I get out of here, I might try to find a job."

"Job?" The word sounded foreign coming from his mouth. For a moment I wondered if the syrup-medicine was making him loopy.

"The other day I was driving outside Providence to pick up supplies for the city and I saw this little office that does income taxes and other CPA work. It was this quaint little building - a house really. And I don't do this much but I like, projected myself into that building. I pictured myself sitting in a small, clean room, up to my eyeballs in numbers, and it just made me really happy. Happier than I've been in a while."

A nurse stepped in, saw Corey's face, and excused herself. These displays of emotion, Corey never had use for them. So for him now to be sitting in his hospital bed, face slicked with tears, feeling something that could not be measured in nails set or tiles laid, was shocking to see.

Corey ended up staying in the hospital for four more

nights, getting out two days after Christmas. This complicated Christmas dinner, where I made only a cursory appearance at the house. I lied to John and Ariel, telling them that Corey had gotten hurt doing electrical work, not wanting to touch anything relating to tent city or James. To his credit, John didn't bring up his theory of economic specialization. My mother's mourning cries had hardened into a bitter stewing over my father's infidelities. When Josette asked what our mother had planned for the new year, she said to the cringe of everyone at the table that she might be trying to find herself a good lawyer. Ariel told me on the phone later that she mentioned several times that she could "get a divorce and no one would blame her." No one had talked about the financial pipe bomb that our mother had dropped on us. Given all the baggage, I was glad not to be there long.

I did take Corey's shirts out of storage. There were button-ups and polos cast in various shades of blue and gray with curled collars. I brought them up from the basement, warm and fragrant from the dryer, and folded them in his bedroom. The laundry basket sat next to a fresh batch of white T-shirts that had lain fallow since Corey had stopped working on the house. I unfolded and refolded those too and when I did, I put the first one up to my face and took a breath in, surrounding myself in salty sweat and spiced deodorant.

During this period, I started receiving strange phone calls from an unlisted number, usually two per day. I don't answer calls I don't know, and at first whoever it was didn't leave voicemails. I worried that it was Seril, or someone from tent city trying to harass me.

I spent most of the rest of Corey's hospital stay cleaning up the house for his return, while at the same time checking Craigslist for new apartments. No one yet had come to show off my house or change the locks on my apartment, and I felt as if I was in the middle of a lake standing with each foot on a different rowboat. Right now the seas were calm, and I was able to maintain my balance. But I knew it was only a matter of time before a lapping wave would cause the boats to drift, and I would have to pick a vessel to jump into.

Before Corey came home, I did my biggest cleanup yet, putting any and all tools in the basement. I also hacked up scrap materials and deposited them in the dumpster in Olneyville, the one that Corey had taken me to on our first day of destroying his plaster ceiling. That night, dog tired, I put on one of Corey's T-shirts and read in bed under two soft comforters. My eyes kept drifting back to the two laundry baskets, each containing a discrete path in Corey's life.

Chapter Thirty-One

ONE MORNING THE anonymous caller left a voicemail. It was a man. He sounded older, and distinguished. His words hung in the air with a high level of education. I still have it on my phone.

He said, "Robin, we have never formally met, but I would like to meet with you. It concerns your father. I think that, well. Anyways. You're likely wondering how I got your number, which was through the nursing home. I'm very sorry to be bothering you on your personal phone. Please call me back and I can give you my address, or send a car if you'd like. I'm sorry I've called you so many times. You must think, well. Anyways. I do apologize. If your phone doesn't hold missed calls, my number is..." and he gave me his number. The fuzzy sound of the wind against the phone suggested that he was outside.

None of the people I called at Shady Brook had any idea what I was talking about. There was, of course, a strict policy about giving away personal information. More calls came in from the number, but I never got another voice mail.

When I finally called back, my conversation with him

lasted under a minute. I said, "This is Robin."

"I'm so glad you called."

His words came across the phone as a great stress to him. His voice, flat and slow, no longer carried its former refinement.

"I don't like that you have my number."

"I'm sorry. Will you see me?"

"What's your name?"

"Bernard."

"Give me your address."

"I could send a car."

"No."

"Okay then. But you have the option."

He gave me his address, and we agreed on a time. I made plans with Ariel to text her when I knew I was safe; Ariel, for her part, would actually keep her phone on her and at the ready, a strong show of support for her.

The road down to Narragansett from Providence broke down into several segments of old, beaten-down former highways, overtaken with high grass and laced with flat farmland set back from the roads. Route 4 changed over to US-1, the old postal road. I pulled off the highway to fill my gas tank and saw cars packed full with belongings, their owners, all college students, gassing up for their trips back to New York and New Jersey for winter break. Off the beach season, it was essentially a college town, except for December and January when it became a ghost town. The students gassing up were tan despite the winter, sunglasses perched on their heads. They looked broad-shouldered and bored, their weight on one foot as they held the pump handles.

I passed Scarborough Beach. The overcast sky had given the ocean its own distinct shade of gray, something close to churning cement. Spurts of rain came in sideways on the wind, hitting my car with a rolling thud. I pressed the printout of the directions against the dashboard and eyed it while driving.

Past the open beach, the road receded from the coastline and wound through a neighborhood of old stone walls and cedar shake mansions. Glimpses of the ocean peeked between trees on one side of the road, but most of the houses were set far back from the hill and surrounded by old oaks that created dense knots of obscuring branch-work. Everything dripped lazily from the on-and-off rain.

The house marked on my map was on the coastal side, past a loose stone wall and down a gravel road that dipped and turned, pocked with standing water. Small white stones had been set into the greater rock wall to mark out the house number on either side of the open gate. My car pitched under each puddle, front wheel then back sending wings of water across the gravel. My arms tensed at the wheel. The road eventually emptied out into a circular driveway with a rusted fountain collecting rainwater in its overstuffed middle.

The rain stopped, as it had been doing on and off for the entire day. The water in the rusted-out fountain settled into a still mirror, and almost immediately birds dipped down to the lip of the fountain to drink neurotically from its waters. There were several birds, all black with a brushstroke of orange and yellow under the wing. Oh, the hell with it, I thought. Stop stalling, just go into the house.

The front door had those lion's head knockers that

must come free with every newly built mansion. I knocked a few times, satisfied by the tremendous sound of the solid wood. After a few minutes without an answer, I noticed a small doorbell off to the side and pressed it. A woman came to the door almost instantly, a maid or cleaning lady, tall and gaunt but with a big smile.

"Robin?"

"Yes."

"Come this way."

She led me through a slant-ceilinged room steeped in natural light. The windows, floor to ceiling, looked out onto white spray and black rocks along the coastline. I followed closely behind the woman, who did not speak again, as she led me into another room, a long, narrow glassed-in porch thrust out onto the edge of the land. The white spray and black rock could be seen on all sides and one had the feeling of being very high up and balanced precipitously on a great edge. A tall, thin man stood at the end of the porch, looking out onto a churning ocean. A pitcher sat on a nearby table next to two upright tumblers. The area looked meticulously set up, the table cloth fussed over.

My guide walked up beside him and touched his shoulder gently, which appeared to startle him. She whispered in his ear and he turned around, embarrassed. I recognized him, but vaguely. His primary traits, a reddened face and smooth gray hair registered in my memory, but I couldn't place where I knew him. He had one of those older, distinguished faces.

"I'm so sorry," he said. "I was out in the waves. Were you standing here long?"

"Not long at all," I replied. "Two or three waves. Max."

"Lorraine, could you leave us please?" he said, and on she turned and walked out the far door.

"You'll want to try this," he said, pouring from the pitcher. "It's my wife's recipe. They say it's a summer drink, but I've drunk it every day for I don't know how long. There are real lemons in there, that's the key."

It tasted like lemonade, but I smiled and complimented it anyway. We sat for a minute in an extended awkward silence. The muscular coastal wind, coming in from all directions at once, caused a loud whipping sound against the house that I recognized as the sound from the voicemails I had been getting

"Your house is beautiful," I said. "It's everything I would want in a house."

"And what do you want in a house?"

I paused. I hadn't really thought of that question before.

"Something solid, like this," I finally said. "This house deserves to be a mansion. It feels like it's existed for a thousand years."

"Ninety," he replied. "Not the first wave of *riche* to come and build mansions in Newport. The second wave, more interested in the land and the beach than the social games happening across the bay."

"I love it." Outside the wind had turned into a full-force maelstrom.

"My wife didn't love it so much. She needs everything just so. She never wanted a creaky old place like this. She wanted me to buy an empty plot on the ocean and build a new house with all the modern stuff baked into it."

"Where is your wife today?"

"That's what I wanted you to talk to you about. If you haven't already guessed, my wife is a permanent resident at Shady Brook."

"Oh no."

"It gets a little strange here. I was told, via cold call, that my wife Beatrice is seeing your father." He paused, looking past me. "Romantically. Of course, I knew before that."

"Listen, Bernard."

"Bernie."

He looked at me intently, his finger circling the rim of his lemonade glass. I could feel the warm rush of my defenses building. I readied myself to tell him that I can't control my father. That a sound mind is needed for any of society's rules to apply. That he shouldn't get bent out of shape about the actions of two people finding some happiness within their rapidly deteriorating mental space. That if their happiness made them live even an extra week we, should bless it as a miracle.

But I didn't say that. Instead I took his hand and said, "I am so sorry."

He grabbed my hand with both of his and gathered around it, squeezing it tight. Tears threatened, but he swallowed and seemed to come back from the brink. "Is your mother still alive?"

"Yes."

"How is she dealing with all of this?"

"Not well," I said, adding, "but she has her own

issues."

"It's an unbearable strain."

"Lots of things are an unbearable strain on my mother."

He looked out the window, then back at me.

"I learned about the date between your father and Beatrice. I believe you were the chaperone, if my sources are not mistaken."

"How did you hear about that?"

"Robin, I could be modest, but instead I'll say that the new wing of the nursing home will be called the Bernard Chapman wing."

"Oh God."

I grabbed the sides of my chair and shifted back and forth. From this far into the porch the view on all sides was ocean. I wished suddenly that I could be out there in the ocean feeling the ice-cold cleanse of salt water. Sunning afterwards until only a fine salty dust remained across the arms. The summer suddenly seemed so far away. I braced myself for his tears, or his anger or, more realistically, a threat of legal action.

"Bernie, you have to understand, I didn't..."

"Thank you."

"I thought Joanie had told me..."

"Robin." He took my arm again. "Thank you. Until now," he continued, "I didn't know how to make her happy. You should have heard her talking about her date. I hadn't heard her so happy in months. I was furious at first – of course I was. She kept shaking her wrist at me, showing me the present she got on her date. Of course I had given it to her years ago. Of course I had."

"Bernie, the date was a disaster."

"I'm sure it was. You can't take dementia patients out of their environment like that. But you have to realize that their perceptions of the event after the fact and the reality have nothing to do with each other. Most importantly, it made her happy. That's the only thing left. I tried everything, every possible thing, to do that for her. But the only thing that's worked is letting go, listening to her talk about her new boyfriend, asking her questions about it. Once I discovered that, it's been remarkably easy. And I have you partly to thank for that."

"Well, I guess I didn't really have a plan for the whole thing," I said. "It was more like a feeling that turned itself into a plan. Some need to try to do something for my father."

"Did you think I was going to invite you here and accuse you of kidnapping Beatrice?"

"The thought crossed my mind for a minute."

"The man I was even a year ago, I may have." He paused for a moment. "She used to write out here. I'd wake up in the night to an empty bed and find her scribbling out on the porch. With the lights on indoors, you couldn't see out to the water, but you still heard the ocean splashing. Even still, she sometimes would put her chair facing in toward the house, the one way there wasn't a window to the ocean. She really was a terrific writer.

"Her dream was always to write her family's history. It was a great history, though I heard it mostly in snatches here or there. Some of it she wouldn't mention unless she had been drinking. Her family was prominent in Poland before they had to flee. She had a hard time getting a start on it, since so much of it was painful.

"Now it's all gone. I hired a ghostwriter to come with me to the home to try to wring some of it out of her, but its all been mushed together in her mind, or else it's gone, like colors mixed together on a painter's board. For a long time that was the most important thing, getting that information out, and it crushed me how badly I failed."

"I was the same way with my dad. I treated his mind like a piñata with memories hidden inside. I still do, I guess."

"Well, I've given up on all that now. Her happiness in the moment is the only thing left that matters. Not for me - for her."

I didn't respond – Bernie looked on the edge of tears again.

"It is so important to me," he said, gathering himself, "so very important that your father and Beatrice continue to see each other. If you ever need any help, don't hesitate to call me. If you move your father to another facility, Beatrice and I will be close behind. You'll find me stubborn in that way."

"Thank you."

"I mean it. Anything. Before you go would you like to see pictures of Beatrice when she was younger. I usually keep an album close at hand."

"Of course. I'd love to."

"I have to warn you, though. You're not going to believe her beauty."

Chapter Thirty-Two

BEFORE COREY CAME home, I finished the kitchen. This was his white whale: a room that had been so covered with refuse the first time I visited that I didn't know it was even a kitchen. A room so decimated that boiling water was a chore, and making coffee a painstaking fight for counter space.

First, I took off all the cabinet doors, sanded them with low-grit paper and touched them up with high-gloss paint. I pulled off the old countertop and attached the new piece, the one that Corey and I had cut a sink hole into a few weeks before. I leveled it out with shims and secured it with liquid nails. The built-on backsplash kissed against the lowest row of tiling, and I connected the two with a thin bead of gray caulk. The scariest part was putting the sink back in. So many things can go wrong when you're measuring into three-dimensional space. But the home improvement gods were with me that day, and everything lined up like new construction. The lip of the sink overlapped the countertop, sitting securely. All the water feeds connected up without so much as a single drop of liquid hitting the linoleum. And I didn't once have to ask anyone for help. It hadn't even come to mind.

With the sink installed, I re-attached the cabinet doors and sat at the kitchen table drinking a beer, admiring my handiwork. I saw imperfections. They existed in any improvement job, and if you did the work yourself you were granted a superhuman ability to see them. I noticed some permanent marker spots at the edges of the countertop, and a few of the hand-cut tiles had dried crooked on the backsplash. I finished my first beer and started another, letting the buzz relax me into the silence that still felt uncomfortable in Corey's house.

The next morning I picked up Corey from the hospital and drove him home. He didn't have a lot to say on the ride. When we hit the highway, he put his arm out the window, letting the brisk winter air bite into his bandage.

Corey's silence lasted until he walked into the kitchen, where he promptly dropped his bags.

"What happened?" he asked. He ran his fingers down the countertop, opened the faucet handles, and ran his good hand under the water. The cabinet under the sink was ajar, and he flicked it open with his foot and watched the water flow down the P-trap and into the basement. He touched the seals and held his fingers up to the light. "Bone dry," he said, more to himself than me.

"I finished it."

"By yourself?"

When I told him I did, he walked over to the kitchen table and sat.

"It's finished," he said, rubbing the side of his head. "I can't believe it's finished."

"Is everything okay? Do you like it?"

"It's perfect. I just never thought it would actually be finished."

I sat down next to him. He opened his cotton bandaging, put it aside, and laid the moon-like expanse of his arm across the table. With his arm resting between us, he gave me a look halfway between serious and scared.

"Would you live with me, Robin? If I promised to be better. Would you just live with me?"

"What do you mean 'better'?"

"I mean just me. No more lunatics in the attic. No more nights in a freezing tent. Just live with me like we're two normal people. The house is done. I can get a job. We can just be normal.

"Wait, don't answer yet." He had started to get teary. "We could get your books back in, and maybe set up the turret with bookshelves all the way to the ceiling, with a ladder to get up there. I'd have to clean up the cobwebs."

"Let me think about it, okay?"

"Just please - please stay with me tonight."

I did. And the night after that. We fell back into a pattern of sorts. James was away, and I still had my book stuff to work on. My stocks had gotten low, so I had to come up with a plan to start buying again and began taking day trips to bookstores in the outer rings of Boston. Corey started going to job interviews, looking for entrance positions with CPAs or law firms. It seemed that the more neutral the office, the larger the stacks of papers, the more abstract the work, the more Corey wanted the job.

Something felt different. The house was finished, but it was more than that. That the house was livable, and not an open construction site, didn't seem good or bad. It just was. I didn't miss the mess. But I missed the feeling of a house in progress. And I never did get used to the quiet. It was like I had been living with a sound machine following me around, playing white noise until it disappeared into the background of my day. It took someone turning the machine off to make me understand how much I'd relied on the noise to blot out uncomfortable thoughts. One morning, Corey came back into bed and read alongside me. When I'd first spied him from my porch, this would have been the best endpoint I could have written for our story: us in bed, quietly reading, sharing a carafe of coffee. But now it was happening, and it made me want to scream.

Sometimes a tinny alarm broke our new silence. It was his flip phone, telling him it was time to do push-ups or get back to work on the house. Corey didn't follow these schedules anymore, but he couldn't figure out how to turn the alarms off, so he just let them ring into the air, feebly calling out reminders of a life that no longer existed.

Corey was out for a job interview on New Year's Eve when I saw a van pull into my driveway. A man got out, a belt of tools jingling from his waist, and began walking around the perimeter of the house. I went down and met him on the porch, where he was crouched in intense investigation of my front door.

"You're definitely going to want to change that," I said, which startled him. "You can open it with a screwdriver."

He was a locksmith, the one I had expected since I heard my house was in foreclosure. I explained my story to him and surprisingly, he was sympathetic.

"Paying all that rent while he lets the house foreclose - that ain't right," he said.

"Who knows," I said, "maybe I'll buy the fucking place."

That made him laugh. He let me go in and pack up the last of my things. It was just a few suitcases of clothes and some small lamps. A few final books. Most of the dishes and furniture were either owned by former roommates or else they weren't worth the effort of moving. I was happy to leave it behind for my landlord to deal with.

As I stood at the end of the driveway, suitcases in hand, I tried to picture what would happen if I walked across the street and up the porch steps. If Corey got a job. What our lives would be like. I thought about small details: me washing a load of his polo shirts. Us together at a restaurant picking an appetizer. I pictured Corey coming home after a day of office work, his body free of dust and debris. He hangs a messenger bag on a hook as I pull dinner from an oven with a large, patterned mitt. I kiss him and instinctively wipe his cheek, finding there's no dirt or salt deposits to brush away.

Then I tried to just picture Corey, period. It was hard to see him in my mind with any clarity. It's like I had never really gotten a mental snapshot because he hadn't slowed down enough to be anything but a tantalizing blur. I could only dredge up small bits: the wells under his eyes, the upper curve of his neck where his stubble began. Flecks of paint on his angular nose. But my mind couldn't integrate these parts into a living, breathing person. I ended up standing at the end of my driveway until the sun began to set and orange, magic-hour hues descended onto the aging houses on my street, showing them in their best possible light. Kids biked past. Neighbors walked their dogs. And I stood there dumbly, trying and failing to see a person I had lived with for months.

Chapter Thirty-Three

AS I SAT at the cafeteria table, my mind kept wandering to the notebooks in my purse. As always, the place was rife with information. Families began filing in for Sunday brunch, unbundling their children and hunting for napkins. Out the window, the first snowflakes of the season drifted lazily down, softening Shady Brook's exacting landscape architecture. An attendant was setting up a keyboard stand, but Bettie was nowhere to be found.

A family decision was imminent, and I wondered how many more of these brunches I would be witness to. I told Ariel about my meeting with Bernie, but I'd left out the most crucial information, that he would pay for our father to keep him with Bettie. I'd been reminded of this when I walked in and almost stumbled into a large placard announcing *The Bernard Chapman Wing - Opening in Late 2010*, along with a computer rendering of a common space adorned with dark wooden chairs and lush carpets. What a piece of information that was: paying to keep your wife's boyfriend close. My notebook yelled out, starving for these facts, but it was a muffled sort of shout, like hearing a voice from beyond a forest thick with pines. I found it easy to ignore.

The patients began filing in, the families raising a hand to call over attendants, John's "auction" that always made me giggle. I saw the usual sad stuff: drool at the mouth, dandruff sprinkled across the shoulders of old blazers. But the small details didn't make me cry the way they did in the summer. Maybe I'd been hardened by my visits. Or maybe it was the new understanding that it didn't matter how these details made me feel.

The auction ended without any sign of my father, or Ariel and her clan. If they hadn't shown by now, they would have been late even by their standards. I walked across the campus to my father's room, hunching my shoulders to keep snow off my neck. I turned the corner into his room with my breath held. When a dementia patient doesn't show up for brunch, anything is possible. But the room was empty, and there were no signs of recent activity.

From there I went down the hallway to the center of the spur, where Joanie sat at the operations desk. I still hadn't spoken to her since the night of Thanksgiving, and I almost turned around when I saw her sitting there. But she saw me first and pointed down toward the recreation room, smiling warmly as she did, as if nothing had transpired between us.

"Thanks, Joanie," I said as I rushed past her, cutting my own path in the short grass.

The automated doors to the recreation room slid open with a squeal in front of me, releasing the scents I had come to know in the last year, the unique mix of clean rubber and thawing vegetables.

A few things happened when I turned the corner.

First, I bumped into Ariel, who was standing alone, using the wall to keep herself upright. And then I saw my father. He was sitting on one of the couches next to Bettie, who looked resplendent in a blue sequined shirt. Her hair was still an unnatural red, but instead of curls it had been straightened and set shoulder length. On another couch that made a corner with theirs, my mother sat alone with her hands on her lap.

Ariel put an arm out to stop me from walking any farther. Dad hadn't noticed me yet, and I watched from the safety of the corner as he and Bettie looked with unusual focus on a nature program on television. They sat perfectly still next to one another, like two teenagers on an awkward date, with my mother as their chaperone.

I couldn't hear the program too well, but the gist of it was a nature reporter visiting a sheer hill on the Pacific Ocean that had caved in. The sandy hill had been used as home for hundreds of birds that had burrowed into the loose dirt and made cubbies. The hill had collapsed in on itself, and swarms of birds were flying around confused, searching frantically for their piece of real estate. Birds who were trapped inside the hill at the moment of impact were stuck. A camera pan revealed dozens of brightly colored tail-feathers in the dirt. Some wiggled frantically, but others had stopped. The reporter tried to lower herself down to free some birds, and her native escorts tried to stop her. I could hear one dark-skinned man say, "Better to let nature take its course."

"Let it take its course next time," the reporter said. "Help me down."

"Is not fair to the scavengers," he replied.

She started scrambling along the loose dirt hill digging out birds. The collapse must have been fresh because the first, a bright yellow bird the size of the woman's palm, immediately flittered the sand from its wings and took off. The next was a tightly packed group with fluffy, lime green plumage. The woman scraped around the edges like a gardener trying to pull up a stone. Not soon after, three lime-green parakeets were flying off into the high definition horizon. Lastly, the reporter found a large red tail, almost a foot long, poking out of the sand. It was much bigger than the others and proved more difficult to dig out. She called for help but her guides would not intervene. "Is not right," they said, more than once. After a few cuts and a lot more dirt on her knees, she pulled a large red parrot from the sand that sat in her hands still as a stone. From the large hole created by the parrot, two tiny red birds emerged, looking nervous. When the light hit them, they immediately took off and added themselves to the swarm around the hillside. The reporter stayed, holding the dead bird for a few more moments, brushing the sand off and giving it a slight shake. Finally she gave it an underhand toss in the hope that it would fly off, but instead it hit the sand with a quiet thud.

I noticed my father had taken Bettie's hand. He said, "Isn't that interesting? You couldn't make this stuff up."

"No, you couldn't," she replied. "If you wrote this into a movie I wouldn't believe it."

Other than that they were silent with each other. My mother kept her eyes forward on the television, occasionally skating across to look at her husband holding another woman's hand. She sat like an observer, taking up as little space on the couch as possible. Her mind was still razor-sharp, but in body my mother did not look out of place in Shady Brook. I don't know if it was the way she sat, but she looked frail in her housecoat, more so even than at Thanksgiving. Eventually she broke the silence.

"Do you know what kinds of birds those are?" she asked. She spoke casually, like they were strangers passing.

"Gee, I don't know," he said. "I lost my bird book so long ago."

I looked for a spark of recognition in my father's eye, but I didn't see it.

"Are you a big fan of birds?"

"Oh, yes. I always was. My aunt gave me my first bird book when I was twelve."

My mother didn't respond, but smiled at him warmly. It was true.

"You know," he added. "Those birds. Something tells me they might be robins."

"You know," my mother said, squinting back tears, "you may be right."

Ariel put her hand on the back of my neck. It was a beautiful moment to me, and the well of tears in Ariel's eyes told me that it was beautiful to her, too. They were so content. So banal.

When I used to cry at Shady Brook, what I was doing was mourning the death of memories. The war on memories is one being waged across every dementia ward in the world. It's a one-sided war - a slaughter, really. But what I saw that day, what Bernie saw before me, was that for my father, memory wasn't necessary for happiness. I had never considered the possibility before, but maybe it's bliss. Not when you're fighting between dementia and lucidity - that was clearly hell. But what about when you lost it completely? Maybe it felt like closing your eyes and lying back into a pool of warm saltwater. I hope it does. The way my father looked that day - I want that for him for as long as his body holds up.

Everything in the recreation room continued unabated. The atonal beeps and buzzes of machines didn't die down. Frail patients continued to be pushed past on squeaking gurneys. The common area, modeled after a doctor's waiting room with fake plants and an empty fish tank, was not worthy of the emotions it was holding.

My mother looked at Bettie.

"So how long have you two known each other?" she asked.

Bettie didn't acknowledge the words at first. She was either fixated on the reporter, still digging out birds, or she was staring blankly into space. But after a beat, she shook out of it and looked at my mother with unblinking eyes.

"Oh, gosh. Who can remember?"

Before Spring

Epilogue

THERE IS A passage at the beginning of Ansel's *Build Your Dream Home* that stands out to me. After a short intro outlining the many uses of a home repair book such as his, Ansel steps out of his didactic mode and says, "The American home is the cleanest, largest, best lit, most efficient machine in the entire world. But even the most perfectly built machine requires repairs." The book's original date of release was 1933, and I can't help but wonder if Ansel knew that his comment could be taken multiple ways.

I had that line in mind on my last walk through tent city. With everything cleared from my apartment, the last thing I had to do was pack up my belongings in my ceremonial tent. I walked down the main thoroughfare of a half-empty city, stepping carefully inside existing footprints to avoid getting snow on my pants. Inside my tent I found a sheaf of notebooks and a few stray items of clothing. I left my camping gear behind, and my hot pot. The biggest find, and the reason I came, was the Ansel's book, which Corey had left behind. It's a book that will, I think, become a signifier of this time in my life. Its frayed, green binding calls to mind more memories than a dozen notebooks filled with facts ever will. I wrapped it in tissue paper, stowed it in my backpack, and stepped back outside. At the end of the row, Seril's wedding tent whipped in the breeze, torn open and sagging from snow.

Just after New Year's, Corey got word from a former associate that Seril had truly lost it. He was seen in the Woonasquatucket, up to his waist in half-frozen water, trying to walk out to a metal torso bobbing in the tide. Hearing the news, Corey trudged into tent city and took him away, holding him in his arms like a child. He drove him to a Veteran's Psych facility down in Groton, Connecticut, as he had done once before. During that weekend, while Corey was away, I removed the last of my belongings out of his house. Some I brought to my storage space, others I brought to Ariel's, where I'm staying until I can move into my new place. I didn't have the nerve for a face-to-face break up.

Ariel and I decided that for now our father should stay at Shady Brook. My mother finally sat down with John and helped him sort through her finances. They aren't great, but they're better than we expected. He can stay for a while, at least. If things do get grim, we may swallow our pride and ask Bernie for help. We brought the idea up to our mother and she didn't like it, but she didn't dismiss it either. To our surprise, she expressed interest in meeting the man.

Next month I move into a new house in a small town south of Providence. The house is old, but it has good bones, and it's situated up on a hill. I'm going to live on the first floor and use the upstairs for my books. The owners are a couple who had to move for work but, like everyone else in 2010, couldn't sell their house without taking a bath. I immediately saw a dozen or so projects I wanted to take on, and told them so. To my surprise, they said I could have at it and take the cost of any improvements out of the rent. I couldn't hide my excitement. One thing I won't change is the creaky wood flooring, which gleams like gold when the light hits it. When I first toured the place, the low angle of the sun revealed some chatter marks on the boards. Of course, it made me think of Corey and the time we spun his drum sander together at midnight.

I owe Corey a lot. Without him, I'd have no idea what my hands are capable of. But I don't suspect I'll ever see him again; one thing I don't owe him is a relationship. I've been texting with James, who's now home on spring break, but I don't owe him anything, either. It's nice to finally understand that.

If I do ever see Corey again, I hope it will be when we're older and have the world figured out. Then we can meet and catch up. I'd like that. We can meet as distant friends, or as old war buddies reminiscing about the battles we fought together: home repair, dementia. Entropy by other names.

Acknowledgements

I'M A JEALOUS person by nature, and more often than not acknowledgement pages invoke a rage in me that I'm not proud of. The casual name dropping - he got John Darniele to proofread? She knows Deborah Treisman? - sends me into an envy-fueled tailspin, and reinforces what I've already long suspected: that there is a raging party happening somewhere, and I was not invited.

So if you are like me, fear not and read on, because I don't know a single famous person. That said, so many non-famous friends and family put in extraordinary effort to help me complete this book, and they deserve their moment.

I'd like to thank my first batch of readers: Brian Gilhooly, Katie Dickson, Elizabeth Kiepert, Leah Springer, and Kaitlin Andrews. Some of you read more than others based on how well my printer was working on a given day, but all of you helped tremendously with what you were given.

Leigh Medeiros, the closest thing to a real editor I've ever had, was instrumental in this book being an actual story and not a series of sentences. I appreciated every minute I had with her. Thanks also to Jason Rosenberg, who taught me a bit about the shady mortgage market circa 2005, though I ended up scuttling most of it.

I'm thankful to the city of Providence, where I lived between 2008-2010 and saw up close the tent city that would inspire parts of the book. The city is a vibrant, quirky place. Dan Barry wrote an article about the tent city in *The New York Times*, and something about the way that piece was crafted triggered my imagination and set the tone for large swaths of the book. He didn't know that he was helping me, but I thank him anyway.

This book was written in many locations, but none more than The Coffee Depot in Warren, Rhode Island, by far my favorite coffee shop in the world. The money I spent on coffee there will far outstrip any profits I make on this book, but I have no regrets. Thanks also to my cousins, Jessica DeBiasio and Ethan Joseph, who let me stay in their house in Vermont and pretend to be a full-time writer for a few days. I also had many great days of writing in my parents' house, though they didn't know what exactly I was working on. For a while, I didn't want to tell too many people about a project that was 80% done and always would be.

I also want to thank my wife, Kristen, though I don't know quite how to do that. What she provides for me is so large and unspecific, I could spend a lifetime of writing trying to get a handle on it. So I'll just try to articulate one thing. She has *never* just told me what I wanted to hear, even when I've told her specifically what to tell me. She is too strong-willed for that. Good thing, too, because it is the only thing keeping my writing from spiraling off into the land of "look how clever I am." I told her in our vows that it's one of the things I love most about her. And now, with a few years of field testing, I can report: I still love it. Every day.

About the Author

ERIC MANCINI IS a novelist and freelance writer. His finance writing has been featured in The Billfold, Business Insider, and GQ Online. He lives with his wife and two daughters in Warren, a small seaside town in Rhode Island.

One American Robin is his first novel.

Eric loves hearing from readers. The best way to connect with him is:

Website: ericmanciniwriter.com
Email: ericanthonymancini@gmail.com
Instagram: ericmanciniwriter